FRIENDSHIP
GAMES

MARK JAMES

DEFIANCE PRESS
& PUBLISHING

Friendship Games

ISBN-13: 978-1-959677-21-5 (Paperback)
ISBN-13: 978-1-959677-20-8 (eBook)

Published by Defiance Press & Publishing, LLC

Bulk orders of this book may be obtained by contacting Defiance Press & Publishing, LLC. www.defiancepress.com.

Public Relations Dept. – Defiance Press & Publishing, LLC
281-581-9300
pr@defiancepress.com

Defiance Press & Publishing, LLC
281-581-9300

info@defiancepress.com

PROLOGUE

I t was 5:00 p.m. and Khalid Husseini wasted no time calling it a day. He didn't have far to go – about two and a half miles as the crow flies – but getting from Point A to Point B quickly in a crowded and bustling city like Manama can be a very daunting task. He had to walk nearly half a mile to the parking lot of the U.S. Naval facility to pick up his car, and then drive out on Avenue 22 heading west before doubling back on the Prince Khalifa Bin Salman Causeway to Muharraq Island. Once on Muharraq, he'd turn north onto Road Number 11 in Al Hidd, and then east on Road 1107. A pretty short trip, all in all, but one that took about 30 minutes in the heavy traffic.

It was Friday, and Khalid had put all thoughts of work behind him just as soon as he stepped off base. The weekend had officially begun, and he looked forward to going to BJ's with friends. BJ's was an upscale nightclub in the Al Asasiin Hotel (the Americans called it the "Assassin" Hotel, but in Arabic, 'Asasiin' was more akin to "Standard") in Adliya. It was more than a little difficult to get inside, but a couple of American Navy sailors from work would meet him there. Americans didn't have any trouble getting into BJ's.

Infidels.

When the young sailors learned that it was his twenty-first birthday this week, they promised to help him celebrate "American style" at BJ's.

His imam encouraged him to go as a way to get in with them.

Khalid had just slipped in the key to the front door of his flat when something caught his attention, and he looked up and down the street. It was a muffled boom; he didn't so much hear it as feel it. He felt it in his hand as he pushed the key in, the door rattling slightly in its frame. He felt it through his feet as he stood in the doorway, the ground vibrating to a deep bass-tone muffle. And he felt it in his ears. It was a subtle change in air pressure mixed with the strange and harrowing rattling of multiple doors and windows. He scanned the scene to both ends of his street. His view was limited by apartment buildings, but movement above the buildings caught his eye, and he looked up.

He saw what looked like a flare, streaking across the dimming sky and leaving behind a dark contrail. It arched downward and disappeared from view as it descended behind the apartments far away. Khalid heard a delayed high-pitched whistling sound from the flare after it passed, and as he gawked, he realized that he heard faint second and third whistles after the first one faded.

Khalid stepped back from his apartment. Still looking up, he saw two more contrails arching in the sky. One stretched far away to the northwest, and the other appeared to sink a mile away to the east.

Then, like Godzilla rising, a large orange and black cloud of fire and smoke and dust billowed high into the sky from behind his building, and it looked really close.

Khalid stood wide-eyed and open-mouthed as he watched the angry cloud rise and expand. Something, however, tapped him on the top of his head, and broke the spell. He looked around. He tilted his head and listened: a pitter-patter filled his ears. He realized that it was falling dust and debris, and when nearby car alarms sounded all at once, he scurried into the doorway to wait it out. Nothing hit his street, but he heard a few bangs and clangs echoing throughout the eerily quiet neighborhood. It was over just as quickly as it had begun.

Khalid walked briskly down the street, his eyes glued to the rising cloud. People cautiously stuck their heads outside their doors and looked around. Others pointed to the sky and covered their faces in horror. As Khalid rounded the street corner and joined a growing crowd heading south along Avenue 11 to the waterfront, he beheld a surreal sight.

Looming offshore was the massive American aircraft carrier, the *Ford*-class USS *George W. Bush,* anchored in the Khawr al Qulay'ah inlet between Muharraq Island and the main island of Bahrain. The enormous ship towered above the apartment blocks of Al Hidd.

The cloud of smoke and dust grew high in the sky. The top half drifted towards the southwest. The bottom half stood upon the middle of the ship's flight deck. Balls of flame glowed red-orange amid the bowels of the ship and cut through the shroud of thick black smoke that poured relentlessly from invisible openings in the ship's structure. Flares intermittently streamed from the flames like bottle rockets, whistling into the darkening sky.

Was this the sign?

Muffled popping sounds reverberated from the ship. A large blinding flash lit up the sky for a couple of seconds. Khalid threw up his hands to protect his face as he felt the heat of the blast, and a massive *BANG* reverberated so deeply that it seemed the air itself was vibrating.

We're too close!

Khalid stumbled backward before he turned and ran. Others around him did the same. As he ran, he felt a searing blast of air against his back – a sudden gust that nearly pushed him down, but he was able to stay on his feet even as others stumbled and fell. Apartment building windows and car windshields twisted and shattered in their frames.

Only after Khalid ducked behind a wobbly apartment building for uncertain protection did he look back. The ship was now shrouded in thick clouds of black smoke and dust, and several buildings nearest the waterfront had collapsed from the force of the blast.

Now, a second yellow-orange flash forced Khalid to turn and run again. This, much larger, blast seemed to shake the entire earth. He stumbled and fell as the shock wave engulfed him, but he gathered himself up quickly and continued to sprint.

A car smashed upside down to his right, then another to his left. Both had literally fallen out of the sky. Flaming debris rained down all around.

This time, Khalid dared not stop to look back. Sign or not, he was running for his life.

PART ONE

THE BURNING BUSH

1

Hector Gonzales let out a deep sigh as he sank into the leather easy chair in front of the large flat-screen television perched on the lounge wall, his feet propped on a cheap coffee table. The Special Warfare Operator Master Chief placed a cold, sweating bottle of beer to his forehead. "Mmmm," he groaned softly.

The room was noisy, but the din faded as he closed his eyes for a moment. He opened them and took a swig of his Yuengling. He looked over at his men gathered around the work benches, taking off their gear and bantering. Drinking beer. They left him to his after-mission ritual. It was how he decompressed, and the men gave him his due.

He took another swig of his beer and closed his eyes again. He breathed deep, slow, deliberate breaths.

It had been a long day. They had successfully completed the interdiction of a Panama-flagged Japanese oil tanker in the middle of the Persian Gulf after it had traversed the Strait of Hormuz and headed toward Shuaiba, south of Kuwait City, to take on its load.

The Japanese and Filipino crew had taken everything in stride. It was the Persian Gulf, after all, and they could at least take comfort from the fact that it was their American allies who had seized their ship and not Iran's Revolutionary Guards or, worse, some variant of Al-Qaeda or another Islamist terror group.

The whole operation took less than three hours – from wheels up in their coaxial Sea Raider helicopters to dropping into the water with their inflatable rubber boats and stealthily boarding and securing the massive ship. They inspected the ship's manifest and cargo spaces; then rappelled right back off the side of the ship and disappeared into the morning darkness from which they'd come.

It was, essentially, an exercise.

Then came the time-consuming part: hours of the operation's post-mortem. Each squad member and supporting staffer up and down the operation chain was debriefed; each questioned about what they thought they could have done better, about what they thought had gone right and what had gone wrong, etc. Every conceivable angle of the operation was scrutinized and analyzed.

And then they began to plan their next interdiction mission.

All in a day's work.

After a moment, Hector opened his eyes and spoke to his men. "Yo, Rook," he said. Henry Avellino, the most junior operator, who had turned twenty just a few days before, looked over. "Come here," said Hector, nodding to the well-worn couch next to his easy chair.

"Uh oh," one of the guys laughed, "Rookie's in trouble."

Henry hesitated. He had his tactical vest slung over his shoulder and grasped a duffle bag and other gear in his hands.

"Put your shit down and come here," said Hector gruffly. He leaned forward, rubbed his head, and looked at Henry.

Henry heaved his bag onto the work bench along with his tactical vest, itself no lightweight piece of equipment, grabbed his beer, and walked over.

Hector held up his beer expectantly, and Henry clanged it with his own.

"You did good today," said the Master Chief. It was Henry's – and the squad's – first ship interdiction since the last one ended two months previous with a ruptured spleen and a shattered right arm for Steven Anderson, prematurely ending the senior chief's esteemed naval career. For his part, Henry spent two nights in hospital at Camp Lemonnier in Djibouti for exposure and dehydration.

The two had barely survived being repeatedly slammed against the side of the ship by twenty-foot waves in the Gulf of Oman after the *Shenzhen Lion* unexpectedly turned during their surprise boarding. Henry and the senior chief were the last two in the netting. The rest of the squad slipped over the ship's rails just as the first wave hit, and they were certain that the senior chief and the rookie were goners.

"We call every rookie 'fodder,' Hector said. "Every man in this squad was fodder when they arrived, including me, not too long ago.

It's the way. You've got to earn your stripes. You've got to earn our reason to care about you. When we saw Steven and you.. . ." He paused at looked down at his feet. "They care about you." Hector looked up to meet Henry's eyes. "The squad. Hell, *I* care about you."

Henry nodded and looked down.

"Welcome to Echo Squad," said Hector, extending his hand.

Henry looked at the master chief's hand for a moment before grasping it. Hector pulled him in for a shoulder bump – and the whole building shook.

"What the hell!" shouted Hector, rushing out the door, his beer left on the coffee table.

Others ran to the door after Hector, including Henry. They made their way out of the special operations warehouse and down to the seawall at the U.S. Navy section of the Mina Salman seaport. To their astonishment, a mushroom cloud stood high above the *George W. Bush* aircraft carrier anchored in the cove between the shipyard and Muharraq Island, about a mile from where they stood.

What looked like welder's sparks poured from the bow of the massive ship into the harbor. Flares like bottle rockets shot out of the black smoke in zig-zagging patterns and produced piercing whistling sounds that reached the men a few seconds after they had already flared out.

Rockets cooking off.

Another massive explosion sent the men sprawling to the ground, covering their heads. The shockwave reached them in less than a second, arriving with a heart-thumping *BANG* and a smashing gust that rattled the warehouse buildings and shattered windows.

"*Jesus!*" shouted Noah Hastings, Special Warfare Operator Second Class.

No one else said anything.

Another massive explosion forced them to stay put and weather yet another shockwave.

"*Fuck!*" exclaimed Chief Petty Officer Buck Bradshaw. Still pressed to the ground, he looked inland and swept his gaze north across the Prince Khalifa Bin Salman Highway, which transected the base from east to west.

"You thinking what I'm thinking!?" shouted Hector, watching Buck.

"If what you mean is, are we under fucking attack, then *yeah!*" shouted Buck.

The SEALs picked themselves up. Hector and Buck looked dockside. Special Boat Team combatant-craft crewmen were already gearing up. Some, pulling on flak jackets and helmets as they ran, headed to their fast Mark V special operations craft. Within a few minutes, they had scrambled aboard, untied the boats from their moorings, and pulled out at full speed.

They raced to the burning *George W. Bush.*

Echo Squad's young petty officers, whom Bradshaw referred to as the Squid Punks – first-class Christian Köllner, second-class Noah Hastings and Danny Liu, and third-class Henry – hovered off to the side of Hector and Buck.

"I don't see anything," said Noah. His eyes scanned inland across Prince Khalifa bin Salman Highway to the other side of the base. "No smoke," he added.

"We have to *do* something," said Danny. The young petty officers were fidgety.

11

"We could break out the Zodiacs," suggested Christian.

Another massive *BANG* warped the air and shook the earth.

"Those motherfuckers are being *cooked* out there. We gotta get out there," Danny pleaded. "They're *fleet*."

Hector could see a flotilla of the Navy port's muscular 40 PB patrol boats already heading towards the *George W. Bush*. Other Navy ships, part of the *George W. Bush* carrier strike group, were sounding General Quarters – you could hear them from the across the shipyard – and untethering themselves from the long quay. A Navy fire boat was now approaching the *Bush*, with several fountains of water being trained on the carrier from what looked like a dangerously close distance.

The fire boat looked pretty big when tied up at its mooring. It was tiny, however, next to the huge supercarrier, and its fountains of water seemed entirely futile.

"Gear up and get the Zodiacs," ordered Hector. "There must be a ton of guys in the water. Bring 'em here. Set up triage. Put your combat medical training to use here on the dock."

Hector's eyes moved to the neighboring warehouses where a group of enlisted sailors were gathered, gawking at the burning *George W. Bush*. "Rook!" Hector barked. "Go corral those guys, and bring them here. *Move* it!" The men scrambled into action.

A bland white Ford sedan base car with "U.S. Navy" stenciled on both front doors approached Hector, and Lieutenant Commander Nigel Wood hopped out of the back seat. He was wearing his summer white uniform with a gold trident pinned to his chest. Wood was commander of Alpha Troop. He took to the field with Echo Squad, and with Hector as his senior enlisted.

"Master Chief," he said. "Gear up, yeah?"

Wood had a habit of delivering his orders in the form of a question, perhaps to soften their impact. He spoke with a British accent though he was born and raised in Maine. He graduated Harvard before attending the even more elite Oxford University in England as a Rhodes Scholar, where he picked up the accent. Then, to his affluent family's horror, he joined the Navy.

Worse, he became a SEAL.

Hector found both the accent and the orders as a question annoying.

"Already on it," the master chief grunted.

"The base commanding officer has ordered a lockdown," said Nigel. "We're to augment base security."

"That's fucking bullshit, yeah?" said Hector.

Nigel had recognized Hector's annoyance with his faux British accent long ago, but it only encouraged him to pour it on even more whenever the master chief was around.

"We're not going to faff about, mate, not if I can help it," Nigel said. "Alpha and Bravo Squad can manage security, but Echo Squad is yours. I trust you have a plan, Master Chief, yeah?"

Thew Bryson worked the night shift, 4:00 p.m. to midnight, at Warehouse Number 1. It was a busy week with the *George W. Bush* strike group in port. It was generally non-stop tedious work to process hundreds – no, *thousands* – of requisitions for replenishing on-board ship supplies, bundling various mixtures of ordered materials on to pallets, plastic wrapping them, and delivering them dockside.

Then there were the aircraft and ship repairs and upkeep. Replacement parts for all sorts of engines, machinery and avionics equipment were ordered and delivered, and the broken parts sent out for repair at the base maintenance shops. They would be cycled back into warehouse inventories when repairs were completed. Some parts awaited component parts of their own. Some were beyond repair and sent off-island, with requisitions for replacements put on order.

The warehouses regularly needed to be replenished of their non-repairable – or "consumable" materials – stuff like nuts and bolts, and even mundane things like boots and toiletries.

When replenishment merchant marine supply ships were in port at the same time as a carrier strike group, like now – the USNS *Cesar Chavez* and USNS *Amelia Earhart* were tied up along the long Mina Salman pier right amid various destroyers and cruisers of the *George W. Bush* strike group – well, then it was all hands on deck for Fleet Support Center (FSC) Bahrain.

Every warehouse replenishment order had to be inspected, cross-listed and signed for by port-based logistics specialists. Meanwhile, strike group orders for materials and replacement parts came in non-stop, 24/7. It was a delicate balance to process both, making sure that incoming fleet requisitions weren't automatically forwarded off-island because the shelves were empty while the warehouse replenishments waited to be added into the inventory. It was also tedious work.

Most of the sailors at FSC Bahrain cursed the days when either a carrier strike group or merchant marine supply ships were in port. When both were in port at the same time? *Fughetaboutit.*

But as a not-long-out-of-bootcamp E-2, eighteen-year-old Logistics Specialist Seaman Apprentice Thew Bryson enjoyed the work. *This* kind of work. As one of the lowest guys on the totem pole – actually Thew was *the* lowest guy on the totem pole – he was assigned to First Lieutenant and tasked with swabbing the decks and cleaning the heads of the FSC administrative offices.

That's mopping floors and cleaning toilets, for you non-Navy readers.

But now, with the carrier strike group and supply replenishment ships in port, Thew got to drive a forklift, moving materials around and building up and breaking down pallets along with his low-ranking colleagues.

Navy work.

He didn't sign up just to swab decks or clean toilets, said no Navy sailor ever.

Nineteen-year-old E-3 Seaman David Skaggs was sitting in the passenger seat, supervising, as Thew managed the controls of the forklift. Thew saw it as his good fortune to be paired with Skaggs. He was a total slacker, through and through, and with a "fuck you, Chief" attitude to boot.

A sudden hot gust of wind slammed into the forklift, knocking Thew into the center control panel, mashing his ribs and driving his head into Skagg's shoulder, which nearly knocked Skaggs out of the forklift.

"Fucking A!" yelled Skaggs.

"I didn't do anything!" protested Thew over the forklift's engine. He braked hard, which produced a loud rattle and jerked the forklift to a stop. He expected another scolding from Skaggs for jerking the forklift to a stop, but when he looked over, Skaggs was staring into the distance, his mouth agape.

Thew looked to his left and did a double take. *"Holy shit!"* he said as he saw the fiery cloud erupting atop the *George W. Bush* aircraft carrier.

A large cloud of dust drifting from the land north of the burning carrier blended with the black smoke pouring from the *Bush*.

"Buildings," thought Thew. Some of the buildings on Muharraq Island had come down from the force of the explosions.

Thew saw a man jogging purposefully toward him from the seaside tarmac area behind Warehouse Number 2 – the home of Naval Special Warfare (Navy SEALs) and their supporting commands.

Warehouse Number 2 was strictly off limits for "regular" Navy personnel like him. A red line was literally painted on the tarmac demarcating the NSW zone. As if that weren't enough, large block letters, also in red, announced: "RESTRICTED AREA: DO NOT CROSS." If you *did* cross the red line, Thew was warned more than once, you'd be swarmed by armed guards and roughed up like a terrorist, and then likely discharged from the Navy altogether.

They didn't mess around, and now a guy in fatigues was jogging toward him from the other side of the red line with a determined look on his face.

A momentary pang of fear gripped Thew. *Did I cross the red line with the forklift?*

Another massive *BANG,* like a nearby lightning strike, caused Thew to drop flat on the ground again. He looked back and saw another mushroom cloud roiling above the *George W. Bush.*

"You two!" shouted the camouflage-wearing soldier-sailor, unfazed by the third shockwave. He was young, not much older than Thew, but solidly built. He was a petty officer third-class, Thew noted. The black eagle, anchor, gun and trident insignia patch of a Navy SEAL was sewn onto his sand-colored uniform top.

"Follow me," he told them.

It had been only two hours since the initial blast on the *George W. Bush,* but the rescue operation was already a well-oiled machine. Thew drove the forklift from one place to another, moving supplies and bulky equipment to wherever they were needed.

When the SEAL master chief first told Thew to bring supplies from the warehouses to the tarmac, Thew helpfully alerted him that he wasn't actually qualified to operate the forklift without direct supervision.

He didn't have a formal Navy forklift license, you see.

The SEAL master chief gave him a withering look and said, *"Drive the fucking forklift."*

Sir yes, sir! Absolutely, SIR!

It was like boot camp all over again, but Thew welcomed it. The *George W. Bush* was on fire and fellow sailors were dying. Everyone was desperate to do something, anything, to contribute to squelching the flames and saving the ship and its crew.

Saving their shipmates.

So yeah, Thew drove the fucking forklift. He drove it all over

Naval Support Activity Bahrain, as the base was officially known. He weaved in and out of warehouses, picking up whatever he was told to pick up and delivering it to wherever he was told to deliver it.

He even drove between NSA 1, the administrative side of the base, and NSA 2, the portside of the base, using the arch flyover bridge that spanned the Prince Khalifa Bin Salman Highway.

The tarmac along the seawall behind the warehouses filled up with wounded and burned sailors plucked from waters around the *George W. Bush* by various ships and boats, including SEALs on rubber zodiacs and Harbor Patrol personnel on fast gunboats. SEALs and combat medical corpsmen did their best to tend to the wounded.

Thew became grateful for the loudness of the forklift's engines and rattling frame. The one time he had turned the engine off to help unload a pallet full of medical gear, the screams and moans of horribly burned sailors put his back up, and he winced. The sounds were animalistic, and left Thew feeling utterly helpless. All he *could* do was stay out of the medics' way and do whatever was needed of him.

2

E ighteen-year-old Jamal Al-Dosari stood among the crowds along
ASRY Beach, astride the Arab Shipbuilding and Repair Yard
(hence, 'ASRY') at the southern end of Muharraq Island. His
heart thumped as he watched the American carrier burning offshore.

This must be the sign.

Jamal was one of the youngest members of Suraya al-Salmeen
(the Salmeen Brigades), one of the cells in the Islamic Front of Bahrain, each of which was unknown to the other.

The Suraya al-Salmeen cell was named after its leader, Imam
Hussein Salmeen, and was composed of almost twenty impression-
able young men selected from the youth outreach program at the
imam's mosque. The program targeted disadvantaged and troubled
youth who were eager to be good Muslims. They were the vanguard
of the Islamic Front of Bahrain.

Or so they were told by the imam.

They were soldiers of God. Imam Hussein Salmeen was their
General.

What they didn't know was that the Islamic Front of Bahrain
was funded and directed by the Quds Force branch of Iran's Islamic
Revolutionary Guard Corps. Other cells of the Islamic Front of Bahrain had staged attacks against the island's Sunni monarchy, the Al

Khalifa family, which had ruled the predominantly Shia island since the late 18th Century. To date, their attacks were minimally effective: a bank robbery in Manama; an attempted small-boat attack on an American Navy ship (disrupted by the Americans' harbor patrol boats); setting a couple of mines in the Persian Gulf that had yet to be struck by a passing ship.

But Imam Salmeen's group had now been given a more impressive mission.

One that promised to make history.

Jamal took out his cell phone and dialed.

"It's Jamal," he said. "Did you hear the news?"

Indeed, the imam had. It was on television screens and smart phones across Bahrain and beyond.

The towering smoke could be seen from every quarter of the island nation.

"You said we would know the sign when we saw it," Jamal said. "This is it, right? It *has* to be!"

"Calm down, Jamal," Imam Hussein Salmeen said. "*Maybe,*" added the imam, nodding as he thought. He sat at a sidewalk table at a cafe in downtown Manama, sipping tea. He had stopped there to gather his thoughts after seeing live coverage of the burning aircraft carrier in stall after stall of a bazaar.

The sun was setting.

The thick black smoke from the burning ship seemed to color the sky dark.

"You said, 'We will know the signal when we see it,'" Jamal insisted. "'A sign from Allah,' you said. If this isn't a sign from Allah, I don't know what is!"

"I said calm down!" said the Imam, his own voice rising. His phone vibrated. It was another incoming call, this one from Mahmoud Rashid, another of the young martyrs at his command.

"I have another call," the Imam said as he disconnected.

"As-salaam 'alaikum," said the Imam to Mahmoud in as soothing and fatherly a voice as he could muster.

"Imam!" said the boy. "This is it! The sign!"

"I'll call you back," said the imam, abruptly hanging up.

He sighed. *Damn it!*

They were eager to be good Islamic soldiers. They wanted to *act,* and right now. If they were martyred, and they each expected to be, their families would receive $150,000 U.S. dollars – the equivalent of more than 400,000 Bahraini dinars. That was nearly ten years' worth of annual salary for the average Bahraini, and most families of the young cell members didn't even rise to the level of 'average'.

Not even close.

Imam Hussein Salmeen's heart raced.

There was, in fact, no sign.

Those were *his* words to the group of young martyrs. His Iranian handler – whom he knew only as the "Commander" via an encrypted cellphone app – had never said there would be a sign. He had merely issued an emergency message, and it was on the very day of their scheduled operation.

It was a single word.

Abort.

Imam Salmeen had been incensed. He had worked his martyrs – or his team, as the Iranian called them – into a religious fervor. They were to a man, or rather to a *boy*, ready to die for the cause.

And then the carpet was yanked out from beneath them.

So he'd had to come up with *something.* The kids were too excitable. And the line "there will be a sign from the heavens, and there will be no doubt when it comes," flowed from his own lips in his comforting paternal voice.

It had placated the young martyrs.

Barely.

But when the Americans locked down their naval base the next day, and the aircraft carrier pulled into port just days later, the imam understood why their mission had been aborted.

The Americans were on to them, or at least on to the fact that something was planned.

The imam's phone buzzed again. It was Talal Abdulemam. At twenty-six, he was the oldest of the martyrs, and leader of the first team.

The mature one.

Which made him a true zealot.

Which scared the imam.

"It's time," said Talal. "Allah has shown us the sign. The Americans are wounded and distracted."

"Perhaps," said Hussein, in a voice as bored and stoic as he could manage.

Contact the Commander. As soon as fucking possible.

"We go tonight," said Talal.

Hussein sat up. *"We must hear from — "*

Talal hung up.

President Cynthia Belle sat quietly, eyes fixed on one of several large monitors in the Situation Room. She silently cursed herself for the sense of relief that she felt – relief that the unrest in Detroit and Michigan would finally disappear from the headlines.

But was it an attack or another goddamn Navy accident? The Navy had suffered a string of accidents over the past decade, including the sinking of a destroyer in the South China Sea after it collided with an oil tanker. Thankfully, most of the crew were rescued before she went down.

More recently, a supply replenishment ship had sideswiped an aircraft carrier.

After that incident, she had fired the Secretary of the Navy, naming Andrew Peck, Maryland's former governor, as the new secretary with orders to clean house.

And now this.

"Ma'am?" It was Admiral Erik Sorenson, Chairman of the Joint Chiefs of Staff. "Force protection?"

Cynthia closed her eyes momentarily and shook off the distraction. "Yes, of course," she said, "do it."

It was easily the fiftieth approval she'd given in the last twenty-five minutes. She'd been bombarded with logistical minutiae, movements of ships and rapid deployment troops to the region: upgrading the military's defense readiness condition, ordering federal law enforcement agencies to expedite and coordinate their investigations into the disaster, and the like, all of which required presidential approval.

The most pressing matter was the emergency deployment of the USS *Barack H. Obama* and USS *Doris Miller* aircraft carrier strike groups to the Gulf of Arabia as part of the force protection contingent, as well as the call up of military reserve forces.

"The Swiss president is on the phone, Madam President." It was Lynn Benjamin, the Secretary of State.

The United States and Iran hadn't had official diplomatic relations since the storming of the U.S. embassy in Tehran and the ensuing 444-day Hostage Crisis in 1979-81. Since then, Switzerland had acted as the protecting power (diplomatic liaison) for the U.S. That meant the Swiss Embassy in Tehran mediated contact between the U.S. and Iranian governments in Iran.

In Washington, Pakistan was the protecting power for Iran, and its embassy mediated contact between the U.S. and Iranian governments in the U.S. In fact, the Pakistani ambassador was currently waiting outside the Oval Office.

Given the long history of hostility between the United States and Iran, President Belle wanted no confusion. She wanted the Swiss and the Pakistanis to convey the same message to Iran: stand down while the United States and its allies conducted rescue operations in the Persian Gulf. Any provocation would be met with military force.

President Belle picked up the receiver, but before pressing the blinking light, she turned to the Secretary of Defense.

"Bernie," she said softly. "The Detroit situation. *End* it."

★ ★ ★

Imam Hussein Salmeen's face was pale, and his palms sweaty.

Answer the damn app!

The Commander was incommunicado, just as he said he would be before ordering them to abort their mission more than a week ago.

But they had to allow for contingencies! For unforeseen circumstances!

Like the young martyrs taking him at his word that there would be a sign.

What do I do?

He couldn't stand in the way of the martyrs. They would lose faith in him if he ordered them to stand down. *Again.*

Worse, he couldn't imagine how Talal would take it. Not well, he surmised.

Besides, Talal was right. The Americans were distracted. So was the Palace. What better time to strike than right now?

A muffled *boom* shook his table as if to emphasize the point. The American carrier was still burning offshore.

The imam sipped his tea.

The mosque was about two and a half miles from the pedestrian gate of the U.S. Navy complex in Manama. A busy construction equipment site occupied the space behind the mosque, so the concrete mixing truck and dump truck parked between the mosque and the equipment site didn't appear out of place.

Besides, the mosque itself was undergoing a renovation, so the trucks appeared to compliment the scaffolding attached to the mosque's facade.

The vehicles had been taken from a busy repair shop in Salmabad, where twenty-year-old Nabeel Haddad, one of Imam Salmeen Hussein's young martyrs, worked as a mechanic. The trucks were supposedly parked in the shop's sprawling storage yard while they ostensibly awaited parts. They wouldn't be noticed as missing until the parts arrived.

It had been over a month since the trucks – according to the paperwork – first went into the yard to await their ghost parts, and one of the construction companies had started to ask about their truck's status.

Yet another contingency the Iranians had neglected.

Sons of dogs. It's on them.

Both trucks were filled with explosives received by boat from Iran via the Arab Shipbuilding and Repair Yard, where other members of the imam's crew, like young Jamal Al-Dosari, worked.

To un-wire the trucks and remove the explosives would be dangerous. But leaving them parked behind the mosque was more dangerous still.

Yet *more* reasons to strike *right now.*

They had to act with or without the Iranians' orders.

3

Talal and his team followed the concrete mixer in a white work van through the streets of Manama to the Prince Khalifa Bin Salman Highway. Within a minute they were taking the exit to NSA 2, the port side of the American naval base.

It was just before 3:00 a.m., and ambulances were still lining up to enter the base and collect injured sailors from the *George W. Bush*. About twenty ambulances, emergency lights flashing, waited their turn to enter NSA 2's main gate, where soldiers meticulously inspected every vehicle.

Two soldiers slowly and methodically passed a mirror underneath the chassis of the lead ambulance, looking for hidden bombs.

The concrete mixer and van sped past the ambulances and pulled into an empty parking lot wedged between Prince Khalifa Bin Salman highway and the base service road, directly across from the NSA 2 main gate.

Talal exited the van and walked to the driver's side of the concrete mixer. Mahmoud Rashid sat behind the wheel, wide-eyed with excitement, but remorseful and petrified at the same time.

Talal stood up on the truck's step rail, leaned in the driver's window, and gave Mahmoud a tight hug.

"See you on the other side, brother," he said.

Tears flowed down Mahmoud's face.

For encouragement, Talal punched Mahmoud in the arm. "You are brave," he said. "God is counting on you."

Talal stepped back off the rail. He patted his heart and nodded. "Go," he said.

Mahmoud brushed tears from his face. He shifted the truck into drive, and it lurched forward.

He aimed for the exit gate and accelerated as fast as he could. He concentrated on shifting gears and calming his fear as he drove.

Dear God, please hear my prayer.

His goal was to smash through the gate and abandon the truck next to the first major building he found. The rest of the team, led by Talal and Khalid Husseini – who worked on the base as a laborer and knew its general layout – would sprint through the opening and join him.

At least, that's what Mahmoud had thought.

He got up to 55 miles per hour despite the short distance and crashed into the gate.

But the gate didn't budge. The truck cab pancaked on impact, killing Mahmoud instantly. The back wheels lifted off the ground as the truck stopped dead in its tracks, and then crashed back down.

There was a sound of tinkling glass – tiny pieces of windshield, cab windows and brake lights – and then silence.

Talal waited behind cover. The silence grew.

He came out from cover and gawked at the wreckage.

He was aghast. The plan had failed.

Then the truck exploded – an enormous, thunderous explosion.

The blast obliterated the gate guard shack, as well as the ambulances at the front of the line, and the shockwave smashed Talal and the work van like an invisible freight train. Talal disappeared amid the dust as the van careened backward into a nearby wall.

The remainder of the team staggered out of the smashed van, disoriented and coughing from the smoke and dust.

It was total carnage.

A yellow haze shrouded everything, punctuated by flaming debris, little fires spread far and wide.

The air was acerbic, pungent.

The concrete mixing truck was no longer recognizable. Only the blackened chassis remained, twisted and torn.

The first few ambulances in the front of the line were also unrecognizable. Behind them, several more were engulfed in flames.

The heat was intense, warping the air.

Isa al-Qurmezi, the youngest of the crew at sixteen, was the last to scramble out of the van, and he didn't stop.

He had glanced around at the chaos, his eyes as big as saucers, and booked.

"Where's he going?" asked Khalid, confused.

"Isa!" Nabeel called after him, but the terrified boy had faded into the yellow haze and disappeared into the darkness beyond.

The others gathered themselves. There were three of them now: Jamal Al-Dosari, Nabeel Haddad, and Khalid Husseini. Each was bruised and bleeding from tiny cuts and abrasions.

"Where's Mahdi?" asked Jamal, looking around.

Nabeel peered back into the van. Mahdi al-Fardan lay twisted in a heap, moaning. "Mahdi!" he called, then climbed back into the van, pulling him out, roughly, and laying him on the ground.

Nabeel recoiled. A bone stuck out from Mahdi's left shin.

"Oh *shit!*" exclaimed Nabeel.

Mahdi moaned again. Blood pooled beneath his broken leg.

"What do we *do?*" asked Jamal. *"Where is Talal?"*

"Over here!" shouted Khalid.

Talal – or what was left of him – lay at the base of a wall. His right arm was torn off and his left leg stuck out at a right angle from his hip and torso. His burnt and flayed face was turned toward the dust-filled sky. His clothes were practically blown off him, and what remained was in tatters.

"Allah akbar," Nabeel and Jamal said, almost in unison.

"What do we do about Mahdi?" Khalid asked out loud and to no one in particular.

Nabeel sighed. "We have to leave him. We still have a mission."

Jamal threw his free hand up to shield his face from the flames and smoke as he approached the gate. It was still intact, but parts of it were broken and twisted, especially where the truck had exploded. The steel fence sagged over the crater left by the blast, allowing the three remaining team members to squeeze through the gaps in the steel fence.

Jamal gingerly turned sideways and slipped through, carefully stepping over and ducking under twisted steel bars.

Khalid led the way, and he and Nabeel were already through the gate as Jamal slipped between the twisted steel bars. Khalid and Nabeel started shooting their rifles wildly as they sprinted onto the base.

Jack-hammer machine gun fire kicked up dust at Khalid's feet, who zigged left, then right, before falling in a hail of bullets.

"Khalid!" yelled Jamal as he dove to the ground.

Nabeel, too, fell to the ground amidst the kicking up of dust from invisible bullets.

He lay face down. He didn't move at first.

"Help me, Jamal," Nabeel pleaded, his voice barely audible over the din of roaring fires and blaring alarms.

Nabeel writhed slightly and a cloud of dust kicked up around him.

When the dust settled, Nabeel lay sprawled on his back, his face turned towards Jamal.

"Nabeel?" Jamal asked, his eyes large.

Nabeel didn't respond. Flames danced in his open eyes.

Jamal sensed movement in the darkness and scrambled to his feet. He was inside the gate but still hidden by smoke. Slipping back through the twisted metal gate, he fled into the night.

Across town, Imam Hussein Salmeen's Team 2 met with better success. Within seconds of the explosion at the NSA 2 gate, Team 2's explosives-laden dump truck crashed the southside gate of the walled Al-Qudaibiya Palace, home of the House of Khalifa, the ruling family of Bahrain since 1766.

The thunderous explosion destroyed the gate, and the team –following in a work van – waited far enough behind not to be demolished in the explosion's shock wave.

The six-man assault team stormed through the openings in the gate left by the truck bomb and entered the compound.

A series of barracks housing soldiers of the Royal Guard was situated to the left of the breach amid rows of palm trees. The explosion threw the soldiers out of their bunks. Scrambling for their weapons, they began spilling outside in various stages of dress.

In the confusion, the assault team sprinted right past the barracks and straight for the sprawling palace itself. The team split in half, with three shooters heading to the front of the palace, and three shooters wrapping around the back.

Hand grenades blew doors open on both sides, and the teams entered the Al-Qudaibiya Palace, shooting anyone they encountered.

". . . I promise you tonight that we *will* get to the bottom of what happened aboard the *George W. Bush*. We will leave no stone unturned.

If it was a terrorist attack, we will respond with furious justice. And if we determine that the attack was state-sponsored or state-supported, we will not shy away from our awesome responsibility to defend this great nation.

I must be clear that as of this moment we have no evidence of an attack. This could very well be a tragic accident. Navy ships are dangerous places, full of flammable chemicals and fuels, and explosive ordinances. That accidents are such rare occurrences is a testament to the professionalism and training of our young sailors.

That said, given the long history of antagonisms by the government of Iran against our interests and the interests of our allies in the region, earlier today I conveyed to the leadership of Iran via the Swiss Embassy in Tehran and the Pakistani Ambassador here in Washington that while the United States is grateful for their formal offer to contribute to rescue efforts, Iran must not interfere in our rescue operations. I want to be crystal clear, and so I am repeating that message here tonight. Further, I am putting the leadership of Iran on notice. Any attack by organizations sponsored by Iran on American or allied interests in the Persian Gulf or beyond will be considered an attack by Iran on the United States of America."

President Cynthia Belle paused for effect, before starting again.

"I want to assure all Americans that we are doing everything in our power to rescue sailors and soldiers aboard the *George W. Bush.* We offer our heartfelt gratitude to our allies Bahrain, Saudi Arabia, and Qatar for their assistance.

Please join me in a moment of prayerful silence for our young men and women in harm's way."

The President bowed her head and closed her eyes. After a long and uncomfortable minute, she opened her eyes and looked directly into the camera.

"God bless our sailors and soldiers, and God bless the United States of America."

The lighting in the Oval Office dimmed as camera lights switched off. President Belle pushed herself away from the Resolute Desk and stood.

"Nicely done," said Madelyn Kumar, the White House Press Secretary. "You struck the right tone. Somber, decisive, and to the point."

"Eighteen minutes and forty-three seconds," Maddie continued. "Not too long and not too short."

"Good," sighed the President, noticing activity in the office doorway. It was Oscar Schwartz, her National Security Advisor, along with some military brass.

"We have a situation," Oscar said in a low voice.

"Jesus, Oscar, what now?"

"What am I looking at?" asked the President.

A string of ambulances, engulfed in flames, filled the television screens along the walls of the Situation Room.

"A car bomb at the front gate of our base in Bahrain," Oscar said.

"No one has claimed responsibility yet," added Vice Admiral Baltzer Oberkirsch, "but we suspect the Islamic Front of Bahrain."

"In the middle of our rescue operation?" asked the President, but it was a rhetorical question.

The President took her seat at the head of the table. "And Iran funds and directs the Islamic Front of Bahrain?"

"Yes, ma'am," said the admiral.

The President sighed deeply and spread her palms on the table.

"You mean to tell me that after warning Iran not to interfere in our rescue mission or cause some other provocation, they directed an attack on our base in Bahrain just a few hours later – *while I was delivering an address to the country?*"

The president's eyes drifted back to the television screens. The news had cut to a reporter outside the Al-Qudaibiya Palace in Manama. Sporadic gun fire could be heard along with intermittent booms that echoed through the night.

4

Rear Admiral Hashemi Ghavam wasn't home even ten minutes before his cell phone vibrated.

It was Rear Admiral Hossein Mousavi, his counterpart as Commander of the Islamic Republican Guard Corps Navy.

"Hash," Mousavi said, "turn on the news."

Hash turned on the television to Al Jazeerah, where he saw the mushroom cloud atop the American aircraft carrier off Bahrain.

The *George W. Bush.*

"What the . . ." he said, his voice trailing off.

"What's happening, dear?" asked his wife as she mixed ingredients on the stove.

Nazanin turned up the heat on the stove and pulled lamb kebabs from the oven. She added them to the stew simmering on the stovetop, and then walked to the living room.

Hash was gone.

Nazanin looked at the television, which Hash had left on. She covered her mouth with dread as she watched the breaking news.

Hash called everyone he could think of on his short drive back to base: his deputy commander of the Southern Forward Naval Headquarters at Bandar Abbas, the base commanding officer, the commanding officer of any ship or squadron he had committed to memory. Once in his office, he called more and ordered his subordinates to track down still others.

The weekend be damned. He wanted all hands on deck. As far as he knew, Iran and the United States were at war.

Or were about to be at any moment.

It had already been a busy week with the *George W. Bush* carrier strike group prowling the Persian Gulf. His missile boats and patrol aircraft, as well as the Islamic Revolutionary Guard Corps (IRGC) Navy's fast attack boats, harassed and probed each American warship as they entered the Gulf through the Strait of Hormuz.

Scores of them would dart straight toward a U.S. ship and then turn away. Another squadron would soon follow and get even closer before turning away. They turned attack radars on and off. They timed each encounter to test how long the Americans responded on the radio, what kinds of evasive maneuvers they made, and under what circumstances the Americans threatened a shot across the bow.

They monitored how American ships and aircraft communicated and coordinated with each other.

Each encounter was recorded by video, and all radar and radio communications were also recorded, for later analysis. The Americans, no doubt, did the same.

The operations persisted day and night, day after day.

Obviously, something had gone horribly wrong.

Hash glanced back at the news on his office's flat-screen television.

Through too many phone calls to count, Hash had ordered every Iranian Navy ship and boat back to port with all haste. He wanted every vessel, missile, drone, sea mine, even bullet, accounted for.

His office phone rang. It was Rear Admiral Amir Naqdi, Commander of the Navy. He worked directly under the Commander of the General Staff of the Armed Forces in Tehran, just beneath the Defense Minister who, in turn, worked directly under the Supreme Leader.

"Good, good," Amir said after Hash briefed him on the status of naval assets at Bandar Abbas and Chabahar, his two main Navy bases.

"Hash, get on a plane to Tehran. I need you. We're having an emergency meeting with all commanders. In the meantime," he added, "make sure your command is prepared to assist the Americans and Bahrainis. The Foreign Secretary is reaching out to the Swiss to offer our help."

The 50-passenger twin-engine turboprop Fokker F27 Friendship aircraft took just under two hours to fly from the naval air station at Bandar Abbas to the Imam Khomeini International Airport in western Tehran. In addition to its ten crew members, the Navy Fokker F27 carried just three passengers, each a VIP: Rear Admiral Hashemi Ghavam and two aides.

It was another 30 minutes by armored SUV to the House of Leadership campus in central Tehran, even with a police escort.

The armored car and police escort slowed as they passed the soaring Azadi Tower and Square, just outside the airport, which served as a western gate of sorts into the sprawling city.

It was always a treat to see the iconic, beautiful showcase of Persian architecture. Lit up at night, like now, and in various colors, it was a sight to behold.

Hash stared at the Azadi Tower with sorrow. The entourage had slowed as it navigated past the Azadi Tower because of the number of people gathering in the square.

Crowds of people, whole families, were celebrating – *celebrating!* – the burning of the American ship in the Persian Gulf.

They clapped their hands and danced, and made the V-sign for victory.

There were more than 4,000 sailors aboard a *Ford*-class aircraft carrier like the *George W. Bush,* Hash knew. Further, a shipboard fire was the worst nightmare of every sailor anywhere in the world.

Images of massive crowds in Iran and across the Muslim world celebrating the *Bush* disaster would fill Americans and the West with rage.

They don't know what they are celebrating, Hash thought.

If they only knew what was coming.

The meeting went better than Hash expected.

Everyone had their knives out.

Major General Hossein Mousavi, Commander-in-Chief of the Army, was the first to draw blood. No sooner had the door clicked shut when he turned to General Mohammad Yaghani, Commander-in-Chief of the Islamic Revolutionary Guard Corps, and demanded, in his soft, calm way, that Yaghani explain "exactly what the *fuck* you've done."

Yaghani was stoic, but his face turned red. "Nobody knows what happened," he offered.

"We know that the Army and Air Force did not attack the Americans," said Mousavi. "Navy?" he asked, and looked to Hash's boss, Rear Admiral Amir Naqdi, Commander of the Navy.

"All weapons systems and assets are accounted for," Amir said, glancing over at Hash. "I gave no orders of any kind to attack the Americans."

"There, you see?" said Mousavi. "We know what *didn't* happen. We know that the regular armed forces didn't attack the Americans."

"Can the IRGC say the same thing?" asked Mousavi.

Yaghani looked at Mousavi with scorn. "What do you take us for? *Cowboys?"*

As a matter of fact.

"Enough," said Major General Gholam Abassi, Commander of the General Staff of the Armed Forces. The entire military – both the "regular" military, and the uniformed but irregular IRGC and its branches – were under his leadership.

"There was no direct attack by Iran on the Americans," Gholam said. "We know this because *I* did not give any such order, and neither did His Excellency," giving Mousavi a hard look.

"What we need to know is if this was some kind of covert operation by proxy, or a fateful accident by the Americans."

Looking at Yaghani, he added, "Mohammed, His Excellency wants a full accounting. Anything that *hints* of the Islamic Republic must be cleaned up."

Nothing unsubtle about that, Hash thought. Cloak-and-dagger stuff. Emphasis on the dagger.

The meeting turned to military readiness and the geography of military units. Eventually, Hash briefed the room about the distribution of regular Navy assets at Bandar Abbas in the Strait of Hormuz, and at Chabahar in the Gulf of Oman.

"I've ordered four of our *Kilo-class* submarines and five of our *Moudge*-class frigates out of the Persian Gulf. They are to seek shelter in ports and Navy bases in Pakistan," Hash reported. "We want to convey to the Americans that we are withdrawing assets from the Strait of Hormuz and toning down perceived threats to their ships. Frankly, I want to put our most capable warships out of range of twitchy American Navy captains traversing the Strait."

"Why?" asked Mousavi, the Army chief. "Doesn't that just project weakness?"

"Maybe," said Hash with a shrug. "Let them think we're weak."

Who cares? Fucking moron.

"How many subs and frigates remain in the Strait?" asked the Navy chief.

"One each," Hash said. "Their continued presence allows us to maintain a potent capability."

Hash paused and surveyed the room. *God I could use some sleep.*

Nearly everyone was a political appointee. Only the actual commanders of military units, regular or IRGC, were not.

No one asked any questions. In fact, they looked bored.

Hash wasn't sure the high-level appointees understood the gravity of the situation.

In fact, he was certain they *didn't.*

It was after midnight when the meeting mercifully ended. Hash was booked at the Ferdowsi Grand Hotel, a mile east of the House of Leadership. Once there, he struggled to fall asleep.

In fact, he was still awake when there was a knock on his door at 4:00 a.m. It was one of his aides.

More breaking news: a terrorist attack at the front gate of the United States Naval Base in Manama. An apparent car bomb. And a possible attack on the Al Qudaibiya Palace in Manama.

Brilliant.

There would be no sleep for Hash.

Instead, he stretched out in a chair next to a window that overlooked the lighted and empty street below, letting his mind wander as he stared out the window.

War is coming.

He could feel it in his bones.

Another morning, another meeting.

Sleep. It had been too long. Too long.

This meeting was bigger than the last one. It was full of ministers and staff members from several government ministries: Foreign Affairs, Intelligence, Defense and Armed Forces Logistics, even the Ministry of Culture and Islamic Guidance. Other staff were from the Office of the Supreme Leader, and still others from the Islamic Consultative Assembly, Iran's Parliament.

With the exception of Defense, most of the senior ministers were mullahs and imams.

These were the principals of government.

Preachers, the lot of them.

With the overnight attack on the American Navy base in Bahrain, plus the American President's belligerent speech, the principals had worked themselves into a frenzy.

They *celebrated* the news of the *George W. Bush* disaster, and of the terrorist attacks on the American naval base and Bahrain's Palace. They talked of victory if war came.

"We will smash the Great Satan."

"We will bring the Great Beast to its knees."

"The sands and wadis of the whole of West Asia will run red with their blood."

The hyperbole was nauseating.

The disconnect with reality was truly frightening.

These bastards will be the end of us.

They spoke as if trying to out-do each other in currying favor with the staff of the Supreme Leader, who hadn't bothered to attend either meeting.

Doesn't he know that the Islamic Republic faces the greatest threat to its existence since the Revolution?

Not only was the existence of the Islamic Republic at stake, but so was the existence of Iran itself.

Sleep . . .

The relatively low-level, on-the-ground military commanders like him sat quietly while the others worked each other into a froth of anti-American religious delirium.

God, it's so hot in here.

Hash eyed the clock on the wall. He eyed the door. He fidgeted.

The meeting dragged on. Hash sweated profusely. He had work to do.

"If the Americans are stupid enough to strike, we'll hit back like a sledgehammer."

Heads nodded emphatically.

They're all insane.

5

Hash made it a point – the central point, in fact – to visit his daughters whenever he was back in Tehran. As Commander of the Southern Forward Naval Headquarters, he found himself in Tehran more than ever before, even though the headquarters were in Bandar Abbas, some 650 miles to the south.

Azadeh, twenty-four, was his youngest daughter, and lived near the University of Tehran, where she studied to be a pharmacist.

He took the Tehran Metro subway to Ab-o-Atash (Water and Fire) Park in northern Tehran to meet Azadeh at the western entrance to Tabiat Bridge.

Tabiat Bridge was a flowing sculpture of futuristic steel-cable. A pedestrian-only bridge, it had won multiple global architectural awards. It spanned the tree-lined Modarres Expressway and ravine, and linked Ab-o-Atash Park with Taleghani Forest Park on either side of the ravine.

The bridge was designed to be a park in its own right, with two decks, lots of benches that overlooked the Modarres Expressway and ravine below, and unhindered views of the snow-covered Alborz Mountains to the north. The bridge was tree-like in its design, with steel cables like roots, and plants and trees adorning the entirety of its length. It even hosted ice cream parlors and food courts.

Tabiat Bridge had become one of Tehran's biggest attractions since its construction in 2014. People and families congregated there at all hours of the day and into the night.

Hash stood astride the lighthouse at the center of Ab-o-Atash Park. A group of teenage boys did tricks on skateboards, leaping onto handrails and jumping off steps. Their tricks were athletic and gravity-defying, but whenever one fell, it was on pure concrete, and Hash winced.

He was glad he had daughters.

Hash saw Azadeh walking to the stairs from the direction of the metro station, the same way he had come. She hadn't seen him yet, and Hash watched her.

She was a beautiful young woman. She was elegantly dressed and walked with the confidence of an admiral's daughter.

Hash smiled, but with a wisp of sadness. His little girl was all grown up.

Her face immediately brightened when she spotted him.

They embraced, and then walked slowly to the Tabiat Bridge. He asked how her studies were going, and she asked about his job in Bandar Abbas. Hash bought ice cream for the two of them and they took a bench in the center of the bridge.

It was a beautiful, sunny afternoon. The ravine below was lush, and the Alborz Mountains were purple with snow on top, and they appeared much closer than they were in the crisp, clean air.

Azadeh cut to the chase. "You look tired," she said.

Sleep.

Before Hash could answer, Azadeh continued. "It's awful – what's happened to that American ship. Is that why you look so tired?"

"It's been busy," he said. "Do I really look that bad?"

Azadeh looked worried for him. "What's going to happen?"

"I don't know," said Hash, truthfully.

Despite the topic, Azadeh was radiant. Hash tilted his head and looked askance at her.

"What?" she asked, shyly.

"What's his name?"

Azadeh blushed slightly. There was no point in denying it. Her father knew her too well.

"Zana," said Azadeh. "He's studying to be a doctor."

"Hmmm, a *doctor*," said Hash, his right eyebrow raised. "I'd like to meet this . . . *doctor*." He smiled.

"How's Mom?"

"Nice pivot," Hash said. "She's good. You should call her more. How's university life?"

Hash liked hearing about Azadeh's life. The gossip about her professors and classmates, which classes she liked, what she and her friends did after class. She told him about childhood friends from the old neighborhood with whom she stayed in touch. He vaguely remembered some of their names.

"I am so proud of you," Hash said in the middle of one of her updates.

Azadeh beamed at her father's adulation. She couldn't help it, nor hide it.

They finished their ice cream.

Hash had another appointment to keep.

"Please be careful, Dad," Azadeh said, embracing him. She held him tight for a lingering moment.

She turned and walked away, and Hash watched her until she disappeared into the crowd.

Hash took the subway to Shoush station, and then made his way to the Darvazeh Ghar neighborhood of Tehran, just south of the city's sprawling Grand Bazaar.

Tehran was a study in contrasts between rich and poor, and like most cities, the division was geographical. The northern part of the city was affluent and cosmopolitan. The southern neighborhoods were poor and religiously conservative. This was the home base of Iran's ultraconservative government.

Paradoxically, the impoverished but religious southern neighborhoods were also home to many of the vices that plagued such neighborhoods anywhere in the world: crime, drugs, alcohol, prostitution.

Even in a semi-theocracy like Iran.

It had been three years since Hash first wandered into Darvazeh Ghar. At the time, he was plagued by insomnia, and the medicines he had managed to secure through his wife's dentist/cousin no longer did the trick. He'd become desperate.

Darvazeh Ghar was a series of densely-packed residential casbahs hemmed in behind industrial compounds, junk yards and repair garages. Hash had meandered through the maze-like streets in a kind of daze, not certain why he was there. After some time, he had rounded a corner and was walking past a courtyard when he stopped.

At the entrance to the courtyard, a young man sat on a stool behind a podium, like a waiter. The young man appeared to be in his twenties, though he could've been in his late teens. He was boyish, but seemed older than his years.

There was something off about him. Some kind of disability, Hash had thought. He couldn't tell if it was physical or cognitive, but it was there.

The kid looked to his left into the courtyard and held his gaze for a moment, then looked back to Hash, but he avoided eye contact.

Hash looked into the courtyard. An older woman was sweeping the floor.

A cleaning lady. Is that what she was?

Hash looked back at the young man. He was peering at the ground, but he held a hand out, keeping it below the height of the podium.

Hash pulled out a wad of cash in a clip and the boy quickly seized it. Then he nodded for Hash to enter the courtyard.

Now the woman held out her arm, bowing slightly and avoiding eye contact. She was directing him to one of three alleyways that opened into the courtyard.

Every fiber of Hash's being screamed for him to stop, turn around, and walk away. But his feet shuffled forward anyway.

He walked past the woman and into the alley, and slowly followed its meandering path.

He scanned the high stone walls lining the alleyway. They cast the length of the alley in shadows. The hairs on his arms tingled as though with static electricity. He felt as if he were being watched.

These walls have eyes, he thought. *Lots of eyes.*

A hard-looking woman sat in a windowsill above the street, looking passively down at Hash.

Hash held her gaze until he passed beneath.

A short, hobbled man stood in the alleyway ahead. He, too, refrained from making eye contact. He stood at the entrance of another alley and held open curtains for Hash to enter.

Hash did so, and the man closed the curtains behind him and was gone.

In front of Hash was a short alley with a dead end. Two pairs of stairways led down into basement entrances on each side of the alleyway.

One of their doors was open, and Hash walked to that stairwell. He descended the stairs and entered a long dark corridor.

His eyes slowly adjusted to the darkness. The wooden floor creaked as he walked.

The woman who had swept the floor in the courtyard waved him forward and gestured to a room.

Hash entered through a curtain of beads.

The room was surprisingly posh.

A Persian rug adorned the floor. Otherwise, the room was empty, except for a large Turkish couch against one wall. Beside one arm of the couch was a night stand with an ornate hookah pipe. The midnight oil was already lit. Beside it was cash – change from the clip he had handed off to the young man on the bar stool.

Hash removed his jacket and shoes and climbed onto the wide couch as if he were in his own living room.

He examined the hookah pipe. He sniffed it, held it out, and looked it over.

He took the end of the hose and placed it between his lips. He closed his eyes and pulled, inhaling the bitter but flowery substance.

Chandoo. Chinese Tobacco. Joy Plant. Midnight Oil.

Pure-grade Afghan opium.

Iran was swimming in it.

Nothing had happened at first. But Hash leaned back on the couch and kept his eyes closed.

He didn't remember when it came, but he remembered *how* it came.

Sleep.

He hadn't dozed off. And it, *sleep*, hadn't come gradually.

It had arrived on a chariot as white as snow.

Four Arabian chargers galloped midair amid a fluffy white cloud the length of the horses and chariot.

In the chariot were four sirens with silky black hair that flowed like a river. They were nude. Their skin was olive-toned and smooth as a baby's.

Sleep, my love, the sirens cooed, beckoning him.

Hash climbed in, purposeful but shy. For some reason, he remembered, there were soccer balls in the chariot, and Hash had to step over them and roll them away as he climbed in.

Sleep, my love, the sirens sang in unison.

That was the last thing Hash remembered from that first visit.

It seemed so long ago.

Now he was a semi-regular. Four or five times a year. Sometimes more.

And here he was again, the well-dressed man with a salt-and-pepper mustache and matching, if balding, hair who owned a commanding disposition that marked him as someone not to be trifled with.

Maybe a cop. And, if so, a high-ranking one. Someone with authority, to be sure.

The young man at the podium in the courtyard tensed as the salt-and-pepper man emerged out of the bustle of the street. It was a different youth this time, a teenager, but someone who already projected a weaselly vibe of deceitfulness. The boy's eyes looked to the woman who swept the floor, the same woman as always. She barely glanced at Hash.

Yesterday's news.

The boy stepped away from the podium to allow Hash through, but studied him out of curiosity.

The salt-and-pepper man's eyes were mournful and glassy with the fever of the pull. He had seen a hard face at first glance, but now it held an expression of longing, a haggard longing that the boy instantly recognized. It was a look shared by the faces of so many patrons.

Indeed.

Hash settled in and took to the ornate pipe with urgent expectation.

Sleep.

He leaned back in the sofa. After a while, he took another pull on the pipe, and as the chandoo took hold, he stared blankly at the wall. Images played on it like a movie screen.

Ships ablaze and half sunk while still moored to their pilings. Young sailors screamed in their berths down below.

"Mind your ship!" a gruff voice commanded.

The dead bodies of young sailors floated amid burning debris in waters thick with oil and gasoline.

Poor Americans.

But they weren't Americans. They were young Iranian conscripts, just out of high school.

Iranian sailors.

His sailors.

"Mind your ship!"

It was a common refrain that Hash often used in his directives to ship captains and low-ranking sailors alike.

Mind your ship, and your ship will mind you.

Explosions erupted left and right, the roar of invisible jets and missiles overhead in the blackness of the night sky.

The scenes morphed as Hash's mind drifted.

Now he saw black American bombers gathering like vultures. At Al Udeid in Qatar; on Diego Garcia and Guam. Skull-faced troops armed with scythes, an army led by Death himself gathered in Qatar, Bahrain, Saudi Arabia, and Kuwait. Thousands at first, in what the Americans called "force protection." Then tens of thousands, even hundreds of thousands, as smiling American diplomats flattered and cajoled their allies and the countries that bordered Iran into building an impossibly formidable "coalition," another favorite word of the Americans – to legitimize the whole enterprise, you see.

The expectation was a killer in its own right. The Americans had time on their side. Maybe they wouldn't come, after all.

Another flurry of diplomacy and a sigh of relief.

You let your guard down.

And then they came, like hunters in the night, the air strikes, relentless and uncompromising.

Stealth bombers and cruise missiles.

Not a city spared.

Death from above.

Azadeh. Nazanin. Fatameh.

Unless . . .

A chasm opened on the floor.

Hash looked down. The chasm was dark and deep.

Deny . . .

Was that a voice? A muffled voice or voices?

Bluish sparkly crystals reflected off . . . *wings?* No. *Hair?*

Female voices, humming a pop song in Farsi. But there was a different voice, underneath, muffled.

. . . the . . .

Sirens! The humming voices. They were the voices of the sirens from the chariot, the chariot from long ago, beckoning him . . .

Sleep, my love . . .

. . . space.

The other, underlying, muffled voice was male and familiar somehow.

"Deny the space!" the voice shouted.

The voice was his own.

The sofa pitched forward and Hash fell in.

Imam Hussein Salmeen walked briskly through the narrow streets and alleyways of Manama Souq, the city's main bazaar, on the way to the mosque.

Manama Souq was eerily devoid of the daily throngs of people who walked its narrow corridors in search of everything from electronics and T-shirts to jewelry and shishka pipes. Those few who *were* on the streets were standing around stalls whose merchants had flat-screen television sets behind the counters to catch a glimpse of the latest news.

After spotting a couple of uniformed Public Safety officers, Hussein ducked into a stall that sold Persian carpets, joining a small cluster of people huddled around a television set.

News reporters spoke rapidly in Arabic as the TV screens showed video of smoke pouring from the Al Qudaibiya Palace spliced with still images of the bodies of the terrorists who were cut down overnight at various locations inside the palace.

All night long, the *pop-pop-pop* of small arms fire punctuated by explosions had echoed throughout the city from the palace. Meanwhile, the *George W. Bush* had burned through the night and small munitions still cooked off on occasion, adding to the cacophony of war.

The massive aircraft carrier was no longer in the cove. American and Saudi tug boats had worked through the night to tow it farther from the shore, even as it continued to burn.

Nevertheless, the pungent stench of burning fuel, munitions, wiring, plastics, even metal, still permeated the air.

'*Bahrain Under Attack*' read a continuous ticker headline at the bottom of the screen. *Bahrain Under Attack . . . Terrorists Storm Al Qudaibiya Palace . . . Car Bomb at U.S. Navy Facility . . . Bahrain Under Attack . . . GW Bush Rescue Operations Continuing . . . Thousands Feared Dead . . .*

The few people walking in the bazaar or huddled around television sets were subdued.

Hussein discreetly turned his head, looking down, but raised his head just enough to get a glimpse of the alleyway. The police officers weren't there and must have passed by. Still, he turned back to the television to wait a bit longer.

King Isa Al Khalifa would be holding a press conference later in the afternoon, headlines promised.

So far, there had been no claim of responsibility for the attacks, but as usual, pundits didn't hesitate to speculate. "All fingers point to Iran," said a prominent Middle East security expert at King Abdul Azziz University in Saudi Arabia.

Imam Hussein stepped away from the stall and continued to the mosque. His heart pounded in his chest.

As he approached a main road, he could see the minarets of his mosque a block away.

Nothing seemed out of the ordinary.

Everything seemed out of the ordinary.

But no police. No obvious surveillance.

Would I even know surveillance if I saw it?

Hussein reached the mosque and slipped into the lobby.

"*Imam!*"

Hussein nearly jumped out of his skin. His breath caught in his throat.

It was young Jamal.

"*Really* Jamal!" exclaimed the imam. "Don't *do* that – you nearly gave me a h-heart attack," he said, breathing heavily.

"Wait, what are you doing here?"

Jamal was amped up. He paced back and forth and his eyes darted about. His face was blackened with soot, his arms slick with sweat and soot, his T-shirt dirty and torn.

"They're all *dead,* Imam," Jamal said. "What do I *do?"* Tears streamed down his face, cutting through the soot, but he wasn't crying. It was adrenaline.

"Come," Hussein said, ushering Jamal into his office. "Let me get you tea; then tell me what happened."

Jamal spoke fast, *too* fast. He jumped around in his narrative, but Hussein got the gist of it. The mission had been a total clusterfuck.

"What of Madhi?" asked Hussein. "You said everyone was dead, but then you said Mahdi was injured."

"I don't know," Jamal said.

"It's important, Jamal. *Think.* Was he dead when you left?"

"I think so, I don't know. If you saw him," Jamal said, his voice trailing off. "Otherwise . . ." Jamal's eyes widened. "The Americans! The Americans must have him!"

Now it was Imam Hussein who jumped to his feet and paced the room. "No, no, *no!"* he said. He bundled a hand into a fist and punched the open palm of the other.

He shook his head. "You were supposed to be *martyred, all* of you!" snapped the Imam.

"What do we *do?"*

"I'm sorry," said the imam, still pacing. He stopped and put a hand on Jamal's shoulder. "I'm sorry," he said again. "We will figure it out. Everything will be alright."

Would it be? Of course not.

"Go home, and get yourself cleaned up. I'll make some inquiries."

Daylight brought the extent of the disaster into sharper focus. At least two apartment buildings in the Al Hidd district had collapsed as a result of the explosions aboard the *George W. Bush,* and another appeared to be leaning.

Emergency equipment had arrived, but it was difficult to get them into place. Hundreds of people climbed over piles of debris that had been the apartment buildings, lifting slabs and pieces of broken concrete and passing them down a line of volunteers in a desperate attempt to reach survivors.

These were family members. Friends.

Across town, smoke billowed from windows in two wings of the Al Qudaibiya Palace, and also from the main gate of the U.S. Navy base.

The *George W. Bush* still burned, some sixteen hours after the initial explosions. But it was no longer in the cove. Overnight, Bahraini, Saudi, and Qatari tug boats had attached long sturdy ropes and chains to the still-burning carrier and slowly towed the ship out of the Khawr al Qulay'ah inlet.

It was a dangerous undertaking, especially in the dark, and slow going. Explosions had still occasionally wracked the supercarrier, and it listed heavily.

American Navy Explosive Ordnance Demolition (EOD) and diver teams had, at one point during the night, successfully penetrated the ship toward the bow, but their stay was short.

The heat was unbearable.

The entire ship had become an oven and no one could have survived for long.

It was so hot, in fact, that the superstructure of the *George W. Bush* was melting.

The entire ship had a glowing reddish tint to it.

Ocean water boiled at the ship's aft.

By midmorning, the carrier was over the horizon and was no longer visible. At almost 20 miles out, the ship had begun to list further, and its aft sank deeper into the water, causing too much drag for the tugboats. They were forced to cut their lines and steam away as fast as they could.

It was only a matter of time before sea water reached the reactor. And when it did . . .

The *BOOM,* muffled only by distance, washed over Bahrain and northern Qatar, rattling more buildings and nerves.

Moments later, the unmistakable mushroom cloud of a massive explosion rose over the horizon and lingered for a time until the trade winds methodically tore it apart.

It was mid-afternoon, and the USS *George W. Bush* – what was left of it – slipped beneath the waves of the Persian Gulf.

In Detroit, a longstanding policy of the regional electric company, Great Lakes Energy Enterprises, or GLEE, of shutting off electricity to residents behind in their monthly payments, had run smack against a particularly brutal winter, even for Detroit standards. With their power turned off, many of Detroit's poorer residents began using hazardous fire-causing portable gas and kerosene heaters to stay warm.

In previous years, the average number of deaths by fire in Detroit was forty-five to fifty, a tragically high number. This year, the number of fire-related deaths had surpassed *400* by mid-February.

When a popular retired teacher and her family had succumbed, a couple of weeks ago, to a house fire after their power was cut off, tens of thousands of Detroiters took to the streets in protest.

Detroit's police department – decimated by decades of budget cuts and layoffs – was overwhelmed. In an effort to protect the city's core businesses and infrastructure, the police had hunkered down in the central business district, dubbed Fortress Detroit, while the rest of the sprawling city descended into chaos.

Law enforcement agencies from across the state, including the Michigan National Guard, were reallocated to Detroit to help quell the unrest.

Various rightwing militia groups stepped into the void and took control of entire counties as the state's authority all but collapsed.

A refugee crisis ensued in neighboring Windsor, Ontario, as Americans fled across the Ambassador Bridge to Canada.

President Cynthia Belle had ordered active-duty troops from the 10th Mountain Division, based at Fort Drum in Upstate New York, into Detroit. They faced unexpected resistance by warring street gangs seeking to expand their territories while the police were holed up in downtown.

It was all quite embarrassing, and America's standing in the world had taken another hit.

Then the *George W. Bush* exploded in the Persian Gulf.

The "Detroit Situation," as President Belle called it, had to end. Events in the Middle East now required her full attention. War was imminent.

She ordered the 10th Mountain Division to take the battle to the gangs in central Detroit. General McIntyre warned that it would require urban house-to-house fighting.

So be it.

The 82nd Airborne, meanwhile, would deal with the militias.

6

President Belle took a seat in the cramped Situation Room. She practically lived there now, it seemed, along with her entire national security staff.

"Ma'am, the *George W. Bush* has sunk." It was Vice Admiral Baltzer Oberkirsch of the Chief of Naval Operations office.

"I can see that," said the President, nodding to the television monitors. "Where do we stand on casualties?"

"We're at just over 900 survivors accounted for, most of them injured in some way, many with serious burns and other injuries. Over a hundred are in critical condition. More than 700 confirmed dead so far, and another 2,500 sailors are missing."

"Jesus," said George Wartmann, the Vice President, looking paler than usual.

Because of his tall, lanky build and gaunt face, Wartmann was widely referred to as Daddy Longlegs. The nickname also alluded to Wartmann's long reach in government. He had served for twenty years as a United States Senator from Ohio before serving as Secretary of State and then Secretary of Defense.

"Are they presumed . . .," asked Longlegs, his voice trailing off.

"Yes, sir," said Oberkirsch.

"So we're looking at over 3,000 *dead?"* asked the Vice President.

"It is the single worst disaster for the United States Navy in history," said Admiral Erik Sorenson, the Chairman of the Joint Chiefs of Staff. "A thousand more casualties than Pearl Harbor."

Bernice Hamandawana sat in the lobby outside the Trauma Center of the Wayne State University affiliated Detroit Medical Center hospital. At her side was Walter Clay, dreadlocked and wearing his trademark sports coat with blue jeans, looking every bit the Physics professor he was studying to be.

The Army had cut them loose after twenty-four hours of hell. Bernice and Walter didn't know it, but there was a huge and growing outcry about their detention. Daniel Rush, Bernice's wunderkind cameraman, captured the whole thing live – including his own near death. The footage had saturated cable news worldwide and briefly stolen headlines from the *Bush* disaster.

Bernice was a twenty-four-year-old graduate student in journalism at Wayne State University and a freelance reporter for *Motown Mirror*. Daniel, a twenty-year-old undergraduate studying journalism and photography, was her cameraman. She had dragged him right into the heart of a neighborhood where three black teenagers were gunned down by National Guard troops, to conduct interviews with friends, neighbors and family members of the fallen teens – in the middle of a days-long riot. A pale, shaggy-haired, slightly-built white kid, Danny had been apprehensive. The all-black neighborhood had been seething.

But Bernice had scolded him. "If you're scared, major in accounting."

Danny was now fighting for his life.

It was her fault.

Walter sensed her guilty feelings and put an arm around her.

She immediately dissolved into a sob and buried her face in his shoulder.

"He's a brave kid," Walter soothed. "He'll pull through."

On the lobby television, local news cut in with a special report. U.S. Army paratroopers were landing in northern Michigan, the Upper Peninsula and near the Ohio and Indiana state lines.

"What about Detroit?" President Belle asked after the murmurs died down.

"General McIntyre's 10th Mountain Division has fully secured Central Detroit," answered Admiral Erik Sorenson, the Chairman of the Joint Chiefs of Staff. "The 82nd Airborne encountered no resistance in the militia counties in southern Michigan and in the Upper Peninsula. The militia groups scattered when the Army moved in, as expected."

"The FBI, Army CID, and Michigan State Police have made several arrests," Sorenson added.

"When can the Army withdraw from Michigan and Detroit?" The question was from Oscar Schwartz, the Director of National Intelligence.

"The Michigan National Guard were unable to deploy to Detroit in the middle of things, particularly after their main rally point at the Olympia Armory was compromised," answered Sorenson. "But they are fully mobilized now and deployed across Detroit and surrounding areas. Major General John Veazey, the Adjutant General of the Michigan National Guard, assures us that they are ready and able to assume command statewide."

"The 82nd Airborne was primarily a show of force," Sorenson continued, "and it did the trick. I think we can withdraw them pretty much immediately. As for the 10th Mountain Division, I think we can pull them back to Selfridge Air Base and wait and see how it goes for the National Guard and Michigan authorities."

"Do it," ordered the President.

A fifty-year-old four-engine wide-bodied Russian-built Ilyushin Il-76 Candid cargo jet plane took off from Bandar Abbas Naval Air Base, and headed west over the stunningly picturesque Zagros Mountains, including the Hormod Protected Area, Iran's equivalent of a nature preserve or national park. No doubt, the plane was tracked by an American AWACS (Airborne Warning and Control System) E-3 Sentry Boeing 707 out of Al Udeid Air Base in Qatar, which was patrolling the skies of the Persian Gulf. However, the Il-76 had all the characteristics of a routine domestic flight, given its flight trajectory.

About an hour and half into its flight, the aircraft made a sharp turn that took it out over the Persian Gulf. As it continued the turn, it skirted roughly 80 miles due east of Bahrain, most likely causing American F-22s out of Al Udeid to scramble. The Ilyushin Candid dropped in altitude and its back cargo door opened. Lines streamed from the back before blossoming into three large parachutes. The sudden change in speeds between the aircraft and the parachutes yanked a second-generation Iranian *Ghadir*-class mini submarine from the plane.

Two more parachutes deployed, slowing the mini sub's rate of descent.

A team of thirteen parachutists followed suit, jumping from the back of the Ilyushin one after the other.

Seconds later, the Ghadir mini sub – built specifically for the shallow waters of the Persian Gulf – splash landed in waters near the center of the Gulf. The thirteen parachutists, armed with Spanish-made Star Model Z-84 amphibious submachine guns and dressed in black wetsuits, flippers and oxygen tanks, circled above. They came in one by one, each landing astride the floating submersible.

The thirteen frogmen of the IRGC Navy's *Sepah* Naval Special Forces, Iran's equivalent of the American Navy SEALs, clambered aboard the vessel and took command of the small submersible. They started the quiet diesel engine, and the mini sub slipped beneath the waters of the Persian Gulf.

The mini sub was slow, with a maximum speed of about 10 knots submerged. But it was quiet. *Real* quiet.

It steered toward the western side of the island of Bahrain.

Twenty minutes later, an American P-8 Poseidon maritime patrol aircraft of the recently recommissioned Patrol Squadron 17 screamed across the surface of the Persian Gulf just feet above the spot where the *Ghadir*-class *Ayatollah Khomeini* mini submarine had submerged.

The P-8 loitered in the area for nearly fifteen minutes, but its crew spotted nothing. They deployed a sonobuoy via parachute which, upon landing in the sea, activated an array of wide antennas and audio sensors.

The P-8 loitered in the area as onboard enlisted Aviation Warfare Specialists, or AWs, listened intently for the telltale signs of a submarine. Two more sonobuoys were deployed to widen the area of interest, but after an hour of patrolling, the P-8 resumed its usual mission: monitoring aircraft and shipping in and around the Gulf.

Meanwhile, 280 miles southwest of Washington, DC, more than twenty U.S. Air Force four-engine C-17 Globemaster cargo planes lifted off from Fort Liberty, North Carolina (formerly Fort Bragg). Each plan ferried one hundred 82nd Airborne paratroopers.

Simultaneously, twenty-plus C-17 aircraft of the U.S. Air Force Air Mobility Command lifted off from Marine Corps Air Station Camp Pendleton just north of Oceanside, California. Carrying marines of the 13th Marine Expeditionary Unit, they headed out over the Pacific on their way to Al Udeid Air Base outside Doha, Qatar.

7

ash returned to Bandar Abbas. Normally he would be refreshed and emboldened by twelve hours of much-needed sleep and the, er, provision of services in the Darvazeh Ghar district of Tehran, even if the relief proved temporary.

Not this time.

Hash's sense of urgency over the situation in the Persian Gulf had not abated. On the contrary, it had only sharpened.

Hash's eyes swept his office when he stepped in. Atop the metal drawers in a corner was a rolled-up rug.

His eyes lingered on the rug as he crossed the room and sat in his chair.

Sleep, he thought, as he looked at the rug.

It wasn't just any rug. It was an intricately woven Persian carpet, passed down in Hash's family for generations.

Hash's ancestors, including his father and grandfather, were watermen. For centuries, they had plied the waters of the Persian Gulf and the Gulf of Oman for tuna, grouper, goatfish and mackerel.

The rug itself was perhaps a thousand years old, and was special to his father, grandfather and generations before.

He sat down at his computer and typed furiously. He was in panic mode.

The American president had announced the deployment of Marine expeditionary units to Bahrain and Qatar as "force protection" troops.

That was just the beginning. Of this, Hash had no doubt. He had seen it in his dreams the night before.

He flipped through pages of notes and articles scattered on his desk, found what he was looking for, then pecked away some more.

Conflict with America had been gamed out a thousand times.

Considerations of how it might start were many. One of them even entailed the explosion and sinking of a U.S. Navy ship – *a goddamned aircraft carrier at that* – as unlikely as that could be.

Other potential sequences of events were also gamed out, but in almost every conceivable scenario, the Americans would deploy "force protection" troops as their first order of battle.

But what had Hash really wound up was the specter of American air strikes – not a week from now or a month from now. But *today,* or tonight or tomorrow.

"Are you okay, sir?" asked a personal aide hovering in his doorway.

Hash blinked and looked up. He was momentarily confused.

"Am I okay?"

Then his eyes regained their clarity.

"*Yes,* I'm okay. *Of course* I'm okay! Why wouldn't I be? Are *you* okay?"

"Am I okay?" Hash muttered before his aide could answer. "*Of course I'm okay!* Everything will – everything *is* okay!"

"What do you *want?*" Hash demanded.

"Um," the young officer stammered. "The maps you ordered."

The young aide nodded to the long cardboard tubes that he carried under one arm.

"Yes, yes," said Hash, rising from behind his desk. "Why didn't you say so? Put them there, on the floor."

As the officer entered the office, the tubes squirted from under his arm, spilling onto the floor.

"Fuck your sister!" Hash cursed. "Get out!"

The aide's face flushed red, but he dutifully retreated, closing the door behind him.

Hash opened the tubes and pulled out the maps. Most were highly detailed depth charts of the Persian Gulf. Many had been marked up with X's, lines and arrows to depict simulated ship movements and attack formations from previous exercises.

There was a knock at the door but Hash ignored it until he had laid out the charts and maps in a semblance of order.

Hash looked to the door. "You again," he sighed. "What now?"

"Sir, special delivery." The aide held another tube.

Hash took the new tube, and the aide quickly scurried away.

The tube was wrapped in candy-cane-striped red and white tape, and marked TOP SECRET.

Hash opened the top of the tube and let the contents slide onto his desk. It appeared to be a collection of high-resolution satellite images. An envelope also fell onto the desk. It was a note.

Hope these are useful. A gift from our friends in the East. Daria.

Hash sat down. A sly smile spread across his face.

Daria.

Hash had once been assigned as a Navy liaison to the Ministry of Intelligence in Tehran. Daria was very pretty, but her beauty emanated from her personality.

She was deliciously mischievous. She was secure in her skin and intelligence and didn't suffer fools gladly.

Daria had taken him to Darmand Trail in the north of the city. The trail followed a steep, whitewater creek, and was lined with restaurants, hookah bars, and shops. Water rushed over rocks just feet from outdoor tables and benches. The trail meandered across foot bridges and over steep drops that linked the shops and stops on both sides of the creek.

Coniferous trees, their roots twisted among the flowing water and rocks, stood tall and kept the ravine shaded in the daytime.

Mist above the flowing water was a permanent feature, and the air was always heavy with the smell of upturned earth and fresh water.

At night, the trees, guardrails, and shops were adorned with string lights, and colored flood lights illuminated the flowing water below.

It was a magical place.

Hash put down the note and picked up one of the satellite photos. He studied it for some time before picking up another.

He held them side by side, gawking at the photos. First one, then the other, then back to the first again.

He stood up, alarmed all over again, and pressed a buzzer on his phone. The aide came to the door hesitantly.

Hash stuffed the photos back into the tube.

"I want high-resolution copies of these *stat* and deliver them personally to Rear Admiral Habibollah Nasirzadeh."

"Yes, sir," the aide said, taking the tube.

"Wait!" exclaimed Hash before the young officer made it out of the office.

Hash went back to his pile of maps on the floor. He picked through the stack and thoughtfully viewed each one before putting them into one of two piles.

After the last map, Hash bundled the left pile into a couple of tubes and handed them to the aide.

"Do the same with these."

"Wait," he ordered again as he went to his computer terminal and slid behind his desk.

He pecked on his keyboard for several more minutes while the aid stood by wordlessly.

Hash stopped and stared at his monitor.

Should I? he asked himself. Then . . . *Why wouldn't I?*

Everything comes down to this.

Hash connected a thumb drive, and copied the file to it. Ejecting the drive, he then dropped it into the tube and sealed it shut.

"Go," Hash commanded.

Hash opened a small cupboard door in his desk and retrieved a bottle of English Scotch and a small glass.

An admiral has his perks, he thought, and grinned.

He poured himself a shot and downed it, then followed it up with another.

He leaned back in his chair and closed his eyes.

Would it be tonight?

Probably not.

The Americans had to do reconnaissance, review satellite photos, model attack runs and responses.

They had to have maintenance crews in place. Search and Rescue infrastructure and operations had to be ready to go in case of the loss of an aircraft or two.

That meant U.S. special forces. Air Force Tactical Air Control parties and para-rescue units, maybe Navy SEAL teams, too.

Still, American B-1, B-2 and B-21 bombers were already on station on Diego Garcia and Guam, according to the satellite photos. U.S. Marine expeditionary forces were setting up in Bahrain, Qatar and Kuwait.

And according to global news media like America's CNN and Great Britain's BBC, the USS *Barack H. Obama* and USS *Doris Miller* carrier strike groups were steaming toward the Persian Gulf.

Hash opened his eyes and sat up.

He reached for his phone, but then paused.

He was going to ask the Commander of the Air Defense Force to stand down their radars in and around Bandar Abbas and the Strait of Hormuz. The Americans had anti-radiation missiles that homed in on electronic radar signals.

He was certain the Americans would launch air strikes against Iran as soon as they were able.

Not a broad and systemic attack aimed at command-and-control centers in a prelude to full scale war.

That would come later.

Rather, Hash foresaw a limited attack against missile batteries trained on the Strait of Hormuz to show the world that they were *doing* something.

It couldn't be about the *George W. Bush* itself, not yet. *That* would be a prelude to war, and they needed more pieces on hand for that.

If the anti-aircraft radars were turned off, it might make it just a little harder for the Americans to target them.

More importantly, it would show the Americans that Iran was actively trying to avoid conflict.

Hash turned back to his computer. He furiously pecked away on his keyboard once again.

Hash eventually made that phone call to Brigadier General Mansour Mirzakhani, Commander of the Air Defense Force.

He was able to get a full ten minutes in before the commander hung up on him. But not before Hash told him to suck his private parts.

He didn't expect the Air Defense Force commander to shut down his air batteries and radars. But he had to make his case for it regardless.

Hash didn't get a wink of sleep that night – as usual. He was overdue for his increasingly regular jaunts to the Chahestaniha district of Bandar Abbas, but it would have to wait.

Anti-aircraft missile batteries, radars, and American high speed anti-radiation missiles, or HARMs, were on Hash's mind as he traversed the sweltering city the next morning.

He sat in the backseat of his government car catching up with emails, news and the latest intelligence reports.

As far as he could tell, the intelligence reports were just rehashed out-of-date news reports. He gleaned more from scanning the current headlines across a range of Western news websites.

His English wasn't great, at least as far as speaking went, but his reading skills were sufficient for news articles. For the most part.

Hash looked up from his laptop and peered out the window. His car was passing the Port of Bandar Abbas. He passed it every day, and it was the low point of his daily commute.

It was industrial and ugly. Gritty ships were anchored alongside blackened oil tanks, piping and rows and rows of shipping containers.

Hash always thought that the shipping containers resembled American Patriot missile batteries from afar.

Or Israeli Iron Dome batteries, or Russian S-500, or . . ..

"Stop the car!" Hash ordered. His young aide and driver, startled, looked at him through the rearview mirror. "I said stop the car, you son of a whore!"

The aide pulled into the right lane, but there was no shoulder.

"I said stop the car *right now*, you dumb Turk!"

The aide stopped right in the middle of traffic.

Horns blared behind them.

Hash opened the door and walked to the waist-high guard rail separating the highway from a rail yard.

He couldn't see enough of the port, so he climbed on top of the car. Row after row of shipping containers stretched to the sea.

That might work, he thought.

He remembered news reports of Serbian tanks and Army forces withdrawing from Kosovo in the Balkans following months of NATO-led air strikes during the 1999 Kosovo War, back when Hash was still in high school. The Serbians had used inflatable replicas of tanks and bridges, among other things, to confuse NATO and the Americans.

And it had *worked.*

Hundreds, if not thousands, of bombs were wasted on decoy targets.

Those reports – what was he then, 15? 16? – had always stuck with him.

Could the Americans be duped again, all of these years later?

Hash stepped down to the hood, then jumped off the car with a new pep to this step despite his lack of sleep.

"We've got a lot of work to do, young pup," he said as he clamored back into the car.

"Chop, chop," he said. *"Let's go."*

8

Imam Hussein Salmeen was in meltdown mode. After dealing with Jamal, Hussein obsessively texted the Commander, but to no avail.

The sons of dogs had cut him off.

He was on his own.

He had no choice but to break it to Fatima, his wife of thirty years: their lives were in danger. They had to leave Bahrain. *Right. Now.*

The Commander had everything worked out, he told her. They just had to get to Iran.

What of their children, she had demanded.

They would be taken care of, he insisted. The Commander had promised both physical and financial security for their two boys.

Besides, they were already doing well on their own. Twenty-eight-year-old Naail was a logistics engineer for Espag Engineering Company, an Iranian marine equipment firm. Kadin, twenty-five, was a junior accountant at a firm in Manama that handled many of the small businesses in the Souq.

Both had young families of their own.

Hussein knew it was risky, but he had purchased two airline tickets to Bandar Abbas, Iran, via Dubai, United Arab Emirates, with a credit card. There had been no indication of police interest in him so far.

The earliest flight he could get was for today. If it were up to him, he and Fatima would have departed for Iran as soon as Jamal had left his mosque two days previous.

They had just crossed the Muharraq Causeway when they stopped at the traffic light at Airport and Busaiteen Avenues.

"I love you," said Fatima, then opened her door and stepped out into the traffic.

"No, no, no!" Hussein yelled.

"Fatima, get back in the car!" he yelled, but she had put her head down and walked briskly across the lane to the small park between Airport Avenue and Khalifa Bin Salman Avenue beyond.

Hussein threw open his car door and chased after her.

"Fatima!" he yelled. *"Fatima!"*

But Fatima disappeared into the morning crowds shuffling into the casbahs of Muharraq along Khalifa Bin Salman Avenue.

Uncertain what to do, Hussein jogged back to his car. A man walked toward him from the traffic, his eyes trained on him.

Hussein froze.

Is he looking at me?

Hussein turned around and walked back onto the sidewalks of Khalifa Bin Salman – right into a very large woman in a full black burka.

She was nearly a foot taller than him, with wide shoulders.

"Dog in your ghost!" cursed Hussein at the woman.

"So sorry," the woman said in a . . . *was that a falsetto voice?*

As he continued walking, he felt a dull pain in his right hip where he had collided with the large woman.

Damn, she was solid, he thought, limping slightly.

Hussein broke into a jog but stumbled, his right leg losing strength.

He grasped the wall of a scooter business for support, and now struggled for breath.

"Oh!" Hussein gasped. His chest on fire, he slid down the wall to the ground.

People gathered around.

"Sir, are you okay?" asked a concerned young man peering down at him.

"Fatima," Hussein whispered.

It was like an invisible elephant was inexplicably sitting on his chest.

"Fatima," he whispered again, and breathed his last.

The past three days had been the longest of Thew Bryson's life.

After the *Bush* was towed from the cove, Thew had become the go-to forklift operator for both NSA Bahrain Supply and the Special Warfare community.

Then came the Seabees.

A battalion of Navy construction builders (CBs, or rather, "Seabees"), had arrived twenty-four hours after the first explosions aboard the *Bush.* They went to work building a tent city to house both themselves and marines of the incoming Marine Expeditionary force protection unit on the tarmac between the warehouses and the seawall at NSA 2. Thew worked with the Seabees' own logistics specialists and helped move equipment and materials.

The Marines had started to arrive not long after the Seabees.

On the seawall next to the tent city was something out of a video game: an Israeli-built and operated Iron Dome missile-defense system was set up there. It had several truck-based missile launchers and one truck with a spinning radar on top.

A Patriot missile battery, meanwhile, was set up on one of the two major piers.

They were both comforting and terrifying.

After a few days of frenzied work, Thew's moment as an indispensable forklift driver had come to an end. His services were no longer required.

The floors and toilets of the administrative offices beckoned once more.

He didn't complain – not after seeing the horrifically injured sailors from the *George W. Bush*. And then came the bodies, so many of them. Torn and burnt and laid out in long neat rows.

Any notion of war as heroic or chivalrous that Thew might have harbored before the disaster was thoroughly exorcised. In their stead was a foreboding sense of dread, of impending danger.

It was early morning, but the sun was up and it was already blistering hot. Thew's overnight shift had ended and he groggily stepped out into the blinding morning light.

He sundered around the warehouse perimeter and walked to the bus stop to await the base shuttle.

Thew was wearing shabby Navy-blue maintenance overalls with his last name stenciled over his left breast pocket. A mere worker bee amid fighters. He didn't even warrant a rank insignia on his left shoulder.

The growing sound of a helicopter caught Thew's attention and he looked up. A gray Seahawk helicopter – the Navy version of the legacy Blackhawk helicopter of the Army and Marines – approached the tent city along the seawall.

It came in slowly and landed in a clearing, its landing-gear shock absorbers bouncing slightly.

A couple of SEALs or Seabees or Marines or whatever attached a grounding wire and wheel chocks to one of the landing gears.

The hiss of a bus announced the arrival of the base shuttle. Thew stepped aboard and took his seat.

He put on his headphones and connected them to his phone. He had playlists that spanned the decades, but after an overnight shift, his favorite music of late was the dreamy, clanging sound of U2's *War* from the 1980s.

Go figure.

Take my hand
You know I'll be there

If you can
I'll cross the sky for your love

As U2 played, Thew looked out the bus window.

The helicopter side door opened, and four suits stepped into the sunlight.

The bus lurched forward and turned a corner, and the view of the helicopter was replaced by the large nondescript NSW warehouse building. Thew leaned back in his seat and closed his eyes.

And I understand
These winds and tides
These changing times
Won't drag you away

"Welcome to NSA Bahrain," said a shaggy haired and tanned Navy lieutenant commander, his hand extended.

The lieutenant commander wore a Navy desert camouflage uniform. The uniform and shaggy hair were the hallmarks of an American Navy SEAL, but he spoke with an English accent.

"You must be Mr. Moe Adil," he said, cheerfully.

Moe shook the lieutenant commander's hand, then turned to face a bearded Navy master chief petty officer with longish hair and wearing desert camouflage.

"Never mind *him*," said the gruff master chief, nodding to the lieutenant commander. "He went to Oxford."

Raymond Cole sat at a small desk in the corner of his office. Not his wide, main desk that backed up to the window overlooking the Pentagon's River Terrace, the Potomac River and Washington, DC, beyond. *That* desk had a picture-perfect view of the Washington Monument and the Thomas Jefferson Memorial in the distance.

This desk was small and faced a corner of the room like a punishment. Raymond wanted it this way. This was his working desk, where he decamped to read and write.

Since the *Bush* disaster, Raymond had made it his mission to know every angle of the Iran Question.

The Iran Question was not new to him. He had staked out his position long ago. He was firmly in the "boys go to Baghdad, but real men go to Tehran" camp during the post-9/11 build-up to the U.S. invasion of Iraq back in 2003.

The Iran plan was sidelined, then scrapped, as American forces got bogged down in the morass of Iraq – a quagmire that Iran had fully exploited.

It was a disaster. He had argued from the start that the U.S. needed to go into *Tehran,* not Baghdad. It was the opportunity to rid the world of the mullahs once and for all and to reshape the entire Middle East according to *American* geopolitical interests.

The current map of the Middle East was shaped by a British Empire seeking a land bridge between the Mediterranean Sea and the Persian Gulf. The idea was to greatly shorten the distance between London and British India by linking the Mediterranean Sea to the Persian Gulf via the land bridge of Palestine and Iraq.

That imperial project had failed. Yet, the map of the modern Middle East still reflected that failed project.

The United States did not seek to connect disparate parts of a far-flung empire. Rather, the U.S. sought to eliminate or minimize real threats to its economic interests in the Persian Gulf – namely, access to oil – and to protect its own citizens from Islamist terrorism at home and abroad.

Oooh, that sounds good, write that down.

Raymond scribbled on the back page of the white paper he was currently scanning. *Star, star, star and underline.*

When he had watched the USS *George W. Bush* disaster unfold on CNN, he wasn't filled with dread and trepidation, but with exhilaration. *Finally,* after decades of brinkmanship, the Iranians appeared to have stepped over the line.

He looked at this watch.

It was time.

His entourage was waiting for him.

Raymond gathered his papers and briefcase. In his excitement, he didn't notice that his *How to Sound Smart in a Meeting* desk calendar had fallen over.

"Welcome to the Sean C-Connery Fan Club," said a paunchy, bespectacled man in his early to mid-thirties. A framed, 1960s movie poster of Sean Connery as James Bond was on the wall over his right shoulder.

"The what?" asked Raymond.

The young man stepped aside to reveal a large photo of Ayatollah Rhullolah Khomeini, founder of the Islamic Republic of Iran. The ayatollah was the spitting image of an older Sean Connery.

Who knew?

"I would've thought you were too young to know who either of those people were," Raymond said.

"N-no way, ss-ssir," said the man. "Who doesn't love J-J-James B-B-Bond m-movies," he said. "And around here, you better know who Aya-t-t-tollah K-Khomeini was. *And* the shah. *And* M-Mohommed M-Mossadeq."

"Damn straight, young man," Raymond said with an emphatic nod.

What the fuck, Ray thought. *What kind of shit show are they running over here?*

"I see you've met Timmy, our human geography brainiac," said Joy Chatterjee, the recently confirmed Director of the CIA. She was walking along a concourse that circled the room and its hundreds of cubicles.

"That kid has the layout and nearly every street in Tehran committed to memory just by studying maps. Same for Qom, Tabriz, Bandar Abbas, Busheur, you name it."

"Really?" said Raymond, watching as the kid disappeared behind a cubicle.

"Don't let the stutter fool you," she said. "The kid is off-the-charts MENSA material."

Joy led Raymond and his entourage down a middle lane that cut through the cubicles and divided the building floor between north and south.

"Welcome to the Iran Desk," Joy said, spreading her hand out to encompass the whole of the fourth floor, "a.k.a., the Sean Connery Fan Club."

"We have over one thousand analysts, cryptologists, aerospace and nautical engineers and data scientists – all dedicated to Iran, its nuclear program, and its general oversight. Not all here, of course, but this is a good chunk of it."

Joy led Raymond and his entourage down the main staircase of the Jonna Hiestand Mendez wing to the first floor and into a large lecture hall. Jonna Hiestand Mendez was a real-life master of disguise whose work inspired movies and television shows like *The Americans* and the Tom Cruise *Mission Impossible* films.

The room filled up with analysts and cryptologists as several teams, including Raymond's, prepared their presentations.

Raymond and his group had just taken their seats when Joy began her presentation.

"Welcome to the Iran Working Group mini-conference," Joy said. Two screens dropped from the ceiling on either side of the podium. On each one was a room-sized headshot of Sean Connery, smirking.

Raymond's two aides took notes as Joy and her team spoke and displayed satellite images.

Much of the talk was focused on Iran's nuclear program, including the location of nuclear power plants, uranium enrichment sites, science institutes, and the like. Charts displayed estimates of how much enriched uranium Iran currently possessed, and varying timelines on how quickly Iran could produce a nuclear weapon.

Raymond already knew most of that stuff.

Next, Joy displayed images of Iranian ballistic missiles, as well as charts with their estimated ranges. Most missiles covered the Persian Gulf, which put nearly all U.S. bases in the region within range. One missile's range was larger and included Israel within its striking range. The last missile, the recently revealed Shahab 5, put most of Eastern and Southern Europe in range, including Paris.

Again, nothing new for Raymond.

Now it was his turn.

Raymond began with a series of maps showing the locations of Iran's Air Force, Navy, Army and Republican Guard bases. Next was a rundown of Iran's military assets.

For the Islamic Republic of Iran Air Force (IRIAF), the largest number of combat aircraft were the domestically-built dual-fin single-engine dual-seat Sa'eqeh fighter planes – a reverse-engineered derivative of the American 1960s-era Northrop F-5 Tigershark – followed by the American-built 1960s-era McDonnell Douglas F-4 Phantom II and the 1970s-era Grumman F-14 Tomcat, the aircraft featured in the popular 1980s film *Top Gun*.

There were approximately seventy Sa'eqehs and their F-5 predecessors, forty-five F-4 Phantoms, and thirty-five F-14 Tomcats.

None of these aircraft were considered even remotely challenging to America's fifth-generation F-22 and F-35 stealth fighters, or even to its non-stealth fourth-generation F/A-18 and F-15 aircraft.

Other aircraft in Iran's inventory included the 1950s-era C-130

Hercules cargo plane, the 1950s-era P-3 Orion patrol plane, the – it was hard for Raymond to continue with a straight face, and he paused.

He held his hand up to the audience in the room to allow him a moment while he tried to stifle a laugh.

Fuck it. He burst into laughter.

"I'm sorry, I'm sorry," he insisted as he struggled to regain his composure. Several analysts in the rows of desks also chuckled. They were on the same page as him.

Thank God there is no press here.

"Look," Raymond said, "my team will share this presentation with each of you. I can stand here and compare planes to planes, tanks to tanks, and so on, but you already know how lopsided any fight between America and Iran would be."

"These guys," Raymond said, gesturing to the screen showing his presentation, "have been savvy enough to avoid a direct confrontation with the United States for *decades.*"

"I don't know what's changed, but clearly the Iranians felt emboldened. And they've stepped over the line."

"They stepped over the line," he said again, gravely.

The room grew quiet.

Stop right there, Raymond told himself. *No need to push for action. Let the realization sink in.*

A hand went up. It was the Human Geography brainiac with a stutter, but Joy interrupted before Raymond could call on him.

"Please, everyone, save your questions until the last presentation. All presenters will be happy to answer your questions then. Also, there will be an informal gathering in the lobby with lots of refreshments provided. All the presenters will be in attendance and everyone is invited."

Next up were presenters from the National Geospatial-Intelligence Agency, or NGA – another of the so-called "alphabet" organizations along with the CIA, NSA, DIA and other military intelligence and investigative units: NCIS, CID, OSI.

"This is for you youngins," said a rugged looking man in his forties. Dr. Bart Colver was head of the Human Geography Unit at NGA.

The stuttering Brainiac should enjoy this *show*, thought Raymond.

"I'm sure everyone in the room is familiar with the Iran Hostage Crisis, when students from the University of Tehran overran the U.S. Embassy and took 52 embassy staff hostage during the Islamic Revolution," said Colver. He had a gravely, smoker's voice.

"The students demanded the return of their king, or shah, Reza Pahlavi, who was in the U.S. for cancer treatment, in exchange for our embassy personnel. The U.S. refused on humanitarian grounds. The standoff lasted 444 days. Ted Koppel led the news off every single night with 'Welcome to Nightline. It is Day 105 of the Hostage Crisis,' and so on. Every. Single. Night."

"A rescue operation ended in disaster." A photo of a burned-out C-130 and an abandoned helicopter deep in the Iranian desert filled the room's two large screens.

Bart continued.

"The wreckage is still there, by the way. Iran turned the site into a memorial. You can even see it on Google Earth.

"The crisis finally ended when Iran released the hostages as President Reagan was sworn into office. But it's hard to convey to you young folks how dismaying and humiliating it was for the United States to be unable to secure the safety of its citizens.

"Many people clamored for war. But the Islamic Revolution was chaotic; there was no actual government to hold accountable. Moreover, Ayatollah Khomeini was highly popular among the population."

"Also," Bart continued, "let's not forget that all of this wasn't long after the Vietnam War. Americans were tired of war. Also: we had no bases nearby; the closest ally was Israel. We didn't really have relations with Saudi Arabia or the Gulf states in those days. So, it would have been a major undertaking to go to war against Iran – one that America just wasn't prepared for.

"This is all before the modern wizardry of stealth planes, smart bombs, satellites, drones, fast tanks, and all that jazz that everyone is familiar with these days."

As Bart was talking, a slide appeared depicting wounded and dead American Marines amid the rubble of their barracks building following a 1983 truck bomb attack in Beirut, Lebanon.

He turned and looked at the photo and paused, then turned back to the audience, his eye glasses perched on the edge of his nose.

"Remember this," he said gravely. "Revolutions are political *earthquakes.*"

"The Iranians were *HIGH,*" he said, drawing some laughter. *"STONED,"* he emphasized again, drawing even more chuckles.

"High on success. High on people power. High on overthrowing a government that was perceived as being thrust upon them by the United States of America."

"They were *ZEALOUS,"* Bart continued. *"EAGER,"* he bellowed. "Eager to export their revolution to Muslims around the world. Eager to *LIBERATE* their Muslim brethren from Western influences. To *LIBERATE* Muslim lands from the *BEATLES* and *FORNICATION."* His eyes were twinkling. He was clearly having fun.

"This was the truck bomb attack on the U.S. Marine barracks in Beirut in 1983. They were deployed there as peacekeepers to enforce a ceasefire between the various combatants."

Bart spoke lower now, the humor gone from his voice.

"Hezbollah claimed responsibility," he said. "Hezbollah is a Shia Islam militant group based in Lebanon. Founded and supported by Iran."

"Iran operates through proxies: Hezbollah, Islamic Jihad and . . . the Islamic Front of Bahrain." He paused, to let that sink in.

The next slide depicted the recent carnage outside the U.S. Navy base in Bahrain.

"To spread their gospel. *TO LIBERATE THE LAND FROM INFI-DELS!"* he thundered, his face turning beat red.

Jesus, thought Raymond.

A new picture appeared on the overhead screen of juxtaposed photos. They depicted the rubble of two buildings destroyed in bombings.

"This was the Israeli embassy, car-bombed in Buenos Aires, Argentina, in 1992," he said, aiming a laser pointer at the first building.

"And this was a car bomb attack on the Jewish Cultural Center in Buenos Aires in 1994," he said, pointing at the second building.

"Islamic Jihad and Hezbollah, respectively."

The next slide was of yet another car-bombed building.

"This is the Khobar Tower in Saudi Arabia in 1996, just across the causeway from Bahrain," Bart said. "It housed U.S. Air Force personnel, mostly maintenance crews, in support of post-Gulf War operations. Nineteen U.S. Air Force airmen were killed. Hezbollah."

The next few slides showed IED (improvised explosive device) attacks on U.S. supply convoys during the Iraq War. More graphic photos of horrifically wounded American soldiers.

Another slide displayed pieces of an IED after an attack.

Another slide. This one screenshots from Google Earth, focused on Iran. A zoomed-in photo of Tehran had yellow pins superimposed over various buildings across the densely populated city.

"We were able to determine the origin of many IEDs during the Iraq War. Right to the factories that made them."

The next side was a now all-too familiar photo of the USS *George W. Bush* aircraft carrier, half of it shrouded by a towering mushroom cloud standing atop the ship's aft.

Bart looked up at the photo for what seemed like a full minute, then looked back to the audience.

He said nothing.

He didn't have to.

"Poor kid," thought Moe Adil when he and Ali Rashidi, his young counterpart in the National Security Agency of Bahrain, were finally able to visit twenty-year-old Mahdi Al-Fardan in the hospital.

But then he corrected himself. *Poor kid, my eye.* Al-Fardan was part of the Islamic Front of Bahrain's attack on the front gate of NSA 2. Although no Americans were killed, twenty Bahraini ambulance crews and medics were incinerated.

Sure, the kid was severely injured in the attack – his pelvis and left hip were broken and both legs mangled – but he had willingly participated in an effort to kill as many Americans as possible.

Although he didn't remember anything from the day of the attack, he *was* able to name his co-conspirators, and he fingered Imam Hussein Salmeen as the leader of the cell.

High on painkillers and truth serum, he sang like a bird.

Moe could imagine what the Bahrainis had in store for the kid, but that didn't concern him.

Ali spoke to Moe softly while the kid continued to mumble. "Imam Salmeen died of a heart attack the other day in Muharraq. It was quite strange. He died after his wife abandoned their car on Airport Highway and he chased after her. She said he was desperate and trying to get to Iran. He wanted her to go, too, but she fled."

"Is that so," said Moe, his voice trailing off in thought.

9

The four-engine turboprop Lockheed Martin P-3F Orion had just passed the one hour and thirty-minute mark into its mission when Baraz's stomach leaped into his chest. He choked on his hot tea and almost sent the fifty-year-old aircraft into a nosedive.

"Fuck!" he exclaimed. He slammed down his mug, spilling more tea onto the control console.

"Oh, shit!" said his co-pilot, looking out the pilot-side window past Baraz before swiveling to peer out his own side window. "How long have *they* been there?"

"Give us a fucking heart attack, you American scum!" Baraz bellowed as he wiped his chest and arms with his bare hands.

"Someone get me a napkin!"

An American F-35C stealth fighter jet flew wingtip to wingtip with the P-3 to the left of the pilot. Another one flew off the wingtip on the right side of the aircraft.

"Is that a new American weapon?" asked the enlisted flight engineer seated just behind the pilot and co-pilot.

"Shot down by heart attack," he said, smiling.

"I've got nothing on radar," said a voice over the headsets. It was the navigator. "Absolutely nothing. Those things really *are* stealthy."

He seemed genuinely impressed by the American fighter jets.

"Fuck you," breathed Baraz, agitated. "Where's my damn napkin?"

He looked over to the American jet off his wingtip. The American pilot was clearly visible behind the glass bubble canopy, and he had a beeline view straight into the P-3 cockpit.

The American pilot waved to him.

"Fuckin' A," Baraz muttered.

General Mohammad Yaghani, Commander-in-Chief of the Islamic Republican Guard Corps, took his seat at the head of the conference room table. He carried with him a series of reports and documents, and placed one particular report in front of him.

He looked straight to Rear Admiral Habibollah Nasirzadeh, commander of the IRGC *Sepah* Naval Special Force. It was Habib, after all, who had forwarded Hash Ghavam's frenzied but powerfully argued report to the men sitting here at the Ministry of Defense complex in Tehran.

"Tell me about Rear Admiral Ghavam, Admiral," Yaghani said. He didn't waste anyone's time with small talk.

He knew that Hash Ghavam and Habib Nasirzadeh had worked closely together over the years.

Habibollah looked around the conference table.

These men were *operators*. Combat-hardened leaders of the Islamic Republican Guard Corps and Iranian Special Forces.

Unlike the two meetings of the so-called "principals" days before, *these* men were not prone to religious zealotry nor were they slaves to ideological dogma.

These men were decision-makers. They were *The Orbit* – the men who mattered in affairs of war and peace.

In matters of war, anyway.

"He's bold, as you can see," Habib said, his finger tapping his copy of the report in front of him. "Thoughtful. He sees the big picture, which I think also comes through here."

"Unlike his predecessors, he has worked very well with us and the IRGC Navy. He bends over backward to avoid direct confrontations with the Americans, just as he advocates here in his white paper."

"At the same time, he never hesitated to run interference for us against the Americans. When we inserted commandos into Oman, he put on a big show with his frigates in the Strait of Hormuz to distract the American Navy. He lit up an American ship and several aircraft with radar targeting, and sent his frigates directly at an American cruiser and set off fireworks, literally," Habib said, chuckling.

"When we were free and clear, he ordered an about face and gunned it for home before the Americans could organize a response."

"The Americans harassed his ships day and night for the next month," he said, still chuckling.

"Apart from the Americans, he doesn't hesitate to stretch his Navy's capacity. When Somali pirates seized an Iranian tanker last year near the Bab-el-Mandeb in the Gulf of Aden – the *Happiness II* – he took command of the *Shiraz* and led a squadron of three ships to rescue the *Happiness*."

"His helicopters opened fire on several Somali dhows and his frigates sank the main pirate ship. His boarding crew killed or captured all the pirates on the *Happiness* and rescued multiple pirates in the water."

"What does he know about the Americans," asked Rear Admiral Parviz Radan, commander of the Quds Force, an irregular paramilitary unit that engaged in guerilla warfare during the wars in Iraq, Syria and Yemen, and against Sunni Islamists and supposed pro-democracy forces supported by the United States and Israel. "Quds" is the Arabic word for "Jerusalem."

"I know he studies them all the time. He pours over every recorded encounter. He's done that for nearly 30 years. He also gets his news in English. BBC, CNN, the Times of London, New York Times, Washington Post."

Habib felt a pair of eyes boring into him, and he looked down the table to Brigadier General Ali Alamouti, commander of the Army's 65th Airborne Special Forces Brigade.

Habib held his gaze and waited for Alamouti to speak. But it was General Yaghani who spoke.

"Our models suggest that there is no going back. The Americans will declare war on us. Full scale war. And they will seek nothing short of the destruction of the Islamic Republic."

"I'm afraid Hash might sometimes be prone to . . . paranoia . . . and overstating things," Habib said, hesitantly.

"The thing is," Brigadier General Ali Alamouti finally spoke, "we have decades of conflict planning and game theory that back up Rear Admiral Ghavam's report. Our models define a particular and de-tailed series of markers that would suggest a war is about to kick off."

"The U.S. is plowing right through them, almost chronologically. The U.S. dispatched force protection troops to Bahrain, Kuwait and Qatar, and deployed a squadron of F-22s and B-21 and B-2 stealth bombers to Guam and Diego Garcia."

"This morning, an Air Force P-3 was intercepted by American F-35 stealth fighters. They were of the Navy carrier variant. Seems the *Barack Obama* and *Doris Miller* carriers have arrived on station."

"What Admiral Ghavam presents," said Rear Admiral Parviz Radan, "is a way forward against the Goliath."

Habib sat upright. If the *Obama* and *Miller* were in theater, along with stealth bombers and F-22s, plus force protection troops hun-kered down on the other side of the Gulf, that meant everything was in place for . . .

Air strikes.

That was a lot of firepower, and any pretext will do.

Just as Hash had outlined. To soften things up beforehand.

Before *what?*

Before *everything.*

It was all happening too fast.

"It's time we brought Hash into the Orbit," Yaghani said.

Moe Adil was the senior agent in the Army's Criminal Investigative Division, or CID. A former Green Beret, he had worked closely with Navy SEALs, Air Force Special Tactics operators, CIA operators and the like, and had experience working across all of the branches of the U.S. armed forces.

Because of this, he was the go-to man to head up the Defense Department's criminal investigation of the *George W. Bush* disaster.

He had just wrapped up investigating multiple raids on federal armories during the unrest in Detroit and Michigan when he got the call.

Ali Rashidi, his assigned partner from the National Security Agency of Bahrain, had texted him before dawn. They had a lead on the possible whereabouts of Jamal Al-Dosari. They suspected he might be hiding with a friend who worked with him at the Arab Shipbuilding and Repair Yard.

Neither Al-Dosari nor his friend had shown up for work the past couple of days.

Moe stood outside the front gate of the American navy base and waited for Rashidi to pick him up. It was still dark. A pair of headlights diverged from the light morning traffic and aimed in his direction.

A silver Mercedes pulled up. It was Rashidi. His window was down. He was smoking a cigarette.

Moe climbed in. Rashidi held out his pack but Moe declined.

It wasn't long before they arrived at an apartment block in the Al Hidd district of Muharraq Island. A three-story building with shops on the bottom, it was surrounded by heavily armed soldiers.

Rashidi nodded to the commander in charge, and the raid was underway.

It was over in seconds.

Before Moe even entered the apartment, he could smell it. He understood before he even saw them.

Two young men lay sprawled on the floor, a single bullet wound in the middle of each of their chests. Their open eyes and expressions of shock told the story.

They had been dead for at least a day.

One lay at the foot of the door: Al-Dosari's nineteen-year-old friend and coworker. The other was Al-Dosari.

Upon closer inspection, Al-Dosari wasn't shot in the chest. He was shot in the back.

Moe scanned the room. A half-eaten pizza lay on a glass table. A video game on the television screen was on pause.

Someone had knocked on the door while the two played Xbox Basketball. His friend answered the front door and was shot.

Al-Dosari got up to run and . . .

Neighbors hadn't reported anything.

Moe walked out the front door. Rashidi chased after him.

"Where are you going?" asked Rashidi.

"Nothing more to see here," Moe said.

"Where do you want to go?" Rashidi asked, a little edge in his voice. He was growing tired of the enigmatic American.

"I can hail a cab," Moe said.

"No, let me take you. Where are we going?"

"To find the boy. Isa al-Qurmezi."

"We don't have any leads yet."

"I know where he is."

As they headed out across the city, the sun had yet to rise, but sunlight had broken the darkness. The sprawling Salmaniya medical complex came into view, its buildings silhouetted dark against the pink and purple horizon.

Moments later, a doctor unveiled the body of a teenage boy listed under the name of Fulano, the Arabic version of a John Doe.

The body had arrived that very evening.

The doctor pulled the sheet back. Rashidi looked at the boy's open, fresh face, then pulled away, agitated.

He paced the room. "How did you know?" he asked Moe.

Moe pulled out his cell phone, took a picture, and then headed for the exit.

Rashidi blocked his path but Moe shoved him aside.

"Fuck off," Moe seethed. He towered menacingly over Rashidi. "I've got a report to write, and you've got an Iranian hit squad running loose in Manama."

"Don't worry," Moe added. "I'm sure they're long gone by now."

Rear Admiral Habibollah Nasirzadeh was back in Bandar Abbas. He had flown aboard the same Fokker F27 Friendship aircraft for VIPs, which just days before, he'd shared with Hash Ghavam.

It was a rare occurrence for the two of them to be on the same plane. So rare, in fact, that it hadn't happened before.

Throughout his career, Habib had been taught to distrust the regular Navy. No doubt, Hashemi had been taught to distrust the *IRGC* Navy, especially the frogmen of Sepah Force.

Habib had learned early in his career about the run-ins between the IRGC Navy and the regular Navy. Things had been openly hostile in the 1990s and 2000s. The IRGC was the favored branch, given its direct connection to the Supreme Leader and its role of protecting and projecting the Revolution.

But Hash Ghavam knew how to read the tea leaves, it seemed, and how to harness circumstances to steer much-needed resources to the regular Navy.

Iran traced the history of its regular navy to the Achaemenid Empire in 550 BCE. That is, if a handful of surface warships, submarines and a meager fleet of small fast boats constitutes a regular "Navy."

Such a smattering of warships with limited range and capability had proved no match for the *American* Navy in confrontations during the Iran-Iraq War in the 1980s. In one day – *one day* – a few American warships sank Iran's entire poor excuse for a naval fleet after an American frigate, the USS *Samuel B. Roberts*, struck an Iranian mine and nearly sank.

The Americans referred to the confrontation as a "skirmish."

Like swatting a fly.

It had set Iran back by decades.

Habib was pretty certain that the contemporary Iranian Navy would, once again, be no match for the vaunted American Navy.

It was the *IRGC* Navy, with its fleet of speed boats and missile boats, that would be the biggest thorn in their side, though they wouldn't be much of a threat in a head-to-head confrontation. The trick was to avoid direct confrontation, and instead swarm attack any American warship that got cut off from the herd or was sailing solo.

Habib rode in the backseat of an Iran Khodro Rah armored SUV. It was almost midafternoon now, and he didn't want to waste time. Things were unfolding fast.

When his plane landed at the Bandar Abbas Naval Air Station, Habib noticed several teams working in the open desert on the far side of the air station. They were blurry amid the shimmering heat of the desert, but he could make out what appeared to be enlisted sailors setting up three separate missile batteries.

Habib was impressed and confused at the same time.

Navy personnel? Missile defense systems were nearly the sole mission of the Air Defense Force, an entirely separate branch of the Iranian military.

Habib instinctively began to walk toward the closest group to inspect their work. They were much farther away than they appeared, probably half a mile at least, and the heat was stifling.

"Sir?" asked his immediate aide, a young lieutenant. But, Habib ignored him and continued walking.

It was nearly ten minutes before he reached the group, who all straightened at attention when they saw he was an officer – and a Rear Admiral at that.

Now Habib saw the missile battery for what it was: two separate shipping containers perched on two old and rusted flatbed trucks, one of which had no tires. It must have been trucked here.

The shipping containers were pointed to the sky at a fifty-five or sixty-degree angle.

What in the world?

"What are you men doing?" Habib asked.

The men were mere kids, conscripts barely out of high school. They looked miserable.

"Admiral Ghavam," answered one pimply youth. "He ordered us to make these things look like a missile battery."

The youth pointed to a series of hills east of the town. "He's there."

The hills were two or three miles away, and Habib squinted. He could make out more teams setting up what he guessed were also shipping containers.

Has he gone mad? Habib wondered.

"Carry on, men."

He texted his driver, and his SUV sped toward him.

His phone vibrated.

It was Brigadier General Mansour Mirzakhani, Commander of the Air Defense Force.

"General Mirzakhani," Habib said.

Habib had to hold the phone away from his ear as General Mirzakhani unleashed a series of expletives preceding and following the name of Rear Admiral Hashemi Ghavam.

"Tell me what happened," Habib soothed.

Habib listened intently.

Now he understood – or thought he did.

"Listen, General," Habib told Mirzakhani. "Do *exactly* what Admiral Ghavam said and do it quickly. *Today.*"

★ ★ ★

Back at the Pentagon, a group of young Navy cryptology officers and intelligence analysts were hovering around a large computer monitor when Raymond Cole entered.

Despite his Executive Schedule pay grade, Ray worked hard to maintain backdoor relations with ground-level junior officers and personnel in order to have access to unfiltered information. It was also a way to learn things before his peers and supervisors.

Backdoor intelligence-sharing was a no-no precisely *because* it was unfiltered, but Ray didn't care.

"Check it out, sir," said a young lieutenant commander.

Ray peered at the screen. It was a zoomed-in satellite photo. Multiple features were digitally circled across the photo.

The lieutenant commander scrolled to the right and up, revealing more circled features. The more he scrolled, the more circled features there were.

"What are they?" asked Ray.

The lieutenant commander double-clicked on one of the features and the computer zoomed in further.

"Is that a missile battery?" asked Ray.

"Yes, sir."

"*All* those are missile batteries?"

"Yes, sir. And look." He clicked something on the side and all the features disappeared. "This was a few days ago."

Either they're expecting us to hit them, or they're sending us a message.

Probably both.

"You know what they call that in ready rooms across the fleet?" asked Ray.

"No, sir," said the lieutenant commander.

"A target-rich environment," Ray said with a wink. The lieutenant commander and his colleagues laughed as Ray took his leave.

★ ★ ★

Habib returned to his office on base and spent the remainder of the day catching up on his duties and scheduling briefings with *Sepah* commanders.

Rear Admiral Ghavam never did return his call, but Habib was too tired to track him down.

In the morning, Habib was back at it. He poured over the latest intelligence reports. He met with *Sepah* commanders. They worked on contingency plans. He spent the afternoon working to coordinate with the Quds units.

Quds and *Sepah* needed to wet their gills. Neither Habib, nor Rear Admiral Parviz Radan, Commander of the Quds Force, liked being blind or sitting still.

Where is Rear Admiral Ghavam?

It was nearing five o'clock and Habib *still* hadn't heard from Hash. On his way home, he ordered his driver to take him to Hash's home.

"He hasn't been home in days," Hash's wife, Nazanin, said. She was on the verge of tears. And then the dam broke.

"Don't be alarmed," Habib said, and hugged Nazanin. "These are extreme times. Hash is personally overseeing quite a lot, and he takes his work seriously."

Nazanin nodded and wiped away tears that kept coming.

"Tell him to call me as soon as he gets home," Habib said.

Back in his car, Habib scanned his contacts until he found what he was looking for.

Gholamreza Gheybparvar. Commander of the local Basij, the paramilitary organization of the IRGC. The Basij were local thugs who beat up protestors and otherwise spied on and intimidated everyday Iranians, including cops.

Fascists. Zealots. Gangsters. *That's what they are.*

Habib practically held his nose when he hit the green call button.

"Habib," Gholam answered. *Fucking ghoul.*

Recognizing his number and calling him by his first name as he answered, Habib saw it as a minor, petty power play.

Fuck you, little man.

"Gholam," Habib sighed. "I need a favor."

"A *favor*," Gholam repeated, savoring the word. "*Yessss . . .*" he whispered.

Habib laid it out.

"Of course," Gholam answered. Habib could almost hear the skull face grinning.

"Gholam," Habib said before hanging up. "Be discreet."

"Dis*creet*," acknowledged Gholam. "*Yesss . . .*" he whispered.

Habib hung up but not before the whispered "*Yesss . . .*" turned into a serpentine hiss.

"Habib."

"Habib."

Habib's eyes snapped open.

"Your phone is vibrating."

It was his wife, Parisa. There was an edge of annoyance in her voice.

Habib looked at the clock radio on the bedside console.

It was 2:30 in the morning.

What the fuck.

Habib rolled over and grabbed his phone next to the clock radio.

A text message from Gholamreza Gheybparvar.

It was an address.

The phone vibrated in his hand and another text message appeared.

"Her name is Leila," it read.

★ ★ ★

Blue jeans and a T-shirt. A light jacket. It gets cool at night in Bandar Abbas. Winds from the desert.

Habib drove himself in his black Khodro Dena Samand four-door sedan.

He drove from his home just blocks from the Persian Gulf in the posh, palm tree lined neighborhood of Hoseyn Abad and headed east along the coastal highway before turning north toward the Chahestaniha neighborhood.

There was no direct route into Chahestaniha. It was a casbah in the northside of town, with winding, narrow streets, surrounded by other casbahs.

At 2:45 a.m., the roads were deserted, which made it easier for Habib to navigate.

He followed Modares Road north along a channeled wadi when a flash, like lightning, lit up the sky ahead. An orange fireball erupted in the hills north of the city.

What the hell.

A delayed *KA-BOOM,* loud enough to wake the whole city, washed over his car and rattled his windows.

"*Fuuck,*" Habib cursed.

Several more lightning-like flashes from behind lit up the night sky, in quick succession, balls of fire momentarily suspended above the city before quickly fading, followed by more deafening *BOOMs.*

Car alarms blared and their parking lights flashed on and off.

House lights were coming on all over the casbah.

Air raid sirens began to blare.

Random wisps of ash drifted from the abyss of the night sky above.

Habib snaked his way through the narrow streets and came to the address.

He hopped out of his car and banged on the main door of a front gate.

After a minute, Habib heard the door unlock. A burly, unshaven man in a wife beater T-shirt opened the door a crack. He was an Arab, Habib could see.

"Leila," Habib shouted over the sirens and car alarms. He stood ramrod straight, his arms folded across his chest.

The burly man didn't budge. No expression crossed his face.

Even the air raid sirens didn't faze him.

Wumph.

The ground shook and the rattling of doors and windows reverberated through the neighborhood.

Habib pointed skyward and tilted his head to listen to and emphasize the *BOOM* that then followed.

"I'm here for Hashemi, not Leila. He's needed."

Jets roared invisible in the darkness above.

Habib's phone began to vibrate incessantly in his jacket pocket. He ignored it.

The burly Arab opened the gate further, enough to allow Habib inside.

Habib was led into a courtyard and then a walkway that curved around two rundown three-story homes. The homes appeared to be divided into multiple apartment units.

Women in various stages of dress clustered at their entrances, looking skyward, their faces contorted in fear.

What is this place?

A massive *KABOOM* caused Habib to stagger as he approached a basement unit to which the Arab gestured.

Habib entered a musty basement filled with rolled-up rugs, lighted candles and . . .

Habib recoiled and flinched.

A shirtless young man sat glassy-eyed among the rugs, staring into space.

The rugs weren't rugs.

They were people beneath blankets. Maybe twenty people. Mostly asleep. Others, like the boy, sat upright, their eyes, too, glassy and dull amid the flickering candlelight.

Somebody was laughing hysterically. It was coming from a room at the far end of the basement and around a corner.

The house shook from another explosion. Dust fell from the low ceiling.

WOO-HOO . . . HA HA HA HA HA . . . AHHH HA HA HA . . .

Habib rounded the corner and stepped through a curtain of beads.

A shirtless man with a bushy mustache sat with his back against the wall. Tears streamed down the man's face.

HA HA HA HAAAA . . .

A topless young woman snuggled against him, her head resting on his wiry chest. She seemed to be asleep, despite the heaving of the man's chest as he roared with laughter . . . *or was he crying?*

"LOOK WHO IT IS," the man bellowed. *"AHHH HA HA HA . . ."*

The man's face glistened in the candlelight.

Is that?

Habib squinted.

"LOOK WHO IT IS," the man repeated. *"HA HA HA . . . AHH HA HA . . ."*

It can't be.

But it was.

It was Rear Admiral Hashemi Ghavam.

PART TWO

FRIENDSHIP GAMES

10

"**M**y fellow Americans . . ."

It was 7:00 p.m. in Washington, DC. Most major networks – CNN, Fox News, BBC, SkyNews, France24, others – carried the American president's evening address to her country live.

Most were split-screen with the U.S. president delivering her address on the left, and live footage from Tehran on the right. It was a beautiful panoramic view of the sprawling city and its nightlights.

It was peaceful, serene.

But a ticker ran below the split screens: *"Air Raid sirens blaring in Tehran . . . U.S. air strikes may be under way . . . Airstrikes reported in coastal Bandar Abbas . . . Airstrikes reported in Bushehr . . . Air Raid sirens blaring in Tehran . . ."*

"Armed Forces of the United States are presently conducting military operations in Iran aimed at protecting our ongoing rescue and recovery efforts in the Persian Gulf.

Last week I had warned Iran against provocative actions while the United States recovered casualties from the USS *George W. Bush* and investigated its cause. That very night . . ."

President Belle's voice cracked and she paused.

"That very night," she continued, "the Islamic Front of Bahrain

– a proxy of Iran's government – staged an attack on American Navy personnel and Bahraini first responders in the middle of rescue operations, and also on Bahrain's Royal Palace."

"Iran – by funding, supporting and directing the Islamic Front of Bahrain – is fully responsible for that group's murderous actions."

"Further, recent satellite images have shown that Iran has stationed up to 100 missile batteries in and around Bandar Abbas and the Strait of Hormuz."

"This is a provocative act that puts our sailors in harm's way and jeopardizes the safety of ongoing rescue and recovery operations."

Cynthia Belle paused again and looked sternly into the camera.

"We are holding Iran accountable for their actions," she said.

Habibollah Nasirzadeh hadn't flown between Bandar Abbas and Tehran as many times in his whole IRGC Navy career as he had in the past week and a half.

Here he was again at a conference table in the bowels of the Ministry of Defense compound in Tehran, this time in a bunker beneath the adjacent Mehran neighborhood, Habib guessed, less than twenty-four hours after *leaving* the city and returning to Bandar Abbas.

And what a crazy 24 hours it had been.

He hadn't slept a wink in almost two days. The adrenaline that kept him going for the past sixteen hours was spent. Habib was crashing. He could barely keep his eyes open.

Rear Admiral Hashemi Ghavam, meanwhile, was fresh and well-rested, despite the state in which Habib had found him during the overnight attack by the Americans.

He sat stoically, his back straight, eyes forward.

They think they have me, Hash thought. Well, that much was true. They *did* have him, and he was resigned to his fate.

He was ready for whatever they would do to him. He thought that accepting what was in store for him would comfort him.

It didn't.

He kept thinking of Azadeh. He desperately wanted to see her one last time.

Both Habib and Hash ignored, or tried to, the flat-screen televisions lining the walls of the bunker's conference room. Four of them were on and displaying different satellite news networks. Each one of them continued to cover the American air raid over Iran during the pre-dawn hours of . . .

Was that today? This morning?

Habib stretched his neck and rubbed his eyes.

CNN showed grainy black-and-white footage from individual attack aircraft with what they described as missile batteries at the center of the crosshairs of target sights.

Then *poof,* the grainy targets disappeared behind a flash.

Another aircraft, another target, same result.

Poof.

Again and again.

The other networks played the same footage, but with the CNN logo blurred out.

General Mohammad Yaghani burst into the room along with an entourage of aides and high-ranking officers.

"Gentlemen," he said, taking his seat at the head of the table.

"Thank you for coming on such short notice."

One of his aides turned on the remaining flat-screen television. Two more aides attached a portable hard drive to the television.

When the TV came on, multiple video files appeared. General Yaghani, using a remote-control laser pointer and mouse, clicked on the first one.

High-definition drone footage from the Bandar Abbas Naval Air Station depicted a large, blackened crater in the landscape with debris strewn about.

"This is from this morning, first light," Yaghani said.

It was hard to tell for certain, but the debris was presumably the remains of the shipping containers.

The footage cut to another site. The land was hilly and dry, suggesting the foothills just north of Bandar Abbas. Several more blackened craters littered with burned and twisted debris pockmarked the ground.

"The Americans reported taking out multiple missile sites in and around the Strait of Hormuz and Bandar Abbas," Yaghani said. "Air Defense reports that our S-400 and HQ-22 missile systems are unscathed. Not a scratch," he said with a grin.

"The Air Defense Force also reports no casualties. *Zero.*"

Hash remained stoic, his back ramrod straight.

The Air Defense general had rejected his pleas to take the Russian- and Chinese-supplied missile batteries offline and stash them.

What is this? Why this strange humiliation? Just throw me in prison and be done with it, you trader of whores!

General Yaghani's friendly eyes lingered on Hashemi, and Hash realized that everyone at the table was gazing at him, awaiting some sort of response.

Hash took a deep, deliberate breath. His heart pounded.

"What do you want?" he asked. He hoped his voice didn't sound as shaky as it did in his own ears.

Yaghani's eyes remained on Hashemi as he processed Hash's question. A shadow of confusion crossed his face.

After a moment, Yaghani chuckled uncertainly.

"Shipping containers," General Yaghani said, and shook his head. "Brilliant."

"I've ordered all of our bases to do the same."

"We've all read your report, Hash. The football angle – or what the Americans call soccer – it's so *pedestrian.* It might actually work."

Hash looked down at the table, then raised his eyes to meet Yaghani's.

"It's a fool's errand," Hash spoke, almost angrily. "We are *incapable.*" He nodded to one of the televisions.

As CNN continued to show footage from the overnight airstrikes *ad nauseam,* the recently named Supreme Leader, Grand Ayatollah Sayyid Ali al-Milani, issued a fiery statement condemning the American air raids and promising that the Persian Gulf would run red with American blood.

General Yaghani looked at Hash with a glare that bored right through him. "You let *me* worry about *them. Your* job," he turned and looked each officer in the eyes, "is to build a plan and to *fight."*

"This is the fight that we all knew would come. In all likelihood, none of us in this room will live to see out the year ahead. So it is for our children and grandchildren that we fight. For Azadeh," Yaghani said, looking directly at Hashemi again. "For Behrouz and Farhad," he said, looking at another officer.

"For *Persia."*

"Iraq is what America thinks of us."

"They have no idea."

Moe Adil held onto the handgrip near his head as the gunmetal gray coaxial Sea Raider helicopter rose and then dropped to hover above the USNS *Grasp,* one of the Navy's two remaining rescue and salvage ships. The *Grasp* was part of a flotilla of rusty U.S. Navy industrial ships, including tugboats and barges.

It had been a smooth ride up to that point. Moe likened the ride to the comfort of a business jet as the helicopter streaked over the waves of the Persian Gulf.

A jolt and a slight bounce marked the landing of the chopper on the aft deck of the *Grasp.*

Like many of the logistics ships in port at Naval Station Bahrain, the *Grasp* was owned by the Navy but manned by civilians – mostly U.S. Navy veterans – in the Military Sealift Command. Hence the

USNS, or United States Navy Ship, designation rather than the USS, or United States Ship, designation of active-duty combat ships.

"Welcome aboard the *Grasp,* sir," shouted the khaki uniformed officer. The insignia on his khaki officer's hardhat marked him as Military Sealift Command. The eagle pins on his collars marked him as the commanding officer of the ship.

"Captain Paul Welling," he said, extending a hand. Moe shook it and the captain handed him a khaki hardhat. "Regulations," Welling quipped.

The Sea Raider helicopter lifted off and banked sharply.

The winds of the rotors were replaced by the winds of the open waters, and the deafening chops of the helicopter's rotors quickly faded.

"Special Agent Moe Adil, Joint Investigative Services Task Force," said Moe.

"JIST," Welling said with a wink. "I get the gist of it."

"The military loves its acronyms," Moe said.

Moe followed the captain up two sets of stairs to the bridge, careful not to smack his head on any of the steel cables or machinery.

On the bridge, nine men in hardhats and overalls hovered around a man seated in front of a computer monitor. They spoke loudly to each other, in what Moe guessed was Dutch.

"Dr. van Aalst," Welling said, and the seated man turned. "This is Special Agent Moe Adil of the American Joint Investigative Services Task Force. They're investigating the cause of the disaster."

"I see," said the seated man.

"Moe, this is Dr. Martin van Aalst of Smit International, the world's premier ship salvage company. They are headquartered in Amsterdam," Paul said as Moe stepped forward and the men around Martin parted. "Martin is based out of Singapore."

"Pleased to meet you," Martin said as he and Moe shook hands.

Paul guided Moe to a large map table in the center of the bridge where a detailed depth chart was laid out.

"Here she is," said Paul, pointing to a handwritten X on the chart.

He picked up a pair of binoculars and looked out over the bow.

Welling pointed to an area southwest of their position. "There," he said, "about a mile."

"She split into five major sections, from what we can tell so far. The flight deck separated from the superstructure and broke in half. The island was ripped off. The superstructure itself was blown apart into at least two sections."

Welling and Moe joined Martin and his men as they watched video footage from an underwater drone. A large and jagged section of the ship emerged from the dark depths of the sea. Plankton reflected in the drone's lights like snow.

"Geeze," said Moe, "that was one hell of an explosion."

"It was," said Martin. "When seawater hit the reactor, the resulting steam explosion was on the order of a Nagasaki – about twenty kilotons."

"The first series of explosions in the Khawr al Qulay'ah inlet were from the weapons storage area, that much we can ascertain," Welling added.

"How can you tell?" asked Moe.

"The interior of the ship is practically gutted. The superstructure held despite the munitions cooking off," Welling said.

"Here," Martin said. The drone came upon a jagged end, then turned to view inside the massive portion of the superstructure. "You can see how gutted the interior is," Welling said.

Walls were warped and floors were twisted. Ladders drooped, partially melted.

It looked like a Salvador Dali painting.

"The entire ship was an oven before it sank," Welling said. "All decks. No way anyone could've survived the heat."

"Can we raise her?" asked Moe.

"It will take time," Martin offered. "We'd have to build scaffolding around the various sections and build a, um, platform to work from."

"We'd have to cut the sections into manageable pieces for lifting," Martin continued. "We'd basically have to deconstruct her."

"How long would that take?" Moe asked.

"Years."

Raymond Cole's black armored Suburban SUV pulled into the crescent driveway in front of Number One Observatory Circle, the Vice President's mansion at the Naval Observatory in Washington, DC.

Several other black armored Suburban SUVs were ahead of him. One by one they pulled to the curb in front of the Queen Anne style mansion and unloaded their backseat passengers.

There was Vice Admiral Baltzer Oberkirsch from the office of the Chief of Naval Operations, and other military officers.

There was Joy Chatterjee, Director of the CIA, and several of her aides.

It was Ray's turn. A uniformed young Marine opened his passenger door and stood at attention, and Ray and his own two aides stepped out.

"This way, sir," said a middle-aged man in a dark blue suit, standing at the top of the mansion's front stairway.

Ray and his aides were ushered into a wide reception room doubling as a conference room.

It was a "smart" conference room, with several screens along the walls that dangled from the ceiling. Google Earth was projected onto the screens and zoomed in to western Iran.

Meanwhile, an assortment of pastries and a breakfast buffet lined the back wall.

The room was loud with multiple conversations that dimmed when Daddy Longlegs entered.

The Vice President shook hands and conversed with various principals.

Eventually, Longlegs made his way to the head of the conference room table, and everyone else found their assigned seats marked by folded name cards.

Low in the pecking order of guests, Raymond found his seat near the end of the table, away from the VP.

Raymond had never met the VP before, and he was a little star-struck. Daddy Longlegs was a legend in Washington. A longtime senator from Ohio, he was a national security stalwart. Though a conservative Republican, he had played a crucial role in the Iran Nuclear Deal struck between the Obama Administration and Iran, and then helped broker the second deal in the Biden Administration.

Paradoxically, he had also helped advise the Trump Administration in labeling the Republican Guard a terrorist organization and in targeting its leader, Qasam Solemeini, for assassination by drone in 2020.

"Welcome, everyone," Longlegs began.

"Despite every effort of this country to normalize relations, Iran continues to behave like a pariah state."

"Now we've got over 3,000 Americans *dead,*" Longlegs said, his face reddening with anger. "This is more consequential than 9/11. If we chalk it up as an *accident,* nobody would believe it. Not the Russians, not the Chinese, not a single goddamn tinpot dictator on the planet."

"An *aircraft carrier!*" Daddy Longlegs boomed.

"The era of appeasement is over."

"We have waited for two decades for Iran's politics to catch up to its demographics. The vast majority of Iran's population was born after the Islamic Revolution, and they are 80 percent urbanized."

"The promised liberalization of a younger and more urbanized Iran hasn't happened."

"Sure, the so-called Hibab Uprising in 2022-23 led to the disbanding of the Morality Police, but beyond that, it didn't really do much, did it?"

"We cannot bomb a few missile platforms, some airport runways, and call it even. No, we have an opportunity here to right past wrongs and reshape the entirety of the Middle East."

"We must *destroy* the Islamic Republic of Iran."

"And that's just the start."

Daddy Longlegs pressed a button on a remote control. Streaks of red, like scratches, appeared on the maps of western Iran and off Iran's coast at the top of the Persian Gulf.

"This is where the majority of Iran's oil fields are," Daddy said. "And this," he said, circling an area that encompassed most of the red streaks near the Iraqi border, "is Khuzestan Province, Iran's lone majority Arab province."

"We can take a page of Putin's handbook and wrestle Khuzestan and neighboring Bushehr away from Tehran. We don't need to occupy large sections of Iranian territory. Fuck Tehran. We don't need American soldiers teaching them democracy or policing their streets."

A pie chart appeared on the screens. "These are Iran's largest trading partners. The vast majority of exports are to China. And these," he said, clicking the remote again, "are Iran's exports."

The exports chart was divided into many different parts, the largest of which was labeled "cars" and the next largest "auto and industrial parts."

No single sector dominated.

Oil and gas accounted for seven percent of Iran's gross domestic product, or GDP.

"This shows us a couple of things."

"First, Iran's economy is more diverse than many realize. Oil and gas are but a small though still significant sector of their economy. But it doesn't really capture the importance of Iranian oil in *China's* economy."

Another click of the remote listed China's sources of energy imports. Iran was third on the list, accounting for nearly twenty percent of China's oil.

"Second, Iran is fast becoming a regional power, thanks to

its increasing trade with China and despite decades of American sanctions."

"Iran *cannot* become a regional power. It simply cannot. Although America can sustainably project power to the other side of the planet – to Iran, for example – it is still a massive undertaking. Supply lines are thousands of miles long. Strategic airlift capabilities are needed to capture and hold territory tens of thousands of miles from our own shores.

"A regional power is the equal of a superpower within the former's area of operation. And *that* is why Iran cannot become a regional power."

Rear Admirals Habibollah Nasirzadeh, commander of the IRGC Navy and a Sepah Force commando, and Hashemi "Hash" Ghavam, commander of the Southern Forward Naval Headquarters (Regular Navy) at Bandar Abbas, shared an aircraft – yet again – on their return flight to Bandar Abbas.

For Hash, it was an awkward flight. Hell, it had been an awkward *day.*

There had been no mention of his . . . indiscretion. Not a peep.

He looked over at Habib, who sat with his eyes closed.

Habib had behaved as if nothing had happened. Did he tell Yaghani or anyone? It sure hadn't seemed like it.

Hash looked out of the window of the Fokker F27 Navy transport plane. The landscape was beautifully desolate. The mountains were awash in browns, oranges and pinks, punctuated by green valleys.

"They're not done, you know," Hash said as he looked out on the landscape below.

"The Americans. Last night was just the beginning. They'll strike again tonight. And the next night. And the next."

"They'll call it something," Hash said. "*Operation* something."

"They seem to like that word," he said.

Habib snored softly.

"Operation *Freedom Shield,*" said Bernie Mentzel, the Secretary of Defense, "is aimed at defending American forces engaged in recovery operations in the Persian Gulf."

He spoke at a podium in the press room of the Pentagon.

"Iranian missiles deployed along its coast and aimed into the Persian Gulf are a direct threat to U.S. operations and civilian shipping."

"Tonight, the U.S. Navy is continuing operations aimed at neutralizing threats against ongoing recovery operations, our ships and the ships of our allies."

Hash watched the American news network in his tiny office in his command building's basement bunker at Bandar Abbas Naval Station.

The TV screen flickered, briefly going black as the bunker shook.

Welcome home.

The bunker was a large steel tube that ran underground away from his command building, or "Quarterdeck." It was accessible via the Quarterdeck basement.

Each of the sailors' barracks had similar bunkers.

He needn't worry about his ships and submarines, nor the sailors who lived aboard them. None of them were moored at Bandar Abbas, nor at the navy base at Chandahar on the Gulf of Oman. He had ordered *all* seaworthy ships and submarines to seek shelter in Pakistani ports and navy bases immediately after learning of the *Bush* disaster.

No doubt, the Americans would soon ask Pakistan to either order his fleet out of Pakistani waters or to confiscate the ships by force.

We'll cross that bridge when we come to it.

Tonight, at least, they are safe.

His bunker heaved and shook as another American missile or bomb found its mark above.

Sleep. I could really use some sleep.

"Welcome to *Meet the Press,* Secretary Peck," said the host, Andrea Mancini.

"Thank you. I wish I was here under better circumstances," said Andrew Peck, the Secretary of the Navy.

"Where do we stand on rescue and recovery efforts?" Andrea asked.

"It has been a very difficult week for the United States Navy," the Secretary said. "The *George W. Bush* went down in relatively deep waters and has broken apart into three main sections. Given the sheer heat produced by the initial explosions and fires onboard the ship, its subsequent sinking and the time that has since elapsed, rescue efforts have unfortunately turned to recovery," he said.

"Will the Navy raise the *George W. Bush?*" Andrea asked.

"We have a salvage team on scene assessing her condition, but it would be a very dangerous and tedious operation, one that could take several years to accomplish. More than likely, we will recommend that the President declare her to be an official underwater grave."

"The *New York Times* reported that the *George W. Bush* disaster could be the most serious environmental catastrophe in the history of the Persian Gulf," said Andrea. "The Gulf States are, understandably, very much worried about the environmental impacts of an exposed nuclear reactor off their shores. What *are* the environmental impacts of the sinking of the *George W. Bush?*"

"The environmental impacts of the sinking of the *George W. Bush* are mostly related to jet fuel and industrial contaminants, not the nuclear reactor. Nuclear fuel is heavier than water and has fallen to the sea floor. Any radiation impact is highly localized and contained. Further, the reactor has cooled to water temperature. Lastly, nuclear powered ships use very highly enriched uranium, which is less of a contaminant than you would find in, say, commercial nuclear reactors."

"I am not an expert on nuclear power and reactors," he continued, "so that's about as much as I can say."

"Was the *George W. Bush* attacked? Or was it some sort of onboard accident?" Andrea asked.

"Naval architects and engineers are conducting a detailed forensics investigation. While it is still very early in the investigation, indications are that the initial explosions onboard the ship occurred in the weapons storage area. Given how secure our munitions are onboard Navy ships and aircraft carriers in particular, that would be indicative of some sort of an attack.

"We have scoured radar tapes and interviewed hundreds of witnesses. There are no indications whatsoever of an aerial or seaborne attack."

"So, terrorism," Andrea said.

"It would seem so, yes. That is our working assumption at this point."

"So somebody onboard," Andrea said. "A saboteur."

"The Joint Investigative Services Team composed of each of the military branches' investigative arms is interviewing survivors and reviewing the ship's various command rosters," the Secretary said.

"How would that even happen? An onboard saboteur seems very implausible, just on the face of it. Wouldn't an onboard accident be a more likely explanation? Is the Navy grasping at straws?" asked Andrea.

Before the Secretary could respond, Andrea continued.

"I mean, the Navy has suffered a string of accidents in recent years. The USS *Daniel Inouye,* a destroyer, sank five years ago after colliding with an oil tanker in the Singapore Strait – thankfully with minimal casualties. The USS *Delaware,* a nuclear attack submarine, caught fire while berthed in Connecticut. Just last year, the USNS *Earl Warren* collided with the aircraft carrier USS *Doris Miller* in the middle of a replenishment-at-sea operation. There have been accidents involving aircraft, too many to list here, that have occurred over the past decade."

"Isn't that why your predecessor was fired? Isn't that why you were hired in the first place, to clean up the Navy?" Andrea asked.

"In short, yes. But here's the thing, Andrea. The Navy is inherently dangerous. It is a testament to the professionalism and training of our young sailors that accidents are such an anomaly. Every single day our young men and women in uniform are in harm's way, keeping our country safe.

"Despite the use and storage of volatile munitions, jet fuel, oil, flammable corrosion control compounds, and the like, in cramped quarters, plus inherently dangerous flight operations and everyday operations in dangerous sea and weather conditions, it is not a *miracle* that we don't have more accidents or incidents like those you listed, but a *testament* to the utmost professionalism and training of our young sailors. The average age of a sailor on our ships is twenty-four . . . *twenty-four,"* he said again for emphasis.

"It is a testament to their professionalism and training that this doesn't happen more often," the Secretary said.

"You've just made my point, Mr. Secretary," Andrea said. "Is it really a leap, given what you've just described, that the *George W. Bush* disaster was an accident and not a terrorist attack?"

"Given the professionalism and training of our young sailors, and the operational tempo that they maintain daily – every day, every month, every year – and the timing of the attack on our naval base in Bahrain? No, it is not a plausible scenario," the Secretary said.

"Here is what we know," he said, continuing. "The Islamic Front of Bahrain is responsible for the attack at the main gate of our naval base in Bahrain, and for the attack on Al Qudaibiya Palace. Iran directly supports and gives orders to the Islamic Front of Bahrain."

"How do you know this?" asked Andrea.

"We have one of the attackers in custody. He was injured in the explosion at the main gate. He identified his co-conspirators, all of whom were killed in the ensuing firefight with the exception of two. Bahraini law enforcement tracked down the two suspects at large. They were found dead, killed by what we presume to be an Iranian hit squad."

"We also have communications and financial records that I can't get into at the moment," the Secretary continued. "Further, the attack was quite obviously coordinated with the attack on the *George W. Bush.*"

"This was a highly sophisticated and planned operation. An operation like this has the earmarks of state coordination and sponsorship. It was most definitely months, if not years, in the making," the Secretary said.

"Last night, the United States launched airstrikes against Iranian targets for the second night in a row. Is the United States at war?"

"I think the *George W. Bush* answers that question, Andrea, don't you think?"

11

G eneral Mohammad Yaghani, Commander in Chief of the
Islamic Revolutionary Guard Corps (IRGC), sat in an ornate reception room at the House of Leadership, the official
complex of the Supreme Leader.

Two of his most senior officers sat with him: Brigadier General
Parviz Radan, Commander of the IRGC Quds Force, and Rear Ad-
miral Habibollah Nasirzadeh, Commander of the IRGC Navy Sepah
Special Forces.

A fourth senior officer accompanied Yaghani and his IRGC officers: Brigadier General Ali Alamouti, Commander of the 65th
Airborne Special Forces Brigade. The 65th Airborne brigade was
part of the *regular* Army, not the IRGC, but they had worked closely
together in Iraq and Syria.

Like the IRGC officers, Alamouti was part of the Orbit.

Yaghani took stock of his command as he and his officers waited.

He had firm command of the IRGC. He had risen through the
ranks of the IRGC, having proved his mettle in the field of battle.
He had fought alongside Hezbollah and Syrian government forces
against the Islamic State in Iraq and Syria, known as ISIS.

He had repelled Israeli commandos during an attack on his unit
in Syria. He had led Shia resistance fighters against the American

occupiers in Iraq, and later against Iraqi Sunni militias.

He had a reputation of fearlessness and ferocity in battle. Beyond the IRGC, his reputation alone commanded the loyalty of rank-and-file regular Army troops, he was certain of that. From their senior officer corps he sensed begrudging respect, perhaps borne of jealousy. He didn't worry about *them*. Besides, he had Alamouti and the 65th special forces brigade.

So he had the Army. That was important because it meant that he basically commanded all of Iran's ground forces.

Okay, not *all* of them. There was the Basij. They were officially part of the IRGC, but they operated independently. They were more of an extension of law enforcement, a paramilitary force used to neutralize any threats to the government's authority.

When called upon, they threatened and intimidated unarmed civilians.

They were torturers and murderers. Thugs. Certainly not highly trained professional soldiers.

They would be dealt with if it came to that.

The Navy? *Bah!* They had no ground forces and, besides, they were far away, based mostly down in Bandar Abbas and Chabahar. They didn't really matter in this situation.

Nor did the Air Defense Force, the anti-aircraft missile component of Iran's armed forces.

The *actual* Air Force was the wild card. They didn't command any ground forces, either, but if a ground unit went rogue and was backed by the Air Force . . . well, that could be a problem.

Would Brigadier General Tajik, Commander of the Air Force, come through?

Guess we'll see.

In the meantime, crack units of the Quds Force – all in civilian clothes – sat discreetly in the back of work vans at key intersections outside the sprawling complex, ski masks and automatic weapons at the ready.

Just in case.

"The Chief of Staff will see you now, General," said the executive's administrator, an elegant woman with intelligent eyes. She seemed wary of General Yaghani and his officers.

Yaghani and the officers followed the administrator to the doorway of the Chief of Staff of the Supreme Leader, Imam Jalil Doran.

Doran looked up from papers on his stately oak desk, eye glasses perched at the edge of his nose, and did a slight double-take as the other officers filed in behind Yaghani.

"This is highly unusual," Doran said. "What can I do for you, gentlemen?"

He rose to accept kisses on his cheeks from General Yaghani.

His face hardened when they weren't forthcoming.

"I need a word with His Eminence," Yaghani said.

"You can't just come in here whenever you *want,*" said an exasperated Doran, pushing his glasses up on his nose. "I don't care *who* you are!" He picked up his phone but Yaghani reached down and disconnected the line.

"Don't," Yaghani said.

"This is a coup!" said Jalil, stepping back from his desk.

Yaghani stepped forward, forcing Doran backward into display shelves on the wall behind him.

"What do you want?" said Doran, his eyes as big as saucers.

"Like I said, a word with His Eminence."

"He's, he's in the garden," Doran said and licked his lips.

"Then take me to the garden."

"It's this way," said Doran, stepping forward, and then stopping.

"Only you," he said.

"Only me," Yaghani agreed.

Yaghani and Ayatollah Sayyid Ali al-Milani, the Supreme Leader of Iran, walked together in the garden at the center of the House of Leadership complex in central Tehran.

"Tell me, General, what has got my chief of staff all in a state?" the Ayatollah asked, the light of a smile crossing his face.

It was a mischievous expression and Yaghani immediately saw the charismatic appeal of the youngish Supreme Leader.

At fifty-five, Al-Milani was the youngest Supreme Leader since Ali Khamanei assumed the title after the death of Ayatollah Rhullolah Khomeini in 1989.

"Your Eminence, may I speak freely?" Yaghani asked.

Ayatollah Al-Milani nodded.

"America is going to war against Iran. They will not stop until you, the IRGC, the Assembly of Experts and every institution of the Islamic Republic are destroyed.

"Our days are numbered," Yaghani continued.

"What we are doing now is allowing the Americans to build up their forces in the region. They will build their coalition, pass UN resolutions and ultimatums, and strike when we don't meet their demands. They will demand that you step down. They will demand that I and other IRGC commanders be surrendered to them for trial."

"They will demand a complete surrender of our nuclear program, even of our Army and Navy."

The Supreme Leader took a moment to absorb Yaghani's words before speaking.

"Let me remind you, General, that my government wanted to retaliate for those air strikes, but I was told that you *vehemently* advised against it."

"It is true, Your Eminence," Yaghani said. "We are not ready to fight the Americans. We cannot go head-to-head with them. They will methodically cut us to pieces while they *still* go about building their forces and their coalitions and their resolutions. Retaliating would only make it easier for them to accomplish their buildup. NATO would more readily join the coalition if Iranian missiles targeted American forces in the Gulf."

"Your government is carrying on as though business is usual," Yaghani continued. "Issuing threats but not going on a war footing. It is *not* business as usual, whatever your advisors are telling you. An American aircraft carrier was sunk, and they think *we* did it."

"We didn't do that!" protested the Ayatollah. "They can blame us all they want, but it wasn't us! They can't go to war with us for something we didn't do!"

The two men walked in silence for a moment.

"The Americans have time on their side," said Yaghani. "They took nearly six months to build their forces during the First Gulf War in 1990. They won't take as long this time. They have prepositioned equipment – tanks, missiles, troop carriers, construction materials, you name it – sitting in the desert in Kuwait. Rows and rows of tanks, Humvees and artillery batteries are just waiting for the Americans to come and put them to use."

"We need to act quickly and stealthily. We need to take the offensive."

Once again, they walked in silence for a moment.

"Thank you for your boldness, General Yaghani. I will meditate on what you have shared with me."

The Ayatollah awaited the General's parting salutation and obligatory kissing of his cheeks, but they weren't forthcoming.

It was an awkward moment.

"I can't leave here with that, your Eminence," Yaghani said.

As if on cue, two American-built Iranian F-14 Tomcat fighter jets roared high in the sky, in formation, over the city and passed right over the grounds of the House of Leadership.

"Is that you?" the Ayatollah asked as he looked up and watched the jets.

Yaghani did not answer.

The Ayatollah was surprisingly calm.

"I see," he said, finally. "And you are certain about the Americans?"

"They do not conceal their intent."

"What do you need?" the Ayatollah asked.

★ ★ ★

"Ambassador," said the sharply dressed, white-haired man with piercing blue eyes. "It's always an honor."

"William," the ambassador said, "it's been a long time."

The Ambassador slid closed the glass door behind him and stepped into the humid Washington air on the brick patio.

They shook hands.

"How are things at Standard & King Investments?" the ambassador asked.

"Very well, very well," William said, his eyes sparkling. "Have you met my nephew, Carlo?" William called to the young scion who held court amid a handful of fellow twenty-somethings. "Carlo, please come and let me introduce you to the Ambassador of the United Kingdom."

"My, my, what a strapping young fellow," the Ambassador said and took the hand of the tall, slender young man in both of his. "The man of the hour," the ambassador said. "Congratulations, young man."

"Thank you, sir," Carlo said.

"And this must be the young bride." A petite young woman shyly sidled up to Carlo.

"Ah, yes. Michelina, please say hello to Sir Jonathan Galloway, the British Ambassador," William said.

"So beautiful," Galloway said. He took Michelina's hand and, instead of shaking it, he bent over at the waist and kissed it.

Michelina purred with sheepish delight.

"Breathtaking," Galloway said, and let go of Michelina's hand.

"Pleased to meet you, Mr. Ambassador," the young woman beamed.

William took the ambassador's elbow and held out his arm, leading him along a brick pathway to a rustic outdoor bar tucked amid the lush trees and shrubbery that shaded the backyard.

Several casually dressed men and a woman sat in lawn chairs around an old brick stove, nursing their drinks.

All but one of the men stood to greet him.

"Senator Burnside," the Ambassador said, extending a hand. Galloway almost didn't recognize the Ohio senator in the blue jeans, untucked shirt, and Cincinnati Reds baseball cap.

"Ambassador," said another man who stepped forward. He was slender but solidly built. His T-shirt sleeves were painted on his bulging biceps.

It took a moment for the Ambassador to recognize Vice Admiral Baltzer Oberkirsch, a Navy SEAL.

Galloway had never seen him out of uniform before.

"Admiral Baltzer," Galloway said. "How nice to see you again."

Next was the woman, with dark eyes and black hair. She eyed Galloway with an expression of amusement.

"Joy," said the Ambassador. "What a pleasure."

"Pleasure's all mine, Ambassador," Joy Chatterjee said.

The group parted and the Ambassador stood before a man still seated. He was smoking a cigar.

Daddy Longlegs.

"Mr. Vice President, it is an honor," Galloway said, stooping slightly as if bowing.

The Vice President stood up from his lawn chair, his long legs and arms seeming to mechanically unfold and deploy in stages until he was towering over the British Ambassador.

"Thank you for coming, Jonathan," Daddy Longlegs said, his lit cigar between his teeth, and shook Galloway's hand enthusiastically.

"Want a beer?" he asked, gracefully withdrawing the cigar from his mouth with a free hand after greeting Galloway. "Whatever whets your whistle, I'm sure Jasmine can swing it."

"There you are!" It was Jasmine Prichett, on cue.

She was the host of this post-wedding reception. It was really a Sean Connery Fan Club meeting, but there are no stenographers or official record-keeping at private residences.

So it was a post-wedding reception if anyone asked.

"I turn my back, and the ambassador wanders off. Should've guessed that you'd find Daddy and Joy and the boys to hang out with," she said as she closed the glass door behind her. She picked up a tray of hors d'oeuvres – a mix of tiny sandwiches, deviled eggs, and Maryland crab cake balls – and brought it to a portable stand next to the brick oven.

Everyone grabbed a snack and took a seat in a lawn chair.

Raymond Cole, Undersecretary of Defense for Intelligence and Security, was, at forty-two, the youngest member of the working group. He laid a large map on the brick walkway in front of the brick oven, around which the chairs were arranged.

"The Pentagon has cooked up some options, and this is what we're leaning toward," Daddy Longlegs said, filling in the ambassador.

"Admiral?"

Vice Admiral Baltzer Oberkirsch picked up a pool cue stick beside his lawn chair and tapped Kuwait.

"We stage here – at Camp Arifjan in the south of Kuwait. Camp Buehring in the north is where we'll set up the offensive line."

"From there, we drive right across the Al-Faw Peninsula south of Basra and take Abadan."

"We split there. Team A heads north, right up the Karun and Dez river valleys to Dezful and Vahdati Air Base. Team B goes east to Omidiyeh Air Base, then south along the coast to Bushehr."

Daddy Longlegs took a swig from his beer bottle.

"And with that, ladies and gents, we have the whole upper Gulf and pretty much all of Iran's oil fields."

"KISS," Daddy Longlegs continued. "Keep it simple, stupid."

"We don't mess around and take over the whole damn country. That would be a whole nother Iraq and Afghanistan rolled into one, times a thousand."

"No, we take Kuzhestan and Bushehr Provinces, and hold. Stay west of the Zagros Mountains, choke off their oil revenues, bomb the shit out of Tehran and the rest, and wait 'em out."

"Take out their nuclear program. Take out their ayatollah and the IRGC, and see who's left that we can negotiate with."

The Vice President leaned back into his lawn chair, looking impossibly comfortable. He puffed on his cigar.

"What do you think, Mr. Ambassador?" asked Senator Burnside. "More importantly, where does England stand?"

Galloway looked down at the map before making eye contact with each member of the circle.

"You have my deepest sympathy for the loss of your servicemen and women. You must know that the United Kingdom stands firmly with our oldest and most dependable ally, the United States of America."

"What about Article 5?" asked Raymond.

"Without a doubt, Article 5 could be – and maybe should be – invoked, and the United Kingdom will stand with you shoulder to shoulder."

A flurry of cables between the British Embassy and London since the first reports of the *Bush* disaster emerged out of Bahrain had anticipated the state of mind of various segments of the American elite, and also a desire to invoke NATO's Article 5 – the provision that an attack against one member of NATO was an attack against *all* members. Galloway was given a lot of leeway on what he could say, at least in terms of unwritten, private assurances.

"However," Galloway, "I anticipate some . . . deliberation . . . in other corners."

"You mean France, right?" asked Raymond. "The fucking French," Raymond snorted.

"Not *only* the French," Galloway said. "The situation in Ukraine and Moldova, and the Russian build-up on its borders with the Baltic States and in Belarus has much of NATO on edge," he said. "Particularly Germany, Poland and, of course, the Baltic States. Any NATO commitment outside of Europe is sure to be met with trepidation."

"I think we will experience quite a bit of pushback in NATO and beyond," Galloway continued, "until there is some evidence that Iran is responsible for the *George W. Bush* catastrophe."

"The point is, we have our work cut out for us," the Ambassador said.

"One step ahead of you, mate," said Daddy Longlegs, blowing circles of smoke. "I fly out tomorrow."

The next morning, Raymond Cole was back in his office in the Pentagon, and Daddy Longlegs was on his way to Europe to shore up NATO and European support for a war against Iran.

Ray knew it would be a hard sell, especially after the debacle that Iraq had become when the U.S. invaded in 2003.

In the meantime, he studied multiple satellite photos of Iranian air bases following three nights of airstrikes. It looked like the Iranians had moved most of their MiG-29s, of which they had about ten – *ten!* Ray shook his head – to Mashhad.

The fighter aircraft were sheltered in a couple of hangars, one of which was now a pile of rubble.

What a joke, he thought.

Ray almost felt sorry for the Iranians.

The MiG-29 was arguably their most advanced fighter aircraft, and they only had ten of them. After last night's air strikes, they might only have five left.

They also had a bunch of American-built F-4 Phantoms – all of which were built in the 1970s.

For all these years – hell, *decades* – Iran was the Big Bad of the Middle East.

Why the fuck are we in Iraq when we should have gone into Iran?

The other major fighter aircraft that they had was the formidable American F-14 Tomcat. Iran had about thirty in operation, and they were also fifty years old.

Neither the MiG-29 nor the F-14 Tomcat were any match for modern F-22 Raptors or F-35 Lightning IIs. It would be almost as lopsided as Japanese Zeros from World War II going up against fifth-generation stealth fighters.

In Tehran, national television cut to an impromptu press conference at the House of Leadership.

Supreme Leader Ayatollah Sayyid Ali al-Milani stepped to the podium.

"The Americans say we sank their aircraft carrier. We did not. It was the Divine Hand of Justice. Nevertheless, the Americans gather like storm clouds. They attack without provocation. We turn to the Divine for eternal protection. We are commanded to serve as Instruments of Allah, to serve as the Rock Upon Which Evil Stumbles.

In Service to Allah, I am declaring a national state of emergency.

I appoint General Mohammad Yaghani as Commander of the Armed Forces. I appoint Rear Admiral Parviz Radan, Commander of the IRGC Quds Force, to Commander-in-Chief of the IRGC.

This Jihad is a Spiritual Jihad, and each and every one of us has our own part to contribute to the Glory of Allah. Not one single assignment is inconsequential.

Our industries of commerce are hereby enlisted into the Great Jihad.

All able-bodied males between age sixteen and fifty-five are ordered to report to their nearest law enforcement office for enlistment into our Great Armed Forces.

Allah is Eternally with Us, and We are Eternally His.

Allah Akbar."

12

Daddy Longlegs walked slowly with Ugo Cervi, the Prime Minister of Italy, along a shaded brick pathway lined with ancient palms. Through the palms and a break in the coastal forest adorning Villa Rosebery, Mt. Vesuvius stood majestic across the turquoise blue Gulf of Naples.

"You and your country have our deepest sympathy, Mr. Vice President," Ugo said. "We completely understand your desire to seek justice."

"You understand that my government – *all* Italian governments, for that matter," Ugo snorted lightheartedly, "is very fragile."

"It will take some time and quite a bit of work to bring the parties on board with your coalition."

"I get it," Longlegs said. He looked down on the slim Italian Prime Minister. He was dressed stylishly, with white slacks and an untucked button-down collared shirt. A blue sweater was draped across his shoulders.

Daddy Longlegs hated how some Europeans wore their sweaters like that. To Longlegs it was . . . feminine.

"I now understand the necessity of such a strong statement like 'You are either with us, or you are against us,' spoken by the namesake of our stricken carrier, President George W. Bush, after 9/11," Longlegs said.

"We need you on board, Ugo. If your coalition can't manage it, then put together another coalition."

"I wish it were that simple," Ugo sighed. "Nothing is ever so simple in this land."

"I need you to be strong, Ugo. A strong Prime Minister. A strong leader who can steer the public discourse and build a consensus."

Ugo nodded. *The arrogance.*

"It is true," Ugo said after a moment. "And that will be a formidable task for any Prime Minister – *whoever* he or she may be," he said with another self-deprecating snort, "particularly because of the 9/11 situation that you refer to," Ugo said.

Daddy Longlegs stopped and folded his arms over his chest. He looked down at Ugo with a raised eyebrow. "Oh?" he asked.

Self-deprecation didn't appear to be going over well with the American Vice President, Ugo noted.

Time for no hairs on the tongue.

"Our intelligence services believe that the Islamic Front of Bahrain acted without authorization from Iran. And we have not seen evidence of an Iranian attack on your aircraft carrier."

"We have conferred with the intelligence services in France, Germany and the United Kingdom, and we are all in agreement."

"If you recall, our intelligence services also did not agree in 2003 with the American premise that Iraq was developing nuclear weapons."

"Evidence?" Daddy Longlegs cut in. "Your service hasn't seen *evidence?"*

"What is Italian for *covert?"* Longlegs said. "You *have* heard the word before, yes? And 'plausible deniability?'"

"Jesus," Longlegs said, and looked away with disgust. "If there was a *mushroom cloud* over Milan, would you wait until you had *evidence* before you acted? Hell, *murder* cases rarely reach a degree of certainty!"

"They sank a goddamn *aircraft carrier,* Ugo. Over 3,000 of our sailors went down. Three *thousand* young men and women."

Ugo nodded. "You have our sympathy and our –"

"I don't want your goddamn sympathy," interrupted Longlegs. "I want your *participation!"*

"You're our goddamn ally," Longlegs said. *"Act* like it."

In Tehran, just west of its Mehrabad International Airport lies an industrial zone that stretches some fifteen miles to Karaj, a satellite city of Tehran in Alborz Province.

The industrial zone, comprising manufacturing facilities, warehouses, train yards and storage facilities, borders the main lines of IranRail's high-speed passenger and freight rail to Tabriz.

Here, the largest manufacturing complex is Iran Khodro. Branded as IKCO, it produces nearly one million passenger cars a year and another quarter-million work trucks, vans and other vehicles.

After the national emergency was declared, however, Iran Khodro stopped producing automobiles for domestic consumption and export. Instead, as in the United States during World War II, Iran's industries were conscripted into the war effort.

At the manufacturing plant, General Yaghani – now the Commander of the General Staff of the Armed Forces – watched as the first twenty-two-wheel supersized truck, a Transporter Erector Launcher, rolled off the assembly line.

Transporter Erector Launchers, or TELs, were mobile ballistic missile launchers.

For purposes of redundancy, two other plants – one in Tabriz, and one in Mashhad – were turning out the same model TEL.

Yaghani looked like a proud father.

"We can produce up to twelve a month," the factory foreman said.

Yaghani figured that the main factory in Tehran wouldn't last a week once the war began. The Americans would, no doubt, target the *entire* industrial zone of western Tehran.

Still, if just *one* of the remaining assembly lines could survive between now and a month from now, it might produce up to fifty TELs by then – TELs that the Americans would have to hunt down and destroy one by one.

How many missiles could each one deliver?

General Yaghani smiled. *If...*

If things went smoothly, which they never do.

Yaghani's smile faded.

No, they needed missiles, too, and a gazillion of them.

Vice President Daddy Longlegs, born George Wartmann, traced his family lineage to the Frankfurt region of southwestern Germany, in the state of Hesse, near the Main River. So, he was pleased to learn that Gyde Baerbock, the youngest ever German Chancellor at 42, awaited him at Ramstein Air Base, just an hour southwest of Frankfurt.

Longlegs was eager to stretch out in a Frankfurt beer hall and talk *politics.* No more of this walking around in ancient palatial gardens and plazas. He wasn't a goddamn tourist, after all. He ordered his staff to do their best to make that happen.

"Welcome to Germany," she had said in perfect American English when Longlegs stepped off the Boeing C-32 designated as Air Force Two.

"I understand that you would like to visit a beer hall in Frankfurt," she said.

"I would like that very much," said Daddy Longlegs.

She chuckled. "Let's go," she said. She twirled a finger in the air and her security detail and entourage swarmed into action.

A convoy of black armored Mercedes pulled right onto the tarmac.

Baerbock led Daddy Longlegs to one of the vehicles.

"I'll let you rest after your flight, and I'll see you in Frankfurt," she said.

Baerbock turned on her heels and walked to another SUV.

Longlegs got into the back of his assigned SUV and let out a long sigh.

Gyde's perfume lingered.

Longlegs smiled. He liked her already. She was just like her persona on television: pretty and charming.

See you in Frankfurt.

General Yaghani flew by helicopter to Chalus, a city on the other side of the Alborz Mountains from Tehran, on the densely settled narrow coastal plain between where the Alborz Mountains abruptly ended, and the Caspian Sea.

Like Tehran, Chalus sat at the base of the Aborz, but on the other side. This was the windward side of the mountains, and unlike Tehran, proximity to the Caspian Sea produced a relatively cool and humid climate. Orographic uplift produced a green landscape of thick, lush forests in the hills and mountains above.

Because of its lush forests and sunny beaches, the Caspian Sea coast and adjacent mountains were among the most popular tourist destinations for all Iranians.

The area was also home to multiple secret assembly plants all along the narrow coastal plain.

In the Jisa industrial district west of Chalus, one plant was of particular import. The site was selected because it was hemmed in by the mountains, which offered a degree of protection from air strikes, particularly from points far south like the Persian Gulf and Indian Ocean.

More than likely, the Americans would have to strike from Incirlik Air Base in Turkey, but even that was a long distance. And during the U.S. invasion of Iraq in 2003, Turkey had refused to allow the base to be used for offensive purposes given the flimsy criteria – nonexistent weapons of mass destruction – for the war in the first place.

American strategic bombers like America's new B-21 stealth bomber, or even its older B-2 stealth bomber, could probably do the job, but even for them it wouldn't be a walk in the park.

And much of the plant was built *inside* the mountain.

Brigadier General Cyrus Kordestani, commander of the IRGC Aerospace Force, greeted General Yaghani at Plant One. They climbed aboard a tracked mine car that took them into the base of Azad Kooh Mountain.

They didn't go far when they came upon the most recently assembled missile, the *Zamburak.*

Yaghani smiled.

'Zamburak' translated as 'wasp' in English, but it was named after the camel-mounted *zamburak* swivel guns developed to deadly effect during the Safavid Dynasty in the 18th Century.

He may not live beyond the next few months, and even the Islamic Republic may not survive as it is beyond the next year or two, but he and Iran were not going down without a fight.

"We have 25 already deployed right now," Brigadier General Kordestani said. "And once all of our sites come online in the next week or so, we should be able to roll out at least 10 a week," Kordestani said.

Ten a week, Yaghani thought.

Would that be enough?

In Frankfurt, Daddy Longlegs and German Chancellor Gyde Baerbock, along with multiple aides, sat on a deck overlooking the Main River in the back of a cozy beer hall.

A hole in the wall.

Longlegs thought it perfect.

"I'm sure you know why I have come here," Daddy Longlegs said. He took a swig from his frosty beer mug and leaned back in his chair. He stretched out his legs and relaxed as the cold beer drained down his gullet.

"America is going to war against Iran," Longlegs said matter-of-factly. "We're going to destroy that murderous regime *finally*, and once and for all."

"The Iranian people are a sophisticated bunch," Longlegs continued. He took another swig of beer. "I don't want to say that they will welcome us as liberators, not after what happened in Iraq a couple of decades ago, but yeah, I think the lot of them will."

Longlegs chuckled.

"They are stifling under sharia law. Imagine an Iran that is free and a full-fledged member of the community of nations. An Iran that doesn't blow up aircraft carriers or pursue nuclear weapons," he added.

"A stable Iran would also mean a stable Iraq, and that Assad regime in Syria would quickly fall, I guarantee it," Longlegs said. "No doubt about it."

"As far as NATO is concerned," Longlegs said, taking another swig of his beer, "Iran is a sideshow, I get it."

"But let's not lose sight of the big picture here," Longlegs continued. "An actively belligerent Iran on the move gives Russia room to maneuver. Hell, who's to say that Russia didn't encourage Iran to act in the first place to fudge things up for all of us up here in Europe?"

"Let's nip that shit in the bud," Longlegs said. "Put on a show of our own down there, shock and awe times ten. Show Russia, hell, China, North Korea, and any other tinpot dictator out there, not to *fuck* with NATO and the United States of America."

Longlegs drained his beer and plopped his mug down on the table. He nodded to a waiter standing by for another one.

The waiter arrived with another frosty mug. Longlegs immediately took a swig from it.

"There's two hundred thousand Ruskies and Belo-ruskies on the Polish and Lithuanian border. They're babbling about some bullshit 40-mile Suwalki Land Bridge between Belarus and Russia's Kaliningrad exclave, and we aren't asking to reposition NATO forces away from that."

"In fact, I told Ugo down in Italy that I could give a rat's ass about Italian or German or Polish troops getting in our way in Iran. America can go it alone, that's not even a question," Longlegs said, feeling the warmth of a buzz take hold.

"Iran," he said, "is a piddly ass little country that should've been slapped down a long time ago."

"We're not asking for NATO to contribute troops. We want NATO to officially sign off and *we* will do the job. We won't even need to pull troops from Europe. We've got enough manpower and firepower from the continental United States, Guam, Japan, South Korea, and the Persian Gulf to accomplish what we want," Daddy Longlegs said.

Gyde was still nursing her first beer as Daddy Longlegs drained his second and slammed it down with flourish.

"Can we count on Germany?" Longlegs asked after he wiped his mouth.

Next up for General Yaghani was the Iran Aircraft Manufacturing Industrial Company, or the acronym HESA in Farsi, in Shahin Shahr, a suburb of Isfahan in central Iran. HESA maintained a sprawling production facility in Shahin Shahr, including its own airport to test its aircraft prototypes.

HESA's main achievement was a series of domestically-built helicopters and fixed wing aircraft. Nearly all of their aircraft were reverse-engineered helicopters and airplanes – mostly American-built – that the Islamic Republic had inherited from the Imperial State of Iran under the Pahlavi Dynasty that was overthrown in the Islamic Revolution in 1978-79.

Others, like the modern IrAn-140 passenger and cargo plane,

was built in cooperation with Ukraine and was based on Ukraine's Antonov An-140.

The HESA Kowsar, or "thunderbolt", was Iran's premier indigenous fighter plane. It was the latest variant of the original knockoff of the single-seat, supersonic American F-5 Tiger light fighter aircraft.

The American F-5 Tiger debuted nearly 70 years ago. Nevertheless, the F-5 was a sleek and very capable and agile aircraft throughout its service in the U.S. and other countries' Air Forces, with a history of combat missions in Vietnam, Kenya, Ethiopia, Saudi Arabia, and Tunisia.

The Iranian version, the Kowsar, had some modifications. It was a two-seater, for one, and it contained the latest avionics technologies, mostly from China.

"It doesn't stand a chance against fifth generation fighters like the F-22 or F-35," said Brigadier General Ali Tajik, commander of the Air Force.

"But she isn't built for that. She's built to support IRGC ops in Iraq, Afghanistan, and Syria, and anti-insurgency ops in Balochistan," Tajik said.

"She is the workhorse of our Air Force," he continued. "We have 50 in service right now. Her production is straightforward and we build most of her component parts right here in Iran. We purchase avionics from China."

"In partnership with Iran Khodro and other manufacturers, we can have 100 more by this time next year," Ali Tajik said.

Yaghani grunted. More than likely, whatever they can produce would be replacing what was lost.

"Supersonic, you say?" Yaghani asked.

"Yes," Ali Tajik said. "Just," he added.

"Can we get all 50 in the air at the same time?" Yaghani asked.

Ali Tajik nodded but looked askance. "For a strike of that magnitude, we would need the element of surprise," Ali Tajik said. "And we probably wouldn't be able to pull it off a second time. It would be murder on our fleet of pilots," he said.

Yaghani looked deflated.

Ali Tajik smiled. "I take it that His Eminence hasn't told you about our Taklamakan Squadrons?"

"Our what?" Yaghani said.

"Well, now," Ali Tajik said, smiling.

13

T*his* was unexpected.

Yaghani could barely contain his enthusiasm.

After a four-hour flight from Isfahan, Yaghani stood on the tarmac of an air base deep in the Taklamakan Desert of Xinjiang Province in far western China.

Everything about Taklamakan Air Base appeared to be new. Even its runways – and there were many, and they were long – looked like they had been paved and painted the day before.

This was China's Area 51.

Fifteen large, reinforced hangars were spread out on the desert floor. Countless mound-shaped single and double aircraft bunkers filled the spaces in between.

General Yang Xiaogang of the People's Liberation Army Air Force, or PLAAF, greeted Yaghani. He was taking both Yaghani and Brigadier General Ali Tajik on a tour.

They rode together in a black van, its air conditioner on full blast, to one of the large hangars.

The desert shimmied beneath a clear, cloudless sky that stretched to the horizons.

The hangar was probably two miles away.

When they arrived, men in blue maintenance coveralls and green flight suits stood at attention. They were a mix of Chinese and . . . *Caucasians?*

"Carry on," Xiaogang commanded, and the men went about their work.

This happened each time they turned a corner.

Eventually they made it to the hangar floor.

Several black stealth fighters were parked side by side. They were sleek FC-31 Gyrfalcons, China's second stealth fighter.

"The FC-31 Gyrfalcon is an export-variant stealth fighter developed by the Shenyang Aircraft Corporation," Xiaogang said.

"The aircraft is designed for both air superiority and strike capabilities. Our two governments concluded a trade pact more than ten years ago. I am unaware of the details, but it involves discounted Iranian oil in exchange for squadrons of FC-31 Gyrfalcon aircraft, including training for your flight and maintenance crews."

General Yaghani was speechless.

"One hundred fifty aircraft," Brigadier General Ali Tajik offered, practically laughing.

"What's that?" Yaghani said, not seeming to believe what he was hearing.

"We have 150 FC-31 Gyrfalcon stealth fighters," said Ali Tajik, smiling from ear to ear.

"And the air and maintenance crews," he added, "all trained and experienced for the last decade, to come with them."

Yaghani stopped and shook his head.

Two fighter planes at the far end of the hangar were getting a fresh bright roundel painted on their fuselage and wings: green, white and red at the center, the roundel of the Islamic Republic of Iran Air Force (IRIAF).

"No low visibility roundels," Ali Tajik said. "Part of the stipulation."

"You said that the HESA Kowsar was the workhorse of our Air Force," Yaghani said. "Of which we have about 50."

Ali Tajik, still beaming with delight, nodded.

"If we have 150 . . . *Gyrfalcons* . . . with trained air and maintenance crews, then . . ." Yaghani trailed off.

"For most missions over the years, the Kowsar does the job," Ali Tajik said. "They also serve as training jets. All of our pilots here started out flying the Kowsar."

"But to go up against Israel, or the United States?," Ali Tajik continued. "The Kowsar doesn't cut it, not by a long shot. Nor the F-4 Phantoms."

"With the Gyrfalcon, we now have a degree of parity," Ali Tajik said. "Not sure how the Gyrfalcon stacks up against the F-35 – the Gyrfalcon hasn't flown in combat before – but Shenyang is confident in its performance."

Yaghani stared at the jets but wasn't really looking at them. He was deep in thought, calculating timelines.

It was just after noon when Yaghani and Ali Tajiki arrived back in Tehran.

An armored IKCO SUV awaited them, and when Yaghani and Ali Tajiki got in, Yaghani was handed an intelligence brief.

Yaghani sighed as he read the report.

"News?" asked Ali Tajiki.

Yaghani looked out the window of the armored SUV and handed the brief to Tajiki.

"Germany has joined with America and the Brits. The rest of NATO will fall in line now."

"Ali Tajiki," Yaghani said, "the time has come to get your personal affairs in order."

Yaghani made eye contact with the driver in the rearview mirror.

"Take us to the House of Leadership," he ordered.

Yaghani no longer needed an appointment to visit the House of Leadership. Once there, he and Ali Tajik found Ayatollah Sayyid Ali Al-Milani waiting for them in his office.

"It is time?" asked the Supreme Leader.

"It is," Yaghani said.

Ayatollah Al-Milani let out a long sigh. He gazed around his office, wearing a mournful expression. "I will do my part," he said.

"As for you, General Yaghani," the Supreme Leader continued. His eyes softened even as an expression of resoluteness hardened his face.

"Shoot for the moon."

The Orbit's so-called Battle Plan against the Americans rested on the premise that the Americans, despite three decades of military involvement in Iraq, did not fundamentally understand Iraq as a country.

Because, on the ground, Iraq *wasn't* a country at all, never mind the clean lines of demarcation on Western maps delineated as "Iraq".

The British Empire had pieced together eastern *viyalets,* or provinces, of the Ottoman Empire and created the Kingdom of Iraq at the close of World War I.

The Emirate of Trans-Jordan was created out of *western* viyalets of the former Ottoman Empire.

Both the Emirate of Trans-Jordan and the Kingdom of Iraq were led by sons of the Emir of Mecca, whose dynasty – the Hashemites – had ruled Mecca from the Tenth Century until the 1920s when Mecca was absorbed into the Kingdom of Saudi Arabia.

The diverse viyalets that the British had forced together into "Iraq," meanwhile, were anything but cohesive. The northern viyalets were largely composed of ethnic Kurds, a subgroup of the Iranian branch of the Indo-European family of languages, while the rest of the country were mostly Arabs.

Moreover, the Arab population of Iraq was geographically split between Sunni Muslims in the north and west, and Shi'a Muslims to the south. The capital of Baghdad, at the center of the country, was split evenly between the two sects.

So Iraq was essentially *three* countries: Kurdistan in the far north, Sunni Iraq in the north and west, and Shi'a Iraq in the south centered on Basra.

After they overthrew Saddam Hussein, who had kept the country together with brute force, the Americans could never put Humpty Dumpty back together again.

Nevertheless, the Americans continued to prop up the fictitious government in Baghdad and maintain military bases in Sunni Iraq and in Kurdistan. Shi'a Iraq in the south – increasingly if informally called "Basrastan" – had *de facto* been ceded to Iran, the cultural heart of Shi'a Muslims everywhere.

And so, when Saadi Yaqoob, Governor of the Iraqi Basra Governorate, was on television in Tehran at the invitation of Iran's Supreme Leader, his appearance was met with a collective yawn in both Baghdad and Washington.

"Pull up Press TV on your computer." It was Joy Chatterjee, calling Ray from the Sean Connery Fan Club in Langley.

Ray did as she told him. Press TV was Iran's state-owned English-language news channel, which broadcast live on the internet.

Iran's Supreme Leader was holding court with Iraq's Basra Governor at a presser at Golestan Palace, the former center of the Eighteenth-Century Qajar Dynasty, in Tehran.

"I wish to thank His Excellency Ayatollah Sayyid Ali-Al Milani for your hospitality," Yaqoob said through an interpreter.

"To celebrate our great friendship and a new era for relations between Iraq and Iran, Basra will host the first annual Friendship Games between our countries. Athletes from all sports will attend, both professional and amateur."

"Amateur games can be hosted as early as this week. For the main event – professional matches for the Friendship Cup – we will coordinate with the Persian Gulf Pro League in Tehran."

"Who are they kidding?" asked Ray. It was a rhetorical question.

"Boy are they desperate. But what is Iraq doing?"

"Basra enjoys a good deal of autonomy," Joy said. "I doubt Baghdad has anything to do with this. But we'll shake some trees to find out."

"This is just stupid," Ray said. "Pure propaganda. Just a desperate ploy to show how peaceful they are," he said.

Ray was wound up.

"Friendship Games!"

Ray shook his head. He started giggling.

"It's *laughable!* Completely ridiculous. No one's going to buy it!"

14

Some thirty miles southeast of Basra was the Ayatollah Al-Sistani International Friendship Bridge, which spanned the Shatt Al-Arab River, linking Iran and Iraq.

Named after the famed Iranian-born Iraqi scholar of Islam, the bridge was a dual span cable-stayed bridge with five spires that drew comparisons with the Viaduc de Millau in Southern France.

It was also multimodal. The northern span was built exclusively for high-speed rail, and the eight-lane southern span for vehicle traffic. Both spans sported Persian blue tiles that made the bridges sparkle in the sunlight, but especially at night when colored lights lit up the spires and cables.

Although the bridge – the recipient of multiple globally prestigious architecture awards – had already been open for several months, Yaqoob and Ayatollah Al-Milani announced a Grand Opening to coincide with the Friendship Games.

In celebration of both the bridge and renewed friendship between Iran and Iraq, Basra would welcome athletes from Iran almost immediately, starting with amateur and semi-professional soccer players.

Boats of the Iraqi Coastal Border Guards patrolled the border between Iraq and Iran along the Shatt al-Arab south of Basra, and also manned the main checkpoint on the Iraqi side of the bridge.

At the southern span of the bridge, hundreds of buses, cars and trucks converged on the Iranian side of the border in the middle of the night just two days after Yaqoobi and Al-Milani announced the Friendship Games.

The first in a long line of buses pulled into the border post in Al Seeba, Iraq, and a Coastal Border Guard entered to inspect the driver's paperwork. The vehicle was full of young men wearing tracksuits.

The guard asked the driver for his passport, passenger manifest and travel authorizations. The driver looked at him blankly, as did the passengers.

"Um, Guard?"

The border guard turned around.

A uniformed soldier awaited him outside the bus. It was an *Iranian* uniform.

A General, no less.

"Who are you?" the guard asked as he stepped off the bus.

"Hey, hey, hey!" he yelled as passengers disembarked from buses behind the first one, and scores of young men jogged to the border post, unzipping sports bags and pulling out . . .

The guard raised his hands.

. . . rifles.

The Iranian General unstrapped the guard's holster, taking his gun.

Within minutes, the entire guard station was commandeered by scores of armed Iranians in athletic gear.

Obstacles to traffic were removed and inbound traffic was allowed to flow unimpeded across the bridge toward the Al Faw Highway northward to Basra.

As they moved north, Iranian soldiers closed off entrances to the south-bound Al Faw Highway, which led to the eastbound span of the bridge, and opened *that* span to Iraq-bound traffic.

Thousands of buses and trucks, all carrying Iranian "athletes," poured into Iraq, following the highway to Basra Sports City, a massive sports complex on the outskirts of the city.

All night long they came.

The centerpiece of Basra Sports City was Basra International Stadium, with a capacity of 65,000 spectators, as well as two secondary stadiums with capacities of 10,000 each. By dawn, a sprawling tent city had sprung on the fields inside each of the stadiums, covering every square inch. More tents were erected in the parking lots. More buses and trucks arrived by the minute.

As the sun rose, city workers strung up banners with the words "Welcome, Athletes!" along the major roads of Basra, and tied the flags of both Iran and Iraq to light poles.

The tent city around the Basra International Stadium complex, meanwhile, sprawled out into the surrounding desert as the day wore on and buses continued to arrive from Iran.

Joy Chatterjee sensed someone at her office door. But when she looked up, there was no one there.

"Timmy, is that you?"

Timmy DiChiara poked his head inside the office.

"I've told you a gazillion times to just walk in or knock."

"Y–y-yes, ma'am."

"What do you have?"

Timmy entered, hesitantly.

"I-I've b-been monitoring Irr-rr-rraqi sss-social mm-mm media. L-lots of Irr-rr-ranians are f-f-flooding B-B-Basra."

Timmy closed his eyes and paused. He took a few slow, deep breaths – just as Joy had encouraged him to do when excited.

"Let me show you," he said, calming down.

He gestured to her computer. Joy rose and Timmy slid behind the desk. He quickly had several windows open with each loading a different website.

The first window was an Iraqi newspaper site with an article, all in Arabic, of course. Pictures showed buses surrounded by thousands of people. They appeared to be sports fans. They wore sports gear and were just about all young men.

"They announced Friendship Games," Joy said. "Propaganda. So what?"

The next window was from someone's social media account. It was cell phone footage of heavy foot and car – no, bus – traffic around a stadium complex. Horns blew.

"N-notice the tents," Timmy said.

Joy's expression was of . . . *yeah, and?*

The next several windows were more social media posts from people in Basra, mostly text.

Timmy translated a few.

"This one says that the Al-Faw Highway southbound was closed, that the highway was u-u-u-uni d-d-directional – all heading n-n-north to Basra," Timmy said.

"Like we do when there's a hurricane evacuation, l-like in Florida or L-Louisiana," Timmy said.

More social media complained of unprecedented traffic jams.

The last window got Joy's attention.

It was another grainy, jumpy cell phone video. But this one showed a tank under a tent, then two more as the car – the video was apparently taken from a car – slowly navigated heavy traffic near the stadium complex.

"I ordered satellite photos of . . .," Timmy gave the grid coordinates and time, then laid out several high resolution black and white photographs.

"This is the Ayatollah Al-Sistani International Friendship Bridge spanning the Shatt Al-Arab River," Timmy said.

Joy looked closely at the photographs.

There was an unbroken line of traffic for over 100 miles to Dezful, Iran, in the north, and another string of traffic from Shiraz, over 250 miles to the southeast.

"This isn't a sporting event," said Timmy, "and those aren't athletes."

"What are you saying?" Joy asked, her heart kicking up a notch.

"They're 'little green men' – like the Russians did in Crimea and Ukraine.

"It's an invasion, ma'am."

"Troops?" said Ayatollah Sayyid Ali Al-Milani. He chuckled at the podium.

"No, no, of course not. No, these are football athletes. Not 'little green men'. Don't believe what the Americans tell you," he said with a wave of his hand.

"They turn a gesture of friendship among neighbors into a military invasion. Please, don't lose your grounding in reality," he continued.

"Your Excellency, there are many reports of Iranian tanks in Basra, including videos and photographs on social media. Do you deny that there are Iranian tanks in Basra?" asked a female reporter from Al Jazeera, the Qatari-based news competitor to America's CNN and Fox News.

"Oh dear," Al-Milani said, looking sheepish. "Yes, there are Iranian tanks in Basra. But this is not part of some nefarious plot the Americans would have you believe."

"Your Excellency, if you allow," chimed in Saadi Yaqoob, Governor of the Iraqi Basra Governorate.

Al-Milani nodded, his eyes still smiling.

"We are planning opening ceremonies for the Friendship Games," Yaqoob said, also smiling. "There will be a parade showcasing cooperation between our two countries."

"We wanted it to be a surprise, but you know how social media goes," he said. Then he chuckled.

The joke, if that's what that was, did not go over well with the international press corps.

Crickets.

"Ahem," Yaqoob continued, "the parade will be composed mostly of Iraqi and Iranian athletes. But a small number of Iraqi and Iranian soldiers and tanks will also take part to highlight our growing friendship and cooperation," Yaqoob said. "There will be a flyover by the Iraqi and Iranian Air Forces," he added.

Daddy Longlegs returned to Washington in a hurry. This time, the principals of the Sean Connery Fan Club gathered at Number One Observatory Circle, and the Pentagon chiefs had joined them.

"How many Iranians are in Basra?" Longlegs asked, wasting no time.

"About 20,000 and growing," answered Joy Chatterjee. "The Israelis estimate 30,000."

Daddy Longlegs grunted. He leaned forward in his chair and stared intently at the large map of the Middle East and Persian Gulf.

"How many troops do we have in Kuwait?" Longlegs asked.

"About 400 force protection Marines at Camp Buehring near the Iraqi border," said Army General Alexander Pitt, Commander of the United States Central Command at MacDill Air Force Base in Tampa, Florida. "Along with a Patriot missile battery with crew. We also have 13,500 personnel at Camp Arifjan and Ali al Salem Air Base, south and west of Kuwait City. Mainly logistics staff and maintenance crews."

Longlegs grunted again.

"How does this change things for us?" he asked.

"It speeds things up," Pitt said. "We need to put the 82nd and 101st Airborne Divisions on alert for deployment ASAP to Kuwait.

I don't like seeing 30,000 Iranian troops just fifty miles from Camp Buehring."

"The XVIII Airborne Division is already gearing up for Operation Freedom Shield. They'll be deploying over the next month."

"The 24th Infantry Division, Mechanized, is also on alert and set to deploy in the coming days."

"Our attack plan was to avoid Basra, cross the Al-Faw Peninsula, and head straight to that Friendship bridge. From there, it was north to Dezful for Team A and south to Bushehr for Team B."

"But I don't want 30,000 Iranian troops, or however many they have, right off our flank," Pitt said.

A moment of silence as Longlegs thought.

"Are you suggesting that we engage the Iranians in Basra?" asked Longlegs.

Before Pitt could answer, Longlegs continued.

"No, fuck that. I don't want to get sucked into Basra. I don't want our boys getting bogged down in Iraq."

General Pitt looked down at the map, his brow furrowed in thought.

It was a long moment before he spoke.

"Maybe we can organize a Team C of coalition forces – Iraqi and Saudi – and engage the Iranians in Basra in a classic pincer maneuver while we provide air support. They'll be cut off and isolated once we move across the Al Faw."

"In the meantime, we stick with the plan of building up our forces and sending Teams A and B to their targets."

Daddy Longlegs stared some more at the large map, his forehead creased in thought.

He took a swig from his warming beer.

"Okay," said Longlegs. "I think that could work. I'll take it to the President."

He turned to Raymond Cole. "Ray, I need a backdoor point man in Kuwait and Riyadh. When can you leave?"

Another damn flight. This time it was almost half the distance, though, so God has mercy after all. Habib had grown tired of the flights long ago.

When he arrived at Isfahan Airport, he was whisked via armored SUV to the Sheik Lotfollah Mosque in the center of the city. The early 17th-century mosque was built during the reign of Shah Abbas I, and was one of the most important showcases of Persian architecture anywhere. It sat across from the Grand Ali Qapu Palace, which itself rivaled the largest and most beautiful palaces in the world.

Habib was surprised to find all the members of The Orbit there, including Hashemi Ghavam.

General Yaghani led the men in prayer, then they walked together across the sprawling courtyard of the Grand Ali Qapu to Char Bagh Boulevard, perhaps the most famous street in Iran, if not all the Middle East.

It was a wide pedestrian-only shaded boulevard lined with rows of mature trees, fountains, and benches.

"The time has come," General Yaghani said as he slowed to a leisurely walk.

"The Americans have their coalition. The buildup has begun. Their media is at a full fever pitch now, ceaselessly making the case for war. *'Remember the Bush'* has become their rallying cry."

"The American President has ordered their rapid reaction forces to Kuwait. They will be arriving in the coming hours.

"Even the Saudis are revving up," Yaghani said.

Yaghani stopped and the men gathered in a wide circle. He looked each of his men in the eye, one by one.

He reckoned that most, if not all of them, including himself, would be dead in a matter of days or weeks. Anything beyond that would be borrowed time.

"Have you prepared as instructed?" he asked. Each man nodded.

"Leadership in Tehran has gone to ground. This is the last time we meet in person."

"Go back to your commands and await my signal. Then give them hell."

PART THREE

OPENING CEREMONIES

15

The night was uneventful. General Yaghani and the Orbit were certain that the Americans would launch a fresh barrage of air strikes, but they didn't.

Not yet, anyway.

Meanwhile, Iranian infantry units, many of them reserve units, had been ordered to muster at Basra Sports City. The Ministry of Defense commandeered buses and taxis from across Iran to ferry the "athletes." Soldiers with private vehicles were encouraged to drive themselves. That meant thick traffic, as private cars, taxis and buses crawled across the Ayatollah Al-Sistani International Friendship Bridge into Iraq.

More than 60,000 Iranian soldiers had gathered by morning. Basra Sports City was in total disarray, but it was, to some extent, organized chaos. Senior officers worked to get soldiers and junior officers to their assigned units and made sure that everyone had the equipment they needed.

It was like the first day of school, but on a much grander scale.

Rear Admirals Hashemi Ghavam of the regular Navy, and Habibollah Nasirzadeh of the IRGC Navy, meanwhile, had returned to their respective commands in Bandar Abbas.

Hash had no fleet in Bandar Abbas. His ships were mostly in

Gwadar, Pakistan. However, the Pakistani government wanted no part of the U.S.-Iran Crisis, and happily agreed to let the fleet depart.

But first things first.

Sleep.

Habibollah had command of over 5,000 low-displacement IRGC Navy speedboats, all of them armed with anti-ship missiles and machine gun turrets. The speedboats were concentrated at points along Iran's Persian Gulf coast, and among several islands in and near the Strait of Hormuz.

Except for the USS *George W. Bush,* which sat in pieces on the seafloor, there were no American aircraft carriers in the Persian Gulf. The *Barack Obama* and *Doris Miller* were both operating somewhere in the nearby Gulf of Oman or further south in the Indian Ocean, but the Americans were keeping them out of the Gulf for security reasons.

Most of the supporting ships of the *Bush* battlegroup still lingered in the Gulf while the Americans investigated the *Bush* disaster and conducted salvage operations. They posed the biggest danger to Yaghani's air and land operations.

Habibollah's IRGC Navy boats and sailors were ready at a moment's notice. But he couldn't guarantee that they could maintain this state of readiness for long.

They would have to launch soon if they were to be effective.

Real soon.

Deep in the Taklamakan Desert of Xinjiang Province, the first of 150 FC-31 Gyrfalcon stealth fighters lifted off into the night sky.

Then the next one. And the next.

One after the other.

Once airborne, the planes flew in six formations of 25 aircraft apiece, a formation much practiced over several months.

The six formations headed for six separate airports outfitted ahead of time for their housing and maintenance: Doshan Tappeh Airbase in Tehran; Ramsar Airport on the Caspian Sea; Tabriz Airbase in northwestern Iran; Gorgan Airport in far northeastern Iran; Shahrokhi Airbase in western Iran; and Isfahan Airbase in central Iran.

After a scramble in Bandar Abbas between home and . . . certain appurtenances . . . Hashemi Ghavam was met at the airport in Gwadar, Pakistan, and quickly ushered to the Islamic Republic of Iran Ship *Sabalan*, moored at Pakistan's Gwadar Navy Base.

The Pakistanis were a bit frosty, and there was no stopping between the airport and the ship.

Nobody inspected his luggage, or the Persian carpet tucked under his arm.

The IRIS *Sabalan* was the newest of ten domestically built *Moudge*-class frigates, and Hash's flagship. With a displacement of about 1,500 tons, they weren't very large, but they were still Iran's biggest warships.

The frigates, five attack submarines and three logistics and landing ships represented the entirety of Iran's regular Navy.

They slipped out of Pakistan's Gwadar Navy Base at dusk and headed due west. The ships lined up behind the *Sabalan* while the submarines stayed out in front and along the flotilla's flanks as it clung to the coast.

"Full speed ahead," Hash ordered. One by one, the ships' hulls lurched upward before settling into a planing speed of about twenty-five knots.

An hour later, the flotilla entered Iranian waters. A few hours more, and they would be entering the Strait of Hormuz.

So far so good.

It was dusk in the Indian Ocean, and aboard the USS *Barack H. Obama* and the USS *Doris Miller,* the first wave of attack aircraft launched from the electromagnetic catapults.

Two hundred-eighty miles southwest of Washington, DC, where it was still mid-afternoon, twenty U.S. Air Force four-engine C-17 Globemaster cargo planes, each ferrying one hundred 82nd Airborne paratroopers, lifted off from Fort Liberty, North Carolina.

Five hundred miles west of Fort Liberty, at Fort Campbell, Kentucky, twenty C-17s – each carrying a hundred 101st Airborne paratroopers, began their takeoffs.

Along the backed-up taxiway at Fort Campbell were additional C-17s, ferrying units of the 24th Infantry Division, Mechanized.

The destination of all three rapid deployment forces?

Kuwait.

16

I n Basra, Iraq, the sky was fiery as the sun sank out of view to the west, and the desert assumed a reddish Martian hue.

Mars.

The Roman God of War.

General Mohammed Yaghani lifted his encrypted phone. He selected the preprogrammed group list of commanders of Iran's armed forces, and texted.

Go.

He looked out on the starkly reddish desert framed by a darkening sky. It was the blue hour now, and the contrast between desert and sky was breathtaking.

Yaghani looked back to the crowded busyness of Basra Sports City behind him. He sighed.

He hit send.

That was it.

There were no fireworks, no earthquakes. Nothing extraordinary.

Nothing at all.

Just the start of a war.

The Taklamakan Squadrons had no time to rest upon their arrival at their assigned airbases.

Not the aircraft, anyway. Fresh flight and maintenance crews had awaited their arrival.

The planes were thoroughly but swiftly inspected, then fueled and armed.

Go, came the order.

As the first squadrons took off, lights off and unseen, explosions began to light up the night skies over Bandar Abbas, and also over Bushehr, Vahdati Airbase in Dezful, and Omidiyeh Airbase in Omidiyeh.

The Americans.

All the initial targets were west of the Zagros Mountains near Iraq and within the provinces ascribed to Teams A and B.

Unbeknownst to the Iranians, of course.

Explosions were later reported at the Natanz nuclear facility in the desert near Isfahan, and other, supposedly secret, sites in the deserts and mountains throughout the Iranian Plateau.

Facilities of Iran's secret nuclear weapons program.

The six FC-31 Gyrfalcon Taklamakan Squadrons, meanwhile, sped to their own targets.

Colonel Ashgar Samii, commanding officer of Taklamakan Squadron 1, based in Tehran, led his comrades south over the Iranian Plateau in supersonic supercruise mode.

When they bolted out over the Persian Gulf, they dove to skim a few yards above the wave tops.

Samii and the pilots under his command had trained in the Gyrfalcon for over five years, and the aircraft had always responded like a dream. But flying it now, over the Gulf and on a real life or death mission, the feeling was indescribable.

Bahrain was almost due south, and within minutes the myriad

lights of Manama appeared out of the darkness before them. Samii and the rest of the squadron dropped out of supercruise and slowed to subsonic speed.

There were no warnings on his display, and he saw neither tracer fire nor telltale signs of a missile.

He almost couldn't believe it. The stealth part of "stealth fighter plane" was living up to its name.

Samii followed the preprogrammed GPS-mapped path around the eastern side of Bahrain before making a sharp near U-turn into the Khawr al Qulayaa cove between the main island of Bahrain and Muharraq Island, which were connected by a short bridge.

Twenty-two warships were tied up alongside the main Mina Salmon pier and along the seawall next to Naval Support Activity Bahrain, headquarters of America's Fifth Fleet, according to the latest satellite photos provided by Tehran's friends in the East.

Just like Pearl Harbor.

Samii immediately recognized the pier and seawall through his night vision visor. It wasn't *exactly* like the virtual simulation he and his comrades had practiced, but it was close.

Samii pressed the targeting button, and four separate targets were instantly selected for him: three ships at the outer reach of the pier, along with the Patriot missile battery in the middle of the pier.

A major feature of fifth-generation stealth Gyrfalcons was that they were networked, much like the American F-35 Lightnings. Their integrated computers immediately and efficiently distributed the targeting of the seventy-five YJ-12 anti-ship missiles.

The Gyrfalcon's computer toned, marking target acquisitions.

Samii pressed fire.

The aircrafts' bomb bay doors opened in sync, and each plane's payload of three anti-ship cruise missiles dropped out and ignited.

With the bomb bay doors open, Samii and the aircraft behind him had lost their stealthiness, if only momentarily.

The bomb bay doors closed and Samii yanked on his control stick. He rocketed skyward, his aircraft perceptibly lighter, as the missiles streaked to their targets.

From the corner of his eye, he was sure that he had seen a missile streaking up from the ground toward him before the missile battery was engulfed in a fireball.

He looked to his right and saw it. The missile had streaked harmlessly out to sea.

For a time, Taklamakan Squadrons 3, 4 and 5 followed close behind Samii's squadron. Then, Squadron 5 made a wide U-turn and cut across southern Bahrain. They swooped down on King Abdul Aziz Air Base in Khobar, Saudi Arabia, just across the King Fahd Causeway from the western side of Bahrain.

Squadrons 3 and 4 crossed into Qatar. They flew over open desert west of the city of Doha before making a U-turn toward the sprawling Udeid Air Base, a joint American and Qatari air base.

The tarmac there was filled with Air Force Boeing KC-46 Pegasus aerial refueling tankers, along with C-17 Globemaster cargo planes and Navy Boeing P-8 Poseidon patrol and anti-submarine aircraft.

At the end of the main runway was another tarmac. Five eight-engine B-52 Stratofortress strategic bombers were parked there.

The crown jewel, a squadron of F-22 Raptors and two squadrons of F-15 Eagles, were hidden from view. They were parked under Quonset hut-shaped hardened aircraft shelters.

Udeid Air Base was the true center of American air power in the Middle East.

While the F-22 Raptors were a threat to the FC-31 Gyrfalcons, they were not the Taklamakan Squadrons' target. Nor were the runways.

Squadrons 3 and 4 were armed entirely with next-generation Eagle Strike 91 anti-radiation missiles. With four missiles per aircraft, and fifty aircraft, 200 missiles screamed across the desert toward the base radars, anti-aircraft missile batteries and Patriot anti-ballistic missile batteries.

The runways and the aircraft, particularly the F-22s, F-15s and B-52s, would have to wait.

It didn't make sense to the pilots, but they had their orders.

"Trust the plan," they had been told.

When the bomb bay doors opened on the twenty-five FC-31 Gyrfalcons of Samii's squadron, the automated Phalanx Close-In Weapons Systems (CIWS, or "sea whiz") radar aboard the four *Arleigh Burke-class* destroyers – the USS *Richard Lugar, Telesforo Trinidad, Sam Nunn* and *Carl Levin* – immediately detected the aircraft and then the missiles.

Seventy-five of them.

The trouble was time. The aircraft opened their bomb bay doors at four miles out, and the missiles dropped and ignited at 3.5 miles. The missiles then accelerated to Mach 1.5 and closed the distance in less than sixty seconds.

The first sign of trouble was the soul-ripping sound of the Phalanx machine guns on the outer two *Arleigh Burke* destroyers as they opened fire.

BRRRRRRRRRRRP. BRRRRRRRRRRRP.

The first ten missiles were destroyed, but the next four found their mark. Two penetrated the hulls of supply ships lined up on the Mina Salmon pier, and two more hit the destroyers. Their Phalanx guns took out three more missiles before both ships absorbed three more missiles between them.

The Phalanx machine guns of *Richard Lugar,* one of the inner destroyers, kicked into action, shredding three FC-31 Gyrfalcons while the *Telesforo Trinidad*, the other inner destroyer, cut down another Gyrfalcon and fifteen missiles before running out of targets. The remaining missiles had already hit their targets, and the squadron of Gyrfalcons was now out of range.

The Patriot missile battery had detected the aircraft, as well, and managed to launch one missile before two Y-12 anti-radiation missiles slammed into it, lighting up the night with a massive explosion.

17

The rugged Zagros Mountains, with their snow-capped peaks and rich, forested steppes, stretch from southeastern Turkey and northern Iraq to the Strait of Hormuz, marking most of western Iran.

Along the roads that follow the fertile valleys and snake through mountain passes were more than 100 trucks mounted with *Raad-500* ballistic missiles, with a short range of 500 kilometers (310 miles), and *Khorramshahr* ballistic missiles, with a medium range of 3,000 kilometers (1,860 miles). They were following algorithm-derived routes that made it difficult to track them in an area of 64,000 square miles.

Further north and east, in the heart of the Iranian Plateau, were seventeen transporter erector launchers (TELs), separated from each other by tens to hundreds of miles.

The TELs carried an even more potent missile: the *Zamburak*. The *Zamburak* was a domestically built replica of the North Korean Hwasong-18 intercontinental ballistic missile, or ICBM.

North Korea had gladly shared its missile technologies – and even its scientists and technicians – with Iran.

For oil, of course.

Some of the *Hwasong-18* missiles test-fired in North Korea to much global handwringing were actually *Zamburak* missiles.

The *Hwasong-18* and *Zamburak* missiles had an estimated range of 9,000 miles, which put all of the continental United States within range. Indeed, *all* states and territories of the United States were in range of the missiles, with the possible exception of American Samoa in the South Pacific.

Trying to track the TELs would be like seeking a needle in a haystack, or worse, seeking a single grain of sand on a beach.

Each TEL had received their own encrypted signal, timed to coincide with the last of the Taklamakan Squadron's time on target.

Go.

Their crews went to work. Each erector was raised perpendicular to the ground. Following a well-practiced sequence of actions, the missiles were armed.

Secondary checks and confirmations were performed.

Near simultaneously, 100 short- and medium-range ballistic missiles in the Zagros Mountains, and twenty-seven ICBMs in the Iranian Plateau, arced brightly into the night sky.

The United States Space Force manages the U.S. Space-Based Infrared System (SBIRS). SBIRS has multiple satellites orbiting the earth in a high Molniya orbit, which keeps them suspended for long periods over the Northern Hemisphere. The satellites maintain a largely geosynchronous and geostationary orbit, which means they appear nearly stationary when viewed from Earth. Many of the satellites "hover" over the Eastern Hemisphere as well, covering Russia, China, India and the Middle East.

Heat sensors aboard the satellites detect thermal radiation produced by the intense heat of a missile's exhaust plume. Each missile class or model produces a unique heat signature, coupled with speed, arc and maximum trajectories, that are categorized by SBIRS computers at several locations: Peterson Space Force Base in Colorado Springs, Colorado; Cheyenne Mountain Space Force Station, also in Colorado Springs; Buckley Space Force Station in Aurora, Colorado; and Redstone Arsenal in Huntsville, Alabama.

Multiple satellites triangulate the missile, while onboard computers calculate its real time arc, speed and trajectory, sharing the data with the computers at Peterson, Cheyenne Mountain, Buckley and Redstone.

As the 100 Iranian ballistic missiles lifted skyward, every single one was quickly identified and categorized by the onboard satellite computers and SBIRS computers at the four bases.

Nestled among the large "golf-ball" radomes protecting the satellite dishes, radar and telecommunications infrastructure of the Aerospace Data Facility at Buckley Space Force Base in Aurora, Colorado, was the United States Space Force 2nd Space Warning Squadron.

The 2nd Space Warning Squadron commanded the space-based infrared system and satellites that monitored the globe for significant infrared events – like missile launches.

Boooop.

It was an annoying sound – one meant to grab your attention.

A map of the Middle East appeared on a big screen covering the east wall of the windowless building. Analysts poked their heads out of their cubicles. A small red circle appeared in the Zagros Mountains.

Five more circles appeared.

On the wall, a rotating red beacon light lit up and started spinning. A klaxon alarm blared.

The map on the wall zoomed out to encompass all of Iran. More red circles began appearing across the country.

The analysts scurried back to their desks and furiously clicked on the icons on their computer screens, unable to keep up as more red circles appeared.

General Yaghani performed his *Isha,* or night prayer, alone in the desert.

It had been almost an hour since he texted his orders.

It was time.

General Yaghani trekked back to the sea of endless tents. Seemingly carefree young soldiers were milling about, chatting with friends, laughing, smoking.

There were too many salutes to return as soldiers snapped to attention. He simply smiled and nodded as he picked his way through the tent city.

He stepped out onto Highway 80, where a convoy of military transport trucks, Safir jeeps and commercial buses were lining up.

Highway 80.

The Highway of Death.

This was the highway that Iraq had used in its invasion of Kuwait in August 1990. It was also the highway along which fleeing Iraqi soldiers tried to escape the advancing American armies in January 1991.

On the open highway, they were sitting ducks.

American and coalition warplanes swooped down, bombing and strafing them.

It was a turkey shoot.

A massacre.

General Colin Powell, then Chairman of the Joint Chiefs of Staff, was so alarmed that he implored President George H.W. Bush to halt the war which, to his credit, he did.

Yaghani eased himself into a Saffir jeep. Soldiers erupted in cheers.

Yaghani stood and saluted, then pointed south to Kuwait. His jeep, which was in the lead, inched forward before speeding up.

The convoy followed.

Thirty minutes later, as the head of the lengthening convoy approached the border town of Safwan, Iraq, the night sky flashed along the southern horizon like far away lightning.

Again and again, nonstop, like a vicious summer storm.

A moment later, the continuous rumble of far-away thunder, muffled by the distance, met their ears.

But there was no lightning. And that wasn't thunder.

Yaghani knew what it was.

Confirmation that the IRGC Aerospace Force had received his orders.

War had begun.

As the convoy passed through the town of Safwan, several green flares lit up the sky ahead. As the flares, dangling from small parachutes, drifted lazily down from the starlit darkness, they cast an eerie green hue over the town.

IRGC commandos of the special forces *Saberin* unit had secured the Kuwaiti border post.

Saberin. *The patient ones.*

The green flares were *the green light* to enter Kuwait.

18

President Cynthia Belle took her seat behind the Resolute Desk in the Oval Office. Bright camera lights trained on her as a makeup artist brushed highlights onto her cheeks.

Here we go again.

It had been almost two weeks since the last round of airstrikes had ended, but Iran had shown no signs of cooperation or backing down.

Sure, they removed their fleet from the Persian Gulf and benched their speedboats, but at the same time they deployed hundreds of new anti-aircraft or anti-ship missile batteries all along the coast practically overnight, and multiple short and medium-range mobile missile launchers. US air strikes barely made a dent in either.

They had sent a hit squad to Manama to tie up loose ends after their terrorist attack on America's Navy base in Bahrain, and on the Al Qudaibiya Palace.

And as Daddy Longlegs secured an international coalition for possible war if they didn't heel, it appeared that they had invaded southern Iraq by stealth.

Maybe Daddy Longlegs was right all along. Maybe it *was* time to remove that backward regime from power, once and for all. It wasn't like they were giving her any other choice.

The President cleared her throat as the digital clock beneath the camera counted down from ten. At zero, a green light came on.

"Good evening. Earlier today, I ordered America's armed forces to strike a broad range of military targets in Iran. Their mission is to attack Iran's nuclear, chemical, and biological weapons programs and degrade its military capacity –"

A commotion behind the cameras caught Cynthia's attention as the camera lights went dark. Secret Service agents burst into the room.

"Go, go, go!" the lead agent shouted, and the men barreled out of the Oval Office, knocking over television lights, the president between them.

A deafening alarm blared.

"What's going *on?"* shouted the President.

She ran, and was half-dragged, down the hall toward the South Lawn.

"We're under attack, ma'am!" the lead agent shouted.

Raymond Cole's plane touched down at Ali Salem Air Base, west of Kuwait City, just before sundown.

He had a scheduled meeting early the next day with the Defense Minister of Kuwait, who also happened to be the Crown Prince. Later in the day, he would fly to Riyadh and meet with defense officials there.

The base commander, Air Force General Sheila Blake, met him at his plane and welcomed him to Kuwait. She gave him a brief tour of the base, which was bustling with activity despite the late hour. Buses and troop transport trucks were lining up at the base terminal. They would ferry soldiers of the 82nd and 101st Airborne Divisions – due to arrive overnight – to Camp Buehring, near the Iraqi border, where a logistics and engineering battalion was building a tent city.

A loud siren sounded, rising in pitch, and then another. They reminded him of the volunteer fire department sirens where he lived in Maryland.

"Is that an air raid siren?" asked Raymond, chuckling nervously.

He looked to the general.

She wasn't laughing.

She was looking at the sky. Raymond followed her gaze, the smile lingering on his face.

A red flare was suspended high in the sky.

Ray's smile evaporated.

The red flare appeared to be moving, gaining speed.

No, it was *falling*.

Several more flares appeared behind it.

"Follow me!" the General commanded, grabbing Ray's hand.

"Get down!" she commanded.

Moving as fast as a meteor, the red flare was quite suddenly upon them. Sheila thrust a leg in front of Ray and tripped him, sending him to the ground. She followed him down to the ground and covered her head with her hands.

A deafening *BOOM was* followed by searing heat on their backs. Sand filled Ray's mouth as he opened it wide and screamed, but his scream was drowned out by the roar of the explosion.

Another massive *BOOM* and the ground bucked. It felt like a kick to the face and then the ribs as they were lifted up and dropped back down.

Another and another. Kicked up, dropped down, kicked up, dropped down, tossed sideways, smashed in the ribs, kicked in the teeth, a mouthful of sand.

Welcome to Kuwait, Defense Guy, Sheila thought and nearly giggled but for a kick to her stomach. A sledgehammer to her ankle.

A hellish, endless roar.

It went on and on until . . .

Nothing.

Thew Bryson was now working in the Material Delivery Unit (MDU). The midnight shift, of course.

MDU was the Navy's version of UPS and FedEx. They even drove the same Isuzu Reach walk-through delivery vans, though the Navy's trucks were usually yellow and had U.S. NAVY and a serial number stenciled on the door.

Some poor bastard got demoted and sent to First Lieutenant to swab decks and clean the heads, releasing Thew to the Supply Department.

Thew was a rare bird among young people. He was a morning person, which meant he was snoring away atop a role of bubble wrap. His immediate supervisor, Seaman Dave Skaggs, could wake him if an order came in for a delivery.

Skaggs was asleep himself, face down on his desk.

Skaggs jumped when the telephone rang. He looked at the printer and saw that a requisition had come through.

As he reached for the phone, a massive *BOOM* shook the building and nearly knocked Skaggs out of his chair.

Several more *BOOMS* sent Skaggs scurrying under his desk.

"What the hell's going on?" It was the MDU driver, that Thew kid, disheveled and bleary-eyed.

"Get down!" yelled Skaggs, and Thew crouched in a corner of the room.

What happened next was like the grand finale of a fireworks show. The *booms* bled into each other, combined with the sound of multiple jackhammers, and the whole building seemed ready to come down on top of them.

Thew bolted for the door, and Skaggs followed.

The main base warehouse – Warehouse 1 – was a long rectangular structure that paralleled the Prince Khalifa Bin Salman Causeway on the dockside of NSA Bahrain, but was separated from the highway by a high wall.

Thew and Skaggs bolted across the street to the wall.

The "grand finale" was over as quickly as it had begun, but the jackhammers continued for a few more seconds.

Thew and Skaggs kept running.

The northeast corner of the base was about 300 yards away; the two slowed and started walking, their eyes glued on the sea.

The jackhammers had stopped. It was a monstrous sound. Like a tear in the fabric of time and space, and God only knew what sorts of beasts and dragons of another dimension had come through.

Flames leapt into the night sky behind their building, and white lights reached to the horizon like a string of pearls.

Tracer fire, Thew realized.

Bernice Hamandawana was exhausted. Mentally, physically, emotionally.

Danny, the young cameraman who had been at her side when they got caught in the crossfire between the so-called Motown Mafia drug gang and the U.S. Army during the Detroit uprising, was released from the hospital on his 21st birthday. Doctors were optimistic that he would make a full recovery, more or less.

More or less? What the hell did that mean?

She was a celebrity of sorts. Her on-the-scene video reports and articles for *The South End,* Wayne State University's student newspaper, and the independent *Motown Mirror*, were picked up by news outlets worldwide. They had even caught the eye of senior CNN executives in Atlanta.

She and Danny were nominated for the Pulitzer Prize.

It was hard to imagine.

Today was her first day in the Washington bureau of CNN. She would soon work at the military affairs desk, but today was a whirlwind of tasks, tours and introductions.

She met Wolf Blitzer and other DC-based CNN dignitaries. Bernice was starstruck.

And now she celebrated in her new apartment in Adams Morgan. Even with four roommates, she could barely afford it.

The kids were enjoying beer, wine and chicken wings from the Georgetown Wing Company down the street. With chips and dip, of course.

Bernice licked her fingers and sipped red wine. One of her roommates turned up the television. Breaking news on CNN.

More air strikes in Iran. The president would address the nation about the situation there shortly.

When she came on, the roommates and friends gathered around.

The President was just a few sentences into her address when the TV lights in the Oval Office went dark.

Men in suits – Secret Service, for sure – rushed into view, but they were more like silhouettes in the dark room.

"Go, go, go!" one of them barked before rainbow bars with PLEASE STAND BY filled the TV screen.

"What the hell?" said Jason, the boyfriend of one of Bernice's roommates.

A CNN reporter now came onscreen, but the sound was interrupted by three squawks followed by a droning tone.

The Emergency Broadcast System.

A recorded message followed.

"The United States Northern Command has detected a missile threat to the Washington, DC, area."

A red banner scrolled across the center of the screen. *"A missile may impact on land or sea within minutes. THIS IS NOT A DRILL."*

"If you are indoors, stay indoors. If you are outdoors, seek immediate shelter."

Outside, sirens near and far began to whine, their pitch rising and falling independently of each other.

"Remain indoors well away from windows. If you are driving,

pull safely to the side of the road and seek shelter in a building or lay on the floor."

Everyone's phone vibrated and buzzed with an emergency alert.

"What's going on?" It was Deborah, one of Bernice's roommates. She worked at the Congressional Budget Office.

"We will announce when the threat has ended."

"Take immediate action. THIS IS NOT A DRILL."

Another of Bernice's roommates, Barbara, started crying. "What do we *do?*" Her hands were shaking.

Jason went to the front door and out onto the street. Bernice and the others followed.

Outside, the air raid sirens were louder. Deafening.

Jason and Bernice ran across the street to Kalorama Park. The rest followed, except for Barbara, who clung to the door of their row house. Bernice noticed people cautiously stepping out of other row houses and onto their porches, looking skyward.

★ ★ ★

A sleek double-rotor Raider helicopter swooped down from the night sky, and landed, its side door already open.

The President was literally shoved into the helicopter, and the Raider – now designated "Marine One" – lifted off.

It wasn't on the ground for more than thirty seconds.

Moments later, the Raider landed at Joint Base Andrews, just yards from Air Force One.

The VC-25B version of a Boeing 747-8 sat at the end of the runway, ready to roll, its four engines already revved up.

President Belle was practically carried by her Secret Service detail to Air Force One. As she ran up the stairs, two more Raider helicopters landed.

Archie Meglowin, America's First Gentleman and one-time playboy son of British billionaire financier Alfred Meglowin, exited one of the Raiders and bounded up the stairs to Air Force One with their 12-year-old daughter Katie in his arms.

Oscar Schwartz, the President's National Security Advisor, Martin Hartshorne, the President's Chief of Staff, and Admiral Erik Sorenson, the Chairman of the Joint Chiefs of Staff, also raced up the stairs to Air Force One.

After Admiral Sorenson entered the aircraft, the door closed behind him and the stairs were pulled away. The pilot was given the green light, and he took the engines up to full throttle.

Air Force One seemed to sink momentarily as the large aircraft rocketed forward.

The nose lifted up followed by the body. The bumpiness of the runway gave way to floating on air.

"What the *hell* is going on, Oscar?" the President asked. She sat at the head of the Air Force One dining room, which doubled as a conference room.

"Madam President, NORAD and Space Force satellites detected 110 individual missile launches in Iran," said Oscar. "Most appear to be short- and medium-range ballistic missiles, but twenty-six appear to be ICBMs," Oscar said.

"Are they nuclear?" she asked.

"We won't know . . . until . . ."

His voice trailed off. He didn't need to finish the sentence.

"Ma'am," said Admiral Sorenson, "I recommend that we go to Defense Condition One *immediately*. This puts all of our armed forces – including our nuclear forces – on emergency alert, ready to deploy at a moment's notice."

"Defcon *One?*" said the President. "That's nuclear war!"

"Not quite, ma'am," said Sorenson. "But if any of those ICBMs are nuclear, we need to be ready to retaliate in force."

"How much time before impact?"

Sorenson looked at his watch, then at the map on the screen in the conference room.

"Seventeen minutes. DEFCON One puts our attack submarines out to sea, ready to respond in . . . in case. It also puts strategic bombers in the air and our silos on alert."

The President looked down at the table, her brow furrowed.

"Okay. Defcon One. But if those missiles turn out to be non-nuclear, we immediately drop to Defcon Two."

The President pulled her chair back and leaned forward. She rested her cheeks in her fists.

Is she crying? Oscar wondered. *Are you fucking crying?*

The President looked up. "What are the targets?"

She wasn't crying.

"We're not quite sure yet –"

The Commander of NORAD, General Jack "Ripper" Sterling, appeared on the TV screen. "Twenty-six missiles total so far, Ma'am. Two missiles have hit Diego Garcia in the Indian Ocean, and four more are headed to Guam in the Pacific."

"That's four," said the President.

"Yes, Ma'am. The remaining twenty appear to be headed toward the East Coast and the Houston area."

Ripper looked off camera and took some papers that were handed to him. He cleared his throat and sat up straight. He thrust his chest out as he skimmed the documents and cleared his throat again.

"Ten missiles are trekking to DC, Ma'am, and ten to Houston, uh, Ma'am." He cleared his throat again.

"How long?" the President asked.

"Fifteen minutes, Ma'am."

The President closed her eyes and rubbed her forehead.

DC I get. Same for Guam and Diego Garcia. But why Houston?

"What's in Houston?" she asked.

Thew and Skaggs rounded a corner and jogged the quarter mile to the waterfront.

The air was revoltingly pungent, and Thew shielded his mouth and nose with his arm.

Ships were tied up side-by-side along the seawall in pairs – two pairs of *Arleigh Burke-class* destroyers and two pairs of smaller *Cyclone-class* patrol ships. Black oily smoke poured from most of them, especially the four outer ships.

The inner *Arleigh Burke* destroyers seemed to have sustained less damage. The crew of one destroyer had managed to pull it into the cove. It was the USS *Richard Lugar.*

The crew on the second inner *Arleigh Burke,* the USS *Telesforo Trinidad,* scrambled to follow suit.

The two outer *Arleigh Burk* were adrift, one listing heavily, thick smoke pouring from its middle.

It exploded in a massive fireball.

Thew and Skaggs fell to the ground and covered their heads.

I am going to die, Thew thought, as his exposed skin burned from the searing heat.

The fireball quickly faded as it rose above the port.

Thew raised his head in time to catch the bow of the ship slip backward and sink beneath a sea of fire.

The remaining *Arleigh Burke,* itself consumed by smoke, seemed to gather steam and fade into the darkness beyond the islands of flames.

Thew looked to Skaggs, who picked himself up.

"Are you okay?" asked Thew.

Skaggs patted himself up and down his body.

"I think so. You?"

Thew nodded.

Three smaller ships were tied up solo, lined up along the seawall. They were the *Cyclone-class* patrol ships.

One was on its side, one was listing heavily, and the third was unnaturally low in the water. Thick smoke poured from each, and shipboard alarms rang out incessantly.

Three quarters of a mile down the seawall was the long Mina Salmon pier, where the big supply ships were moored. Each of them remained upright but belched heavy black smoke.

Sailors and soldiers appeared, tentatively emerging from buildings and cover before springing into action.

Thew and Skaggs jogged to a group of sailors who were trying to string out some hoses to battle the shipboard fires.

Air raid sirens sounded.

Everyone stopped and looked up.

A red, falling star. Then ten of them. Then countless more.

Straight overhead.

Thew dropped his hose and backpedaled, still gazing at the sky.

A chief petty officer followed Thew's gaze and did a double take.

"Run!" he yelled.

Half the neighborhood seemed to be outside looking at the sky.

It was a cloudless, starlit night. The sirens had stopped, but the warning was still in effect.

The collective mood, from what Bernice could tell, was oddly festive.

Everyone seemed to think that the missile warning would turn out to be a mistake.

In the meantime, party like it's 1999.

"What's that?" asked one of the roommates' friends, pointing east.

Bernice followed his finger and spotted the white star. It was moving south, with four others right behind it.

Now, three *red* stars appeared simultaneously.

The three red stars became six, then nine.

The white stars flickered and disappeared. The red stars grew brighter. Bernice could make out contrails behind each of them.

They seemed to be reaching out, like fingers, reaching down . . .

Everyone started running.

"Get in the basement!" someone shouted.

They ran back inside and sprinted down the stairs to the basement.

Like a gymnast, Bernice used the handrails to propel herself down the stairs, taking four at a time. When she reached the basement, she felt a deep bass *wump* in her chest. The basement seemed to rock side to side.

Somebody screamed. *Probably Barbara.*

A strong scent of sawdust permeated the air.

Another *wump,* then another. Then . . .

Wump   wump   wump   wump-wump-wump-wump-wump-wump-wump . . .

The house shook. Bernice could hear glass breaking upstairs.

The lights flickered and went out. They came back on, then went out.

. . . *wump-wump-wump-wump-wump* . . .

Lights on again.

It was quiet.

Is it over?

The lights flickered again.

Someone was whimpering.

Bernice stared at a lamp near a stationary bike. When it stopped flickering, Bernice stood and brushed herself off.

She could hear sirens. They were of the firetruck or ambulance variety, not air raid sirens.

Bernice raced up the stairs. The gang followed her, tentatively.

The house was fine. Bernice's glass of red wine had fallen and broken on the hardwood floor. Some books had fallen from a shelf.

She went to her purse, fished out her press credentials, and ran to the front door.

★ ★ ★

Lippo Cichetti turned to his right and sprinted. The sound of the ball off the bat meant a solid hit, and he could tell right away that it was in the gap.

Run on your toes, he reminded himself. The coach preached it at every practice.

Lippo glanced up, found the ball sailing fast through the air, and it was headed over his head.

He looked down at his feet and let loose. He sprinted as fast as he could and looked up again over his shoulder.

There it was. Over his head still, but . . .

He extended his arm up and leaped. He felt the ball land in his glove in the middle of his stride.

Squeeze, he commanded himself, and the ball was secure in his glove.

The fence was right before him, but he had just enough room for a couple more strides to carry his momentum, and that was it.

It was a good catch to end the game.

The few people in the bleachers who had stuck around through the rain delay erupted in cheers. His teammates high-fived each other on their way to the dugout.

"Nice catch," said Devin, the center fielder.

"Thanks!"

Lippo entered the dugout and absorbed several slaps on his head, shoulders, back, and backside.

He was glowing inside. He loved game days. And it wasn't just the game and playing it. He would be excited the night before. And in the morning, he couldn't wait to get dressed.

He got to wear his baseball jersey to school all day long, in all of his classes. He didn't know if anyone else felt it like he did, but it was an amazing feeling to be seen in his jersey and identified as a player on the varsity baseball team.

He was just a regular kid any other day, but on game days, he was a *baseball player.*

He ran cross country, too, in the fall, but it wasn't the same. They didn't wear their running gear to class on days they had a meet. And even if they did, nobody would care. It wasn't baseball.

Lippo grabbed his sports bag and sat in the dugout. He took off his cleats and exchanged them for sneakers.

Tornado sirens started to sound off.

That wasn't unusual. It was southeast Texas, after all.

Lippo and his teammates glanced around. It has humid, of course – it always was this time of the year – but there was no lightning or storms. Maybe a storm was a county or two away.

Lippo exchanged his uniform for a T-shirt and sweats and slung his sports bag over his shoulder. Devin, too, was ready, but they waited on Alex, the second baseman, who leaned on the fence and talked to a pretty blonde girl.

While they waited for Alex, Lippo made his way to the bleachers where Sara waited for him.

"Good game," she said. Lippo wrapped his arm around her neck and pulled her in for a peck on the top of her head. She pinched his ribs and giggled, and he pulled away.

"Ouch!" Sara said, rubbing her head. "You pulled my hair!"

"Ahhh!" exclaimed Lippo, his hands at his mouth.

"Your hair got caught in my braces!" he said. He dabbed a finger on his teeth and examined it. It was smeared with a bit of blood.

"I'm *wounded!"* he said.

"Let me see," Sara said, and Lippo pulled his lower lip.

"Oh my God," Sara exclaimed, and giggled.

"Geez," Lippo said, and spit. "Your hair is a lethal weapon."

"You're the one who tried to eat my hair," Sara said, still laughing.

Devin and Alex caught up and the four of them made their way to the commercial Center Street. It was dark now. The lights of the former Shell, now PEMEX (Petróleos Mexicanos), oil refinery on the other side of Pasadena Freeway shone brightly behind them. The lights of the baseball field were still on, too.

There was a lot of traffic. It was backed-up, even, with a line of cars waiting to get into a Circle K gas station. Another line was waiting to get into an Exxon a block away.

They made their way across the street towards a Dairy Queen. Something caught Lippo's eye as he looked both ways for traffic.

"Whoa, check that out," he said, looking north passed the refinery.

A series of red lights flickered high in the sky.

"What is it?" asked Sara.

"Are they airplanes?" Alex asked.

"Aliens!" Devin said, smiling.

"I don't know," said Lippo.

They stood on the corner in front of the Dairy Queen watching the lights. People in the parking lot of Circle K also watched. Another cluster of people stood outside a Whataburger across the street, also watching the lights.

The lights appeared to grow brighter. They seemed to be stationary before . . .

"I think they're falling," Alex said. He was right. They *did* look like they were falling.

As they fell, the lights flickered out.

"That was cool," Lippo said. He lost interest and turned around.

He didn't see the massive fireball erupt in the distance over the refinery. But he did see Sara's and Alex's faces fill with awe, and then the *BANG* washed over them.

He *did* see the next five, all near simultaneous, and the ones after that, as he looked back.

The entire PEMEX refinery was blowing up.

19

General Yaghani was surprised – or *would* be surprised if he allowed himself to be.

He was parked in the desert, southwest of Kuwait City.

They had sped right past Al Jahra, the western reach of Kuwait City, and faced no resistance. Nothing at all. Then, just eleven miles from the city center, they turned south and bypassed Kuwait City altogether.

The horizon glowed orange to his south, directly in front of him. That would be Ahmed Al Jabar Air Base, one of the major targets of the Aerospace Force's many short- and medium-range *Shahab* ballistic missiles.

But what was the status of Al-Diwan Al-Amiri, the seaside royal palace of the Emir of Kuwait?

Yaghani waited.

After he and his lead assault force turned south, away from Kuwait City, Brigadier General Ali Alamouti led two Karrar "attacker" tank brigades from the 92nd Armored Division into the city, while another group aimed for the international airport. Both were supported by Toufan helicopter gunships and *Saberin* commandos.

Rear Admiral Habibollah Nasirzadeh, meanwhile, led an assault team of nearly 100 *Sepah* IRGC Navy Special Forces commandos all the way from Bandar Abbas. They were transported by a Russian-built Iranian Ilyushin Il-76 strategic airlift cargo plane. As the plane neared Abadan at the top of the Gulf, it banked hard to the west, over the Al Faw Peninsula of Iraq and northeastern Kuwait, before heading back out to sea toward Abadan again.

Nothing nefarious about it, except for the 100 frogmen bailing out of the back of the plane.

The *Sepah* commandos fell from high in the night sky. In the distance, the golden lights of Kuwait City twinkled like jewels.

Below them was Kuwait Bay, which brightly reflected the waxing crescent moon.

It was a HALO – high altitude, low opening – jump. The teams landed in Kuwait Bay, three miles north of the city.

As they inflated their zodiac rubber boats, the horizon before them erupted in a series of bright flashes – dozens and dozens in mere seconds – that in turn produced massive mushrooming fireballs.

The commandos started their boats' engines and headed toward the fire.

It was awe inspiring, at first. Falling stars trekked across the southern sky, arcing down over the horizon. One after another, in an almost linear fashion.

Then came the angry flashes and the rumbling of thunder.

Another shower of falling stars followed, this time to the north.

That made the Emiri Guards spring into action. Obviously, something wasn't right.

The Emir and his wife were in their suite, watching "Bridges," a popular Egyptian romantic comedy, when the Emiri Guards burst inside.

"Your Excellency!" shouted the Commander, startling the seventy-six-year-old Emir.

"What is it?" he asked, rising quickly.

The building shook violently.

Blood drained from the Emir's face. He looked at the night guard almost accusingly.

"Is it a coup?"

Before the guard could answer, the gates of hell opened from above.

Habib and his men came ashore at the helicopter pad 200 yards south of Seif Palace. They sprinted across the distance, rifles at eye level, scanning for targets.

The plan was to use the seawall path to breach the sprawling complex at three locations: the Emir's wing, the Crown Prince's wing and the Grand Lobby in between. But the Emir's suite and the Grand Lobby were nothing but a pile of concrete slabs and twisted rebar. Flames and smoke poured from countless openings.

The *Sepah* frogmen sprinted to the front of the Al-Diwan Al-Amiri complex. From there, it was apparent that the Crown Prince Diwan suite was, likewise, a pile of rubble. The air was warped by the heat of the fires burning beneath the wreckage.

Another 500 yards north was the Ministry of Foreign Affairs, a massive complex as big and sprawling as the Al-Diwan Al-Amiri Palace compound. The front facade of the building was intact, as though nothing had happened, but thick voluminous clouds of black smoke billowed into the sky behind it.

Habib and his mean continued their sprint north. They spilled out into the main thoroughfare. Their target now was a smaller, non-descript building, the headquarters of the Kuwaiti National Security Bureau.

Habib spotted a soldier sprinting for cover behind a parked car.

Habib opened fire, shattering the car windows. Soldiers and security officers returned fire from the windows of the headquarters, and Habib and his team took cover themselves.

To his right, Habib spotted movement. It was a line of tanks rumbling down Arabian Gulf Street. Iranian *Karrar* tanks.

The calvary had arrived.

Habib conferred with Brigadier General Ali Alamouti.

Time was of the essence. Instead of storming the headquarters, which would be dangerous and time-consuming, they decided to station tanks on all sides and then level the building.

Security officers fled from of the back of the building.

They didn't get far.

The security building was systematically obliterated – one piece at a time – as the tanks took turns firing.

Habib walked to the center of Arabian Gulf Street and allowed himself to look around.

This was the center of Kuwait's government, and it lay in ruins. The Emir and his family could not have survived the missile attack.

The government of Kuwait had been decapitated.

Yaghani refused to accept the news from Kuwait City as good. There was no such thing as good news in war.

But it was welcome news nonetheless. They were making better-than-expected progress, at least for now.

Yaghani looked through binoculars across the desert at Camp Arifjan. Massive fireballs continued to erupt over the northwest corner of the base. The missile barrage had apparently hit the munitions caches. The rest of the base was a mass of burning and charred vehicles. In fact, the entire base – all five and a half square miles of it – was primarily a vehicle boneyard of sorts. *The* Boneyard, at

Davis Montham Air Force Base in Tucson, Arizona, was perhaps the most famous of vehicle graveyards in the world. It was, of course, composed of aircraft. As new aircraft like the Navy's P-8 Poseidon replace older, less capable aircraft like the P-8's predecessor, the P-3 Orion, the older aircraft are flown to Davis Montham Air Force Base's Boneyard for retirement or storage.

The dry air of the desert means very little corrosion, so aircraft can be maintained for either future use, or harvested for replacement parts. Scores of various models of aircraft, from the P-3 Orion to Vietnam-era F-4 Phantom fighter jets, and so many more, were parked in the desert Boneyard outside Tucson.

The boneyard at Camp Arifjan was composed of various types of military vehicles and equipment: humvees, transport trucks, tanks, artillery pieces, Himars, and other equipment.

And, like the Boneyard in Arizona, the military vehicles and equipment were parked in neat rows out in the open desert. *Thousands* of them.

Unlike the Boneyard in Arizona, however, these were *not* retired vehicles or equipment. Rather, they were prepositioned material that were regularly maintained and ready to be put to use. It would save the Americans a good deal of time and money to keep the equipment 'in theater' if a conflict broke out. It wouldn't take them nearly as long to deploy troops as it did in 1990 during the buildup to the Gulf War.

Hence the need to strike now, Yaghani thought.

Somewhere in the inferno of exploding weapons caches and thousands of burning and charred vehicles and equipment were 10,000 American soldiers stationed there.

Yaghani wanted nothing to do with them, so he ordered a Fajr-6 "Dawn" long-range multiple rocket system squadron to rake over the rows of prepositioned vehicles and equipment once more.

Yaghani and the remaining brigades of the 92nd Armored Division and *Saberin* commandos pressed ahead. A long convoy of Army transport trucks, buses, and even personal vehicles, along with fuel trucks, artillery, and munitions supply units followed.

An hour later – at two o'clock in the morning – the vanguard of Yaghani's troops approached the northeastern border of Saudi Arabia.

Forward scouts and a drone showed no signs of Saudi defenses. Encrypted communications informed Yaghani that the Taklamakan Squadrons had returned to their bases. Refueled and re-armed, they were ready to assume their new mission: air support for Yaghani and his army.

There were other matters, though.

Yaghani was essentially the acting head of state while the government in Tehran went to ground.

It was time to turn his command over to Brigadier General Ali Alamouti.

Yaghani gave the go ahead with a nod. Alamouti had his orders.

The 92nd Armored Division rolled across the border into Saudi Arabia.

20

President Belle and her staff were still aboard Air Force One. "We have reports of impacts in Washington, Ma'am," General Sterling said. "Nothing nuclear."

"Do it anyway," the President ordered.

"It" was an emergency executive order activating the Continuity of Operations Plan (COP) to ensure the continuation of government in the event of extraordinary circumstances – like a nuclear attack on Washington, DC.

Congressional leaders – the Speaker of the House, the Majority and Minority Leaders of the House and Senate, members of key Congressional committees, etc., were already being evacuated from Washington as part of the Secret Service attack response protocols. COP authorized the relocation of all of Congress to the Mt. Weather Emergency Operations Center under Blue Mountain in Virginia, twenty miles west of Dulles Airport. It also moved White House and Pentagon operations to underground bunkers at Raven Rock, just north of the Maryland state line in rural south-central Pennsylvania.

Air Force One had landed at Hagerstown Regional Airport, where several Raider helicopters awaited, one of which was designated "Marine One." Minutes later, they landed at Raven Rock.

President Belle and her family were introduced to their living quarters. Then the President was off to the Raven Rock Situation Room.

"What's the damage in Washington and Houston?" she demanded.

"More than twenty-five impacts in both Washington and Houston," said Oscar Schwartz, her National Security Advisor. "Probably thirty each."

"So," the President rubbed her forehead, "we're talking sixty impacts?"

Oscar looked to Space Force General Sterling on one of the TV screens.

"Ma'am," Sterling said, "it appears the missiles contained three multiple independent reentry vehicles, or MIRVs, each. In other words, each missile had three warheads, and it seems that the warheads were each aimed at individually designated targets."

"A couple of warheads fell in remote areas. The rest were accurate to within eight square miles of their targets. Which means we were lucky. There was no direct hit on the White House or Capitol Building despite multiple impacts in their vicinity. Same for the NSA and CIA buildings."

"The Pentagon sustained at least one direct hit. Damage might rival 9/11."

"Casualties?" It was Daddy Longlegs, on a different TV screen. He was in a bunker beneath the Naval Observatory in Washington.

"Very few. No deaths reported, but that might change."

"Tell me about Houston," Cynthia said.

"It appears that all the missiles targeting Houston were aimed at the big oil refineries there," Sterling said. "Deer Park, Bay Town, Texas City. Satellite imagery suggests very significant damage."

"Ma'am?" It was Joy Chatterjee on yet another TV screen.

"Kuwait has gone dark."

As the missiles – that's what they were, Thew was sure – fell from the sky, there was nowhere to run. No time.

And where would we go?

Instinctively, Thew darted to the seawall, and jumped into the water. He grew up in Ocean City, Maryland, where he'd surfed and boogie boarded since he was eight years old.

Thew was comfortable in water, and it offered at least a degree of protection.

Skaggs was startled to see Thew jump, but he followed suit, hitting the water just as the first missile struck the port side of the base, producing a massive fireball and a deafening roar.

Thew and Skaggs clung to the algae-covered pilings as the blast wave blew right over their heads and into the cove.

The bay erupted. One, two, three, four plumes of water jetted high into the air.

And the sea is a dragon's tail.

The water turned angry, with heavy chop that nearly washed Thew and Skaggs back up onto the seawall.

Instead, they were tossed against the wall and pilings, scraping their bodies against the barnacles.

It was all over in minutes.

Thew and Skaggs couldn't see over the seawall, but they could hear the cackling of fires. Smoke drifted into the cove.

The smell of burning plastics and chemicals was pungent.

Thew and Skaggs looked for a way up the seawall, but there were no ladders. They swam along the wall to look for a rope, anything they could climb up.

It was hard to swim with steel-toed boots. Thew thought about removing them, but decided against it. Instead, he and Skaggs clung to the seawall, calling out when they heard people running past.

A soldier came to the seawall.

"We can't get up there!" Skaggs yelled.

More men came to the seawall. They tossed down the hose.

Thew grabbed hold of it and tried to "walk" up the wall, but it was too slippery. The men had to pull him up. His body scraped against the barnacles the whole way. Once he was high enough, a soldier on either side of Thew lifted him up by his armpits.

"Thank you," Thew said.

Skaggs was next.

Thew looked around. They were on the tarmac in front of Warehouse 2. There wasn't much fire except for scattered pieces of burning debris, but thick smoke poured out of several buildings, including Warehouse 2.

A bearded, shaggy-haired man peered at Thew and Skaggs.

It was that "Drive the fucking forklift" Master Chief.

"You two!" he shouted.

"We work over there," Skaggs said, motioning to Warehouse 1 on the other side of the smoking building.

The master chief shot them a withering look that was familiar to Thew. "And now you work for *me,*" he said.

Thew and Skaggs were incorporated into a work detail locating injured and dead sailors in Warehouse 2. They had to move a lot of debris to get to them. The building had caved in at the center.

Thew and Skaggs once again operated a forklift to move fallen shelves, heavy machine parts and scattered ceiling debris.

The work was grueling and nonstop.

Marines from the Expeditionary Force Protection tent city joined them. The tent city housing them was unscathed, miraculously, and even shielded from missile shrapnel by Warehouse 2, a garage and smaller buildings that surrounded it.

Bodies were laid out on the tarmac. There was no avoiding it this time, and Thew did his best to compartmentalize what he saw and experienced.

Besides, any one of those bodies could have been *him.* They deserved his utmost attention.

Thew did his best by doing what he was told and doing it with purpose.

Night began to fade. The eastern sky went from dark blue to blood red as the sun broached the horizon.

Thew viewed the morning sky with a sense of trepidation.

Red sky morning, sailor's warning.

Can it really get any worse?

The adrenaline that fueled Thew through night had waned, and Thew yawned as the tug of exhaustion took hold.

He drove a forklift now, separating identifiable parts and supplies from the twisted metal and rubble.

He spotted Skaggs pulling boxes from the rubble by hand. Thew parked the forklift and walked over.

"Fucking A," said Skaggs. "Here comes that Master Chief again."

Thew looked up and, sure enough, there he was. The SEAL Master Chief stood on the tarmac by the seawall, hands on his hips. He spotted Thew and Skaggs and walked over.

"Fuuuck," Skaggs sighed.

"Is that yours?" the Master Chief asked.

The Master Chief pointed to Thew's white T-shirt. He and Skaggs had partially pulled off their coveralls and folded them down to their waists, leaving only white T-shirts as their tops. It was common practice for sailors working in hot conditions.

"The *blood,"* the Master Chief clarified.

Thew looked down at his T-shirt. It was wet with sweat, but also pinkish from blood. So was Skaggs' T-shirt.

"Um, . . ." Thew stammered.

"Lift up your shirt," the Master Chief ordered.

Thew did, and looked down. His abdomen sported several long scratches, as though he'd been slashed by Freddie Kruger.

Skaggs did the same. He had similar scratches on his abdomen. His looked even worse.

Right. The barnacles.

"It's from the seawall," Thew explained. "Barnacles," he added.

The Master Chief barked at another SEAL and waived him over.

"Clean them up," he ordered, and walked away.

Thew was embarrassed at the attention he and Skaggs got from the SEAL medic. Barnacle scrapes seemed so minor, even if they covered their abdomens, knees and elbows.

Surely others required more attention.

"You don't want to mess with underwater cuts, especially barnacle scrapes," the SEAL medic told him. "They need to be thoroughly cleaned and dressed right away," he said as he worked. "*Vibrio vulnificus* is a bacterium that thrives in these waters. It is very aggressive and can kill you in days."

Oh shit. Thew was embarrassed no more.

"You're all set," the SEAL said. "Go report to the Master Chief."

Thew and Skaggs walked toward the tarmac. They were exhausted, but so was everyone else.

Thew heard a rumble of thunder and scanned the sky. There were a few clouds overhead, but nothing like a storm.

It was daylight now. The sun had broken through on the horizon.

The Master Chief scanned the sky to the northwest.

"Are you all cleaned up?" he asked without looking at them.

Thew followed the Master Chief's gaze. The Master Chief snapped his head, catching a glimpse of movement out in the cove.

Thew saw them, too.

A pair of stealth fighter planes dropped in out of the north over the island and banked hard. They traversed the length of the Navy base and adjacent industrial zone.

They were so low, Thew could see the pilots.

They continued their hard bank, to the north now, and out of view. It was a full U-turn, affording the pilots unimpeded views of the base.

"About freaking time," the Master Chief said.

"Cool!" exclaimed Skaggs over the delayed roar of the jets.

"Uh, they're not ours, Master Chief," Thew offered.

"The hell they ain't," the Master Chief said. "Those are stealth fighters, son. F-35s," he said with pride.

"They had two engines," Thew said matter-of-factly. "F-35s have only one."

"And those markings," Thew continued, scanning the sky for more planes. "Did you see those markings?"

The roar of jets nearby continued, but neither Thew nor Master Chief Gonzales could spot them.

A *BOOM* rolled over them. An ugly cloud of sand and smoke billowed high into the sky. It was close.

Here we go again.

Air raid sirens sounded anew.

21

Blue jeans and an untucked, black button-down collared shirt, and sunglasses.

You'd never know that he was a General.

Mohammad Yaghani sat at a table overlooking the Mediterranean at Jiyeh, Lebanon.

It was just after dawn, and a group of young men began to arrive, all in black wetsuits. First two, then four, now seven.

They were *surfers,* Yaghani realized. They each carried a board tucked under an arm.

Yaghani had never seen surfers before.

He watched intently as, one by one, they paddled gracefully into the sea.

They ducked under breaking waves, and emerged on the other side, paddling farther out.

The sea was calm, and Yaghani could see them now – sets of ripples that approached the shore from afar. As they got closer, they grew in size before breaking into waves out where the surfers sat bobbling in a line parallel to the shore. These waves were bigger than those closer to the shoreline.

A wave built to the right of a surfer, who turned and paddled toward it. Just as the wave crested, the surfer turned toward shore, paddled, and sprung to his feet.

He dropped down the face of the breaking wave and cut back toward it, rode up the face of the peeling wave and, with a hard twist, sent water spraying like a Japanese fan.

The surfer gracefully turned back to the sea and lay on his board to paddle out again.

The next surfer caught another of the breaking waves, dropped down the face, then pumped his board midway up the face before disappearing. The breaking wave appeared to have swallowed him.

But not. The surfer shot out the side of the wave like a canon along with a burst of air and spray.

The other surfers whooped. Yaghani smiled.

God, it was a scene both peaceful and yet exhilarating.

Someone cleared their throat and Yaghani turned his head.

A tall, fit man stood before him. The file said that he was fifty-two, but he looked a decade younger in person.

Major General Ari Benjamin, Agency Executive of Aman, Israel's Military Intelligence Directive.

He was once an officer in *Sayeret Matkal,* Israel's equivalent of the British Special Air Service, which no doubt had teams within binocular range of Ali Alamouti and his army at this very moment.

Like Yaghani, Ari Benjamin was dressed in a button-down shirt – his was white and also untucked – and a pair of chinos.

Yaghani rose and extended his right hand. Ari only looked at it.

"Please," said Yaghani. He gestured for the man to sit with him.

Ari looked around, scanning for threats, before he pulled out the chair and sat down.

A man of few words.

"America was going to war against us," Yaghani said. "Of that, we have no doubt. And, like the Six Day War, we took a page out of *your* book and struck preemptively. It was a matter of national preservation."

"Our war is with America. We have no interest in a conflict with Israel," Yaghani said, cutting to the chase.

"Our goal," Yaghani continued, "is to deny America the space and bases in the Persian Gulf from which to wage war against us. That is all."

There was no reaction from Ari. He just continued to look at Yaghani, his eyes blank. The moment dragged on.

Yaghani looked out on the surfers again. They seemed to not have a care in the world.

I would like to have been a surfer.

Ari finally spoke. "I am authorized to say *this*. My country is fully mobilizing. *Today.* We will undertake whatever operations are necessary to ensure our people's safety and survival."

"Whatever happens, do *not* move westward. Not one step. No little green men. If you do, your country will cease to exist."

Yaghani continued to look out on the surfers.

Ari stood and walked away.

Yaghani sipped his tea and winced.

It was cold.

Alamouti didn't know what to think. Was it luck? Was it Saudi incompetence?

Had they really caught Saudi Arabia by surprise?

They had traveled more than 100 miles into the Kingdom, right down Highway 95, without encountering any Saudi forces.

No aircraft, no helicopters, no artillery, no drones.

Nothing.

Traffic was light, as expected – it was the overnight hours, after all. So, they just drove.

Northeastern Saudi Arabia is entirely desert, with a smattering of oases and villages further inland.

It wasn't until they approached Jubail, the second-biggest city in eastern Saudi Arabia, that they even encountered a police car.

It was a jeep-like Toyota FJ Cruiser, the vehicle of choice for the Saudi national police, the Department of Public Safety.

It was parked in the desert, facing the highway.

General Alamouti rode in an Iranian *Toofan,* an armored vehicle modeled after the American *MRAP* to withstand roadside improvised explosive devices (IEDs). He had his driver toot the horn as they passed the police car.

Every vehicle in the miles-long convoy would do the same.

The police car didn't budge, but it undoubtedly radioed the regional headquarters in Jubail.

Highway 95 bypassed Jubail by over eight miles. It was a compact city on the Persian Gulf, and by simply driving on, the convoy enveloped it. Jubail was now cut off from the rest of Saudi Arabia.

They just didn't know it yet.

Alamouti led the convoy forward. They detoured south along Saudi Road 6374, the bypass of eastern Saudi Arabia's largest city, Dammam, and the first major objective for Iranian forces after Kuwait.

Like Jubail, Dammam was compact. But it was *twice* as big, with a population nearing two million.

Still no signs of resistance.

Alamouti's heart raced. He wished they could go faster.

Just after passing the junction with Highway 80, the main Riyadh-to-Dammam highway, Alamouti's Toofan pulled off the road and into the desert.

This was it.

The Staging Area.

The convoy split here. Tanks took up defensive positions in the desert on both sides of the convoy.

Soldiers disembarked all along the length of the miles-long convoy west of Dammam.

It was like Basra Sports City all over again. Organized chaos.

Long-range artillery pieces were quickly set up, along with state-of-the art S-500 anti-aircraft missile batteries.

The S-500 could hit targets as far away as 300 miles. *Riyadh* was in range. *Al Udeid* in Qatar was well within range. *Abu Dhabi,* capital of the United Arab Emirates, would be at the outer fringe of the S-500's range.

Soldiers worked up and down the convoy. They set up defenses. They formed into attack positions.

Saberin special forces, meanwhile, continued to press south to Half Moon Bay on the Persian Gulf.

Once there, Dammam – like Jubail – would be cut off.

Dammam was really a conurbation of *three* cities: Dammam, Dahran and Khobar. It was on a wide spit of land jutting into the Persian Gulf. Khobar was located on the eastern side and was connected to Bahrain by fifteen miles of causeways and bridges.

Dawn had broken. The sky to the east was blood red.

The *Saberin* units had reached Half Moon Bay.

A second convoy snaked its way through the staging area, led by General Behzad Toussi.

Alamouti had passed the baton.

Alamouti would lead an assault, if it came to it, on Dammam and Bahrain. Toussi, meanwhile, would continue to press further south along the coast of the Persian Gulf.

It was a multi-stage offensive.

Toussi's objective: Doha.

Everything was set.

The sun broke over the horizon.

Alamouti ordered his artillery to fire.

The target was the sprawling King Abdul Aziz Air Base astride Khobar, which had already been raked by stealth bombers and ballistic missiles.

A secondary target was the obscure Islamic Liberation Army of Al-Ahsa (ILAA). It was not an attack *on* the ILAA, but an attack *in support of* the ILAA.

Like the Islamic Front of Bahrain, the ILAA was a creation of the Quds Force, the irregular unit of Iran's IRGC that specializes in military intelligence and unconventional warfare.

Al-Ahsa was the name of an oasis in southeastern Saudi Arabia, home to most of the kingdom's Shi'a Muslims. The Shi'a have faced persecution in Saudi Arabia for decades, so it wasn't hard for the Quds Force to find a core of disaffected youth to form the ILAA. They also had no trouble in identifying a leader: Ayatollah Fahad Al-Ghamdi of the Al-Anood Mosque in central Dammam.

In recent years, the Al-Anood Mosque had suffered four terrorist attacks by fundamentalist Sunni Muslims, as well as multiple raids by the Saudi secret police.

The most recent attack on the mosque, a car bomb in the parking lot that killed and maimed multiple *jamaat,* or members of the congregation, may or may not have been orchestrated by Quds Force to stir up anti-Saudi sentiment. Whoever was to blame, the result was, in fact, a fierce anger aimed at the Saudi government and majority Sunni Muslims in general.

The kids that comprised the ILAA were worked up into a religious fervor following the *George W. Bush* disaster and the subsequent attack on the American naval base across the causeway in Bahrain.

Not long after that, Ayatollah Al-Ghamdi laid out Allah's plan for an Islamic Republic of Al-Ahsa.

Allahu Akbar.

★ ★ ★

Hashemi Ghavam and his twenty-ship flotilla made it to the Strait of Hormuz unmolested.

This was where the flotilla divided into parts. Much of the Persian Gulf was too shallow for submarines to operate freely, so Hash stationed the five attack submarines near the Strait of Hormuz in the Gulf of Oman. To guard the rear.

The three logistics and landing ships were not essential to the immediate mission. Hash ordered them back to port in Bandar Abbas.

And then there were twelve.

It was full steam ahead.

Aboard the *Sabalan,* Hash led the ten *Moudge*-class frigates and two smaller *Alvand*-class frigates westward into the Persian Gulf.

Multiple large surface ships returned signatures on his ships' radars. The Persian Gulf was usually a busy place, full of oil tankers, tenders, fishing boats and combat Navy ships of multiple countries, mostly American.

Hash paused. He ordered the *Sabalan* and its convoy to idle. He couldn't tell what the ships were, and he didn't want to risk running into any American Navy ships one-on-one.

As an Iranian, Hash was proud of its domestically built frigates . . . but they didn't stand a chance against an American ship.

So his mission was a supporting one.

Rear Admiral Habibollah Nasirzadeh's commander of the IRGC Navy speedboat fleet, Commodore Abbas Sarafpour, came on the radio.

"We've got three American Navy ships confirmed," Sarafpour announced. *"Confirmed, I say! Go, go, go!"*

Prince Saud bin Salman Al Saud, Governor of the Eastern Province and brother of the King, was frantic. King Abdul Aziz Air Base was in flames, and the army garrison there was a pile of rubble.

Hundreds had been killed. The whole city was unnerved.

He contacted Al Yamamah Palace in Riyadh, but the government there was in disarray.

He couldn't reach his brother, the King.

Riyadh Air Base and the sprawling Eskan Village army base had also suffered air strikes. They were talking more than a thousand casualties. *More than a thousand!*

Rumors abounded.

All of Saudi Arabia's air bases had been attacked, it seemed, and the status of the Air Force was unknown.

Riyadh was working on the assumption of a surprise attack . . . *by Israel.*

This was the greatest catastrophe ever to befall Saudi Arabia.

Al-Jazeera, the news network out of Doha, Qatar, reported attacks at *Qatar's* major base, Al Udeid.

CNN was non-stop focused on missile strikes *in the United States. It's World War III!*

Yousef, Prince Saud's chief bodyguard, came into his office.

"Your Highness, the police report a large convoy of military vehicles approaching the city."

Prince Saud let out a deep sigh.

"Good. We're going to need them to – "

"Your Highness," Yousef interjected. "They're *Iranian.* We have to *go.*"

The blood drained from the Governor's face.

Sepah and *Saberin* special forces went in first.

They drove anti-IED Toofan armored trucks. They weren't taking any chances, and they meant business.

It was a three-pronged assault. *Sepah* and *Saberin* forces moved in from the north, south and west, and sped into the city.

General Alamouti followed in a Toofan. He noticed that the streets were empty, despite the early hour. The attacks, the news – he got it. And he was grateful. Empty streets meant a faster assault.

Alamouti held on as his Toofan took a hard turn through a roundabout. A police FJ Cruiser was in the middle of the roundabout. Its doors were open, and nobody was inside.

It was abandoned.

Then something else caught Alamouti's eye. A few feet beyond the open doors on each side of the Toyota Cruiser were piles of clothing. Police uniforms.

He saw two more abandoned police FJ Cruisers as they turned onto a major thoroughfare heading toward the Qasr Khaleej Royal Palace. Again, he saw various bits of police uniforms discarded on the ground.

"There!" said the driver. He pointed to a palace compound at their two o'clock. Qasr Khaleej.

"We have a motorcade leaving the Palace, heading east," an excited voice said on the radio.

"We've got 'em," said another voice.

Alamouti's Toofan sped past the Governor's Palace, then came to a screeching halt.

A caravan of black armored SUVs – Chevrolet Suburbans – had been trapped between Iranian Toofans.

Saberin commandos swarmed the motorcade.

"We've got him, we've got him. We have the Prince."

Alamouti exited his Toofan and walked over.

It was a motorcade of fifteen SUVs. Men exited the SUVs at gunpoint, their hands in the air. *Saberin* commandos screamed at them in Arabic to get on the ground.

They did – forty of fifty men, along with ten women.

Most of the men were dressed in crisp black suits. *Palace Guards,* Alamouti surmised. His soldiers tied the men's hands behind their backs with zip ties.

One middle-aged man stood out. He was wearing a brilliant white thawb, with a red and white checkered keffiyeh, for a headdress.

Two soldiers lifted him. He wouldn't stand on his own.

"Please, please," he begged.

The man was visibly shaking. He was not *refusing* to stand on his own. He was *petrified*. His legs were noodles.

"Please, please," he continued. He was crying.

Alamouti peered at him closely. It was subtle, but the man bore a resemblance to the King of Saudi Arabia.

IRGC Navy Admiral and *Sepah* commander Habibollah Nasirzadeh was fresh from Kuwait City. He, too, rode in an Toofan armored truck.

His convoy sped south, though, through the mostly open desert between the suburban developments south of Dharan.

They skirted past the south end of the massive King Abdul Aziz Air Base. Columns of black oily smoke filled the horizon where the base and its hangars were.

This was Highway 80 again, the Highway of Death. It cut through the north side of Khobar and became the fifteen-mile King Fahd Causeway to Bahrain.

The convoy blew right through Khobar, then the toll plaza, and out onto the causeway.

Habib's heart rate ticked up. They were out in the open now . . . *for fifteen miles* . . . and he knew there were American Navy SEALs on that island.

They could've have wired the bridge.

Hash half-expected – no, *more* than half-expected – the bridge to suddenly disappear in front of him. Or to ride it down to the sea as it disappeared beneath him.

General Alamouti assured him that Quds Force had a team on the island and *they* reported that it was all-clear.

Burn in hell if you're wrong, Ali Alamouti.

"Check it out," the driver said.

A formation of low-lying fighter jets approached the bridge from the north. More aircraft followed.

"Just keep driving!" said the soldier in the front passenger seat.

And so, it ends, Habib thought. He leaned back and closed his eyes.

The first formation of jets roared past.

"They're *ours!*" exclaimed the soldier. "Holy shit, they're *ours!*"

"Look!" he said as the second formation of jets flew past.

And then a third.

Habib opened his eyes and looked.

The red-white-and-green roundels of the Islamic Republic of Iran Air Force stood out against the black fuselages of the aircraft. The white letters "IRIAF" next to the roundels especially popped.

Habib exhaled in relief.

Might we make it to the other side after all?

22

More jets appeared.

The kid was right, Master Chief Hector Gonzales acknowledged.

Black jets, two-engines, red-white-and-green roundels, and "IRIAF" painted as clear as day on the sides of the aircraft.

Iranian.

God knows it doesn't make any sense, but here we are.

The jets were focused on a target about two miles from the base: Al Qudaibiya Palace, the other target of the Islamic Front of Bahrain on the night they bombed the front gate to NSA 2.

The Patriot missile defense system was knocked out overnight, and the surviving ships had pulled out to sea. There was no protection from the air for Naval Support Activity Bahrain. Besides, the jets were stealth.

The SEALs and Special Warfare Combat Crewmen (SWCCs, or 'Swicks") had salvaged multiple rigid-hull inflatable boats and zodiacs from their bombed-out warehouse. The Swicks' Mark V fast patrol boats were still intact.

Communications had been largely destroyed.

NSA Bahrain was blind and deaf.

It was time to get some eyes out there to see what was happening.

Echo Squad's young petty officers – Special Warfare Operator (SWO) First-Class Christian Köllner, SWO Second-Class Noah Hastings and Danny Liu, and SWO Third-Class Henry "Rook" Avellino – were *dying* to do something other than ducking and covering and cleaning up debris.

Chief Petty Officer Buck Bradshaw was right there with them. He took the lead.

The five SEALs boarded a Mark VI fast patrol boat, and the Swick boat captain – a Chief Special Warfare Boat Operator – gunned it. There was no time to waste.

The boat paralleled the base seawall as it headed into the Khawr al Qulay'ah cove, then banked north. They passed under the Prince Khalifah bin Salman Causeway bridge to Muharraq Island and into Muharraq Bay.

From here, Bradshaw and his SEALs had a clearer view of what was happening in Manama. The jets were like angry bees, swooping down one at a time. They pounded the Al Qudaibiya Palace. Other columns of smoke punctuated the city skyline, but Bradshaw couldn't tell what had been targeted.

A few minutes more and they were north of the island of Bahrain.

There were lots of boats in the water – fishing boats, pleasure boats, yachts, you name it – and Bradshaw felt a little less conspicuous once they were among them.

Thirty minutes had passed by the time they got close enough to the end of the King Fahd Causeway to see traffic on it.

The crew kept Hector Gonzales appraised of what they saw as they went, which was nothing except for the aircraft in the sky – which, given the sounds behind Gonzales, seemed to have expanded their dive-bombing targets to include the base. *Again.*

The Swick boat chief throttled the engine from full speed to idle.

It was the closest thing on a boat to a brake.

The boat stopped almost on a dime, then pitched forward and backward, forward and backward, as its own wake overtook it.

"What's up, chief?" Bradshaw asked.

The Swick chief nodded to the southern span of the two-span King Fahd Causeway bridge that linked Bahrain with Saudi Arabia. A steady stream of sand-colored armored trucks, tanks and troop transport trucks passed onto the island.

Bradshaw clicked his mic. "What's going on, Buck?" Hector asked. Buck and the SEALs on the boat could hear another explosion through the radio.

"It's an *invasion,*" Bradshaw said. "Like Red fucking Dawn."

"What's going on *here?*" Captain Paul Welling muttered to himself.

He could see the smoke for miles, but figured it was some kind of industrial fire. Maybe at an oil refinery.

As he steered the USNS *Grasp* past the Khalifa bin Salman Port and turned north into the cove of Khawr al Qulay'ah, he brought his binoculars up.

"What *is* going on here?" he muttered again.

It was clear that the source of the multiple pillars of smoke was dead ahead.

"What *year* is this?" he asked himself. It was like he'd slipped through a wormhole and was stumbling into Pearl Harbor on December 7th, 1941.

"Boatswain!" Welling barked.

"Aye," responded fifty-nine-year-old Tony Bourgeois, a native of New Orleans and a former Mississippi River pilot. He was a fourth-generation waterman.

He looked up from his book of depth charts. *Captain never calls me that,* he thought.

"Better take down that flag up on high," Welling said.

"Sir?" asked Bourgeois.

"You heard me, Tony. The sooner, the better," Welling said. He never took his eyes away from the binoculars.

"Aye," Tony replied. He went to work, barking orders to younger crew members.

Welling idled the ship and considered his options.

From above, the USNS *Grapple* probably – *maybe* – didn't look like a Navy ship. The large cranes fore and aft made it look like an *industrial* ship. But the gray hull and bridge configuration made her look like a Navy ship – which, of course, she was, if only a supporting craft.

He scanned the sky for threats. He didn't see any Japanese Zeros. *Well, that's good.*

He also thanked Heaven – and the Navy, for once, for their years of budgetary negligence. No self-respecting professional Navy captain in the world would mistake a rust bucket like the *Grapple* for part of a fighting fleet.

Where to dock, though? *That* was the question. The whole point of returning to port was to refuel and re-supply after nearly a month on site at the *George W. Bush* wreckage. Normally, that would mean tying up at the long Mina Salman pier. But the pier was burning or smoldering along most of its length.

He aimed for a gap in the seawall, putting the ship in reverse to swing the aft around, then alternated between forward and reverse to bring the ship alongside the seawall in a slow, deliberate fashion.

Sailors came out of apparent hiding and helped tie him in.

Then came a team of black-faced armed commandos. They jumped aboard and swept forward. They screamed orders at his mean to hit the deck.

Oh shit. What have we just gotten ourselves in to?

Habib *did* make it to the other side. And, like Dammam, the high-way was devoid of traffic.

The convoy ahead had reported no resistance whatsoever. Moments later, they surrounded Al-Qudaibiya Palace.

Habib's convoy arrived, and he stepped out. He surveyed the Palace with binoculars. It was in shambles. Fresh fires burned amid the rubble from the latest round of airstrikes just minutes before.

Sepah units swept the Palace grounds. The Palace Guards barracks was mostly intact. Its windows were blown out and the facade was pockmarked by shrapnel. But there were no actual Palace Guards. In their stead were piles of Palace Guards uniforms. They had apparently shed their uniforms in favor of civilian clothes, and gone home.

Self-preservation. Could you blame them?

There was no King or Crown Prince. They were either dead, buried in the rubble, or they had fled.

More soldiers arrived by the minute. The Palace grounds were secured.

Habib turned his attention a mile to the southeast: the American naval base.

"Sorry for the dust up, mate, but we've just come through a bit of a kerfuffle. And then you show up all proper jammy."

Welling *saw* a black-faced, camouflaged, armed-to-the-teeth shaggy haired *commando,* and the world aflame – hell, the *apocalypse* – behind him. What he *heard* was a cheery English gentleman apologizing for a spilt drop as he delivered him tea.

It didn't compute.

"Um, come again?" Welling asked. He was face down on the deck with a boot on the back of his neck.

"Never mind *him,"* said another black-faced camouflaged commando, this one bearded, older and fiercer-looking. "A fooking fake English *twat* is what *he* is," he sneered.

Um, okay . . .

"*What's* going on?" Welling asked.

"It's an invasion," the bearded one said.

"Welcome to World War Three, mate," said the English guy.

It was old hat for Hector Gonzales, and pretty much everyone else on NSA Bahrain, by now. Nobody strayed too far from the few small bunkers on the base.

Gonzales surmised, they weren't built to protect more than a hundred people, but the base sailors were packed in like sardines.

Nearly 4,000 of them.

The planes bombed whichever buildings seemed to be intact, and there weren't many of those left.

The force-protection Marines – there were 400 of them, plus Hector and the remaining SEAL platoons – sought shelter where they could, but their primary focus was defending the base.

Hector had taken up a concealed position with his faux Englishman boss, Lieutenant Commander Nigel Wood, on the roof of a two-story shopping center just off base.

It was eerily quiet. The jets had departed, and the normally bustling streets were empty.

Horns blared in the distance and interrupted the silence. A flock of pigeons, obviously startled by the sound, took flight.

The horns grew louder. A black SUV – no, two; no, *four* – came tearing down Awal Avenue, each weaving like a drunkard.

The SUVs were shot up, dented and covered in dust.

Hector gripped his Colt M4A1 carbine and peered through the aim.

"Easy, Master Chief, yeah?" said Nigel as he watched through binoculars.

The SUVs screeched to a halt outside the gate. Fifteen men, most of them heavily armed, got out of the vehicles with their rifles held over their heads.

"Get on the ground, on the ground now!" yelled several Marines who came out from behind cover and swarmed over the armed men.

And older man, unarmed, was pulled out of the SUV by the Marines and practically thrown to the ground. He wore a handsome gold colored thawb and red and white checkered keffiyeh.

It was the King of Bahrain.

"What does it look like?" asked Captain Prescott Smedley, Commanding Officer of Naval Support Activity, Bahrain.

Smedley sat behind his desk in his working khaki uniform. His executive officer stood behind him. The rest – Nigel Wood, Hector Gonzales and Captain Timothy Lee, commander of the force protection Marines – stood or sat in chairs salvaged from elsewhere.

The room was cluttered with broken glass and smashed book shelves and furniture. The walls were filled with holes and scorch marks.

"They're out in the open," said Nigel. "Whole convoys are taking up positions. I imagine we'll be hearing from them quite shortly, yeah?"

Smedley walked to the window, which was now a gaping hole from floor to ceiling, his hands behind his back.

"Okay," he announced, "I'll go out there and negotiate our surrender."

"The hell you will!" exploded Hector. Nigel held his hand against Hector's chest, urging restraint.

"Sir," Nigel said, "you've got 400 Marines and fifty SEALs trained to *fight*. The best trained fighters in the *world*, yeah?"

"If we fight," Smedley said, "it will be a bloodbath. A massacre. How long can you hold out against *ten thousand? Twenty* thousand? I'm a *supply* officer. My sailors are logistics specialists, yeomen, mechanics – hell, *cooks!* We're *pencil* pushers!"

"They're *military*," Hector seethed. "They shouldn't have signed up if they weren't willing to *fight!*"

"This isn't a *movie, goddammit*," Smedley said, disgusted. "We're not in *Rambo!* We don't even have guns. I've made my decision."

"What about the King?" Hector asked.

Smedley stared out the hole, then looked to Hector and shrugged.

"You can't be siding with that *coward*," spat the Master Chief as he, Nigel and Timothy navigated the rubble of the bombed-out Quarterdeck administrative building.

"*I'm* not going down without a *fight*," Hector fumed.

"No, Master Chief," Nigel said, "I'm afraid that I am unable to accommodate the Captain on this matter."

A look of confusion came over Hector's face. "Can't you fucking speak English?"

Despite the damage to the base, the sailors were able to refuel the *Grapple*.

But the sudden war had changed her supply needs, since Captain Welling didn't foresee a return to the *Bush* wreckage.

When he saw the SEALs return, a chill went down his spine.

"Barbarians at the gate, mate," Nigel said. "And I mean that *literally.*"

"What he means," said Hector, "is that we need your boat. Like *right fucking now.*"

Chief Welling didn't say yes or no. They were *SEALs* for fuck's sake. They wanted the boat? Well, then, it was theirs.

"How many crew do you have?" Hector asked.

"Seventy-five," Welling said.

"Seventy-six," said a tall black man entering the bridge. He had sad, friendly eyes and a lanky build. "Hand me a rifle and count me in. Moe Adil, Sergeant Major, Army Ranger, 30 years," he said.

"Well ain't that the bee's knees, yeah?" Nigel said. "Welcome to Mission Impossible, Master Sergeant Moe Adil."

Captain Welling looked out on the cove and back again.

"This is a *tender,*" Welling said. "A salvage ship. Not a fighting ship."

"It's a boat that floats, innit?" Nigel said. "Leave the fighting bit to us, mate. We just need to get across the way there to Qatar."

"How fast can you get there?" Hector asked.

"Three hours, maybe" Welling said. "More or less. Probably more."

"Not much of a speed boat, is it, mate?" Nigel quipped.

"Fifteen knots," Welling said.

"Let's get going then," Hector said. "Captain Courage over there is giving away the base as we speak."

23

"I wonder what's going on," Skaggs said, as he and Thew watched a bunch of Marines who seemed to be taking up positions.

Like *combat* positions, right there on the tarmac, as others ran to a rusted old work ship.

Thew looked to the still smoldering Naval Special Warfare warehouse. SEALs were dragging out rubber boats.

They were all dressed in desert combat fatigues and their faces were painted black. They each had a machine gun rifle in one arm as they worked.

"Come on," said Thew.

"Where are we going?" Skaggs asked as he followed Thew.

They jogged to a crew of SEALs dragging a boat to the seawall. Thew grabbed onto a side and helped.

"Thanks, shipmate," a black-faced SEAL said.

"What's going on?" Thew asked as they got the boat to the wall and the SEALs pushed it over.

"We're getting out of Dodge," one of them said. "Your captain is surrendering the base."

"What?" asked Skaggs, alarmed.

"To who?" asked Thew.

"You guys don't know?" asked one of the SEALs. "Iranians, man. They're at the front gate."

The SEALs chucked their gear into the rubber boat as other squads dragged out two more boats.

A SEAL walked non-nonchalantly onto to the tarmac, then turned his back to the seawall and scanned the base through the aim of his rifle.

"Move out, yeah?" he said in an English accent, his focus still on the base in front of him.

"Get the fuck out of here, sailors." It was the Master Chief.

Goddamn. He looked even meaner than before.

"Where are we going to go?" Thew asked.

Are the Iranians going to kills us if we stay? All of us?

"Go ask your Captain," the Master Chief said. He tossed his gear into the rubber boat and clambered down a ladder.

"Let us come with you," Thew stammered. "We can fight."

The SEAL crew laughed.

"I would if I could, but we've got no room. And you'll slow us down," Hector said.

"Those two kids been bustin' their asses since the *Bush* went off," one of the SEALs said. It was Christian Köllner, Special Warfare Operator First Class (SWO1).

"Yeah, they helped us move equipment around. They did fire detail. They even helped us with the boats," said the rookie, SWO3 Henry Avellino.

"Skipper?" Hector asked, turning to the last SEAL on the tarmac.

"Afraid the Master Chief's right, lads," the Englishman said. "How about you board that boat over there with the Marines, yeah? Better hurray. Looks like they're about to shove off."

Habib was anxious. This American Navy captain was just too . . . *soft*. Nothing at all like he had expected.

Which made him suspicious. *The man seemed like a . . . civilian? And too confident for . . . whatever he is.*

He wanted to negotiate terms for . . . *how did he put it?* "*Co-existing.*"

A fool. That was the word.

Over 4,000 sailors were there, including 400 heavily armed U.S. Marines and Navy SEALs.

This Captain Smedley had ordered *all* of them to stand down, and for the Marines and SEALs to disarm.

But Habib couldn't just walk onto base on the Captain's word. No, he had to work out a way to verify that the Marines and SEALs were, in fact, disarmed.

A soldier ran up to Habib.

"Sir, a tender and several speed boats are leaving the base."

Habib turned and slugged Captain Smedley in the face.

Smedley stumbled to his knees, his Captain's hat flying. "Oh!" he stammered.

"You deceived me!" Habib yelled.

"No, no, I didn't," Smedley pleaded. "*They* deceived *me!*"

Habib turned to his *Sepah* commander and nodded. The commander spoke into a radio.

"Take the base," he ordered.

The *Grapple* and its escort of speed boats was a mile out – which put them halfway to the mouth of the cove – when the first *BOOMS* were heard.

Flash grenades, Hector surmised.

The Iranians were taking the base.

They must know by now that the SEALs and Marines had left.

Hector shifted his focus to the sky.

Three and a half hours at sea – without air cover – was a freaking long time.

Too long.

Köllner worked on establishing satellite communications with Central Command at MacDill Air Force Base in Tampa, Florida.

Come on, Köllner. Do you want to make Chief or not?

President Belle took her seat in the Raven Rock Situation Room. It was practically a closet compared to the Situation Room at the White House, which itself wasn't all that big.

"Ma'am," Oscar offered, "Dr. Emily Yorke, chief economist at the St. Louis Federal Reserve, has joined us remotely.

"Go on, Dr. Yorke," Cynthia said to the TV screen on which the economist had appeared.

"Ma'am," Yorke began, "roughly one-third of the world's liquefied natural gas and thirty-five percent of its seaborne oil shipments, exit the Persian Gulf through the Strait of Hormuz *each day.*"

Yorke cleared her throat.

"With the presumed closing of the Persian Gulf, even if temporarily, oil prices have risen a thousand-fold."

"Please, Dr. Yorke," Cynthia interrupted. "I really don't have time for a lecture on global economics."

"Yes, Ma'am," Yorke said. "I just wanted to layout –"

"Please get to the point, Dr. Yorke."

"Right," Yorke said and adjusted her glasses. "The Houston area alone accounts for twenty-two percent of crude oil production in the United States. So, in combination with the presumed closing of the Strait of Hormuz, we can expect oil prices to –"

"What will gas prices be at the pump, Dr. Yorke?" Cynthia asked.

"Twenty dollars a gallon by end of the week."

The room erupted in heated discussions until Martin Hartshorne, Cynthia's Chief of Staff, smacked his palm on the table.

"Bernie," Martin said, as in *you're next*.

"Madame President," Bernie Mentzel, the Secretary of Defense began. "Yesterday evening, Iran seized Kuwait. Overnight, they invaded eastern Saudi Arabia and Bahrain. Bahrain has fallen."

"Missiles away!" shouted Captain Cyrus Farsad. Farsad was the actual captain of the *Sabalan,* but with Hash, a Rear Admiral, on board, he was relegated to being Hash's executive officer.

The captain was peering through binoculars at the other nine ships in the convoy, eight of which fired their load of missiles.

Each of the ten *Moudge*-class frigates in the convoy carried four *Qader* sea-skimming anti-ship cruise missiles.

Thirty-six missiles streaked skyward in a high arc before diving to the wave tops.

Hash didn't want to fire all of his missiles at once. He wanted to keep some arrows in his quiver, just in case.

He ordered his ships north around Greater Tunb Island at the western end of the Strait of Hormuz.

Hash knew that the island offered zero protection from missiles fired from the American ships, but it was like child's blanket of sorts. It still provided him a degree of comfort, even if it was infinitesimal.

The American ships were ninety miles away.

Hash looked at his watch and waited.

24

That English SEAL was right. Thew and Skaggs had no sooner jumped aboard the rusted work ship when the ship's crew untied her and they were on their way.

It was a small ship, and 400 Marines were crammed into every space.

The SEALs circled their ship on patrol boats as they slowly pulled away from the seawall.

"Get down!" a Marine sergeant yelled, shoving Thew and Skaggs.

Fuck you, man, Thew thought, and he almost said it aloud. It was then that he heard several *BOOMS,* and all the Marines on the back deck suddenly raised their weapons and aimed them at the sea wall.

"Don't fire!" the sergeant that shoved them bellowed. *"Do not fire unless I tell you to!"*

A Marine crouching beside Thew looked out with a pair of binoculars.

"May I?" Thew asked, and the Marine handed them to him.

There were soldiers on the sea wall, several of them aiming rifles at the ship.

Iranians.

One soldier stood at the center, his hands on his hips.

He looked pissed as he watched the ship slowly sail away.

Once the Navy base and the Arab Shipbuilding and Repair Yard began to fade from view, the soldiers eased up.

Thew and Skaggs found a place on the floor and sat down.

Thew closed his eyes. It had been a *long* night.

He was nudged, but Thew ignored it.

He was nudged again, harder, and Thew opened an eye.

A young Marine, probably no older than himself, stood over him.

"Wake up," he said, "we're unloading."

"What do you mean?" Thew asked.

But the soldier had shuffled off. He was now in a line of Marines who were . . . *walking off the ship.*

They were docked.

I just closed my eyes!

It had been almost four hours since they left Bahrain, according to Thew's watch.

"Where are we?" Thew asked anyone as he stood.

"Qatar," a Marine said.

Nigel Wood contacted the U.S. Special Operations Command at MacDill Air Force Base in Tampa, Florida, via encrypted satellite phone.

He shared everything he knew. The air strikes. The doomed ships. The missile strikes. Chinese FC-31 stealth fighters with Iranian markings. The Iranians at the front gate. The SEALs and Marines stealing across the Gulf of Bahrain to Qatar aboard the *Grapple.*

"Keep us posted," said the officer on the other side of the line before hanging up.

What the hell?

After they docked at Al Ruwais, Nigel's phone vibrated.

"Woods," he answered.

"Nigel, this is General Alexander Pitt." *Holy shit.* Pitt was the Commander of the Special Operations Command. The Top Dog.

"Listen, son," Pitt said, "I'm giving it to you straight, no sugar coating. It's a fucking mess. We have no assets in the vicinity to get you out. Where are you now, Commander?"

"We just docked at Al Ruwais, Qatar," Nigel said.

"Al Ruwais," the general repeated to others.

"Okay," Pitt said. "Get down to Al Udeid. I don't care you how you do it, just get down there."

"Stay out of Doha," the general continued. "Just got off the phone with the ambassador there. People are panicking, rushing the stores and gas stations. The airport's been bombed. There's no police. Roads are clogged. Do what you can to defend yourselves and facilitate movement, and call me when you get there."

The line went dead.

Thew's phone was all but ruined after he and Skaggs jumped into the Khawr al Qulay'ah cove.

Most of the Marines, though, had their phones. Thew and Skaggs hovered over the shoulder of the kid that had woken him up.

Private Clay Stevenson.

Stevenson brought up the Google Maps app on his phone. It immediately zoomed in on the northern tip of a large peninsula – the country of Qatar – that jutted north 100 miles into the Persian Gulf from the east coast of Saudi Arabia.

The port of Al Ruwais, Qatar.

"Welcome to Al Rue-waze, I guess," said Clay.

"You, Marine!" barked a familiar voice. "Give me your phone."

It was the SEAL Master Chief. They, too, had arrived at *Al Rue-Waze.*

Clay looked up. He wasn't about to hand over his phone to some *Navy* guy dressed as a soldier.

"All of you," the Master Chief commanded, eyeing the Marines.

"Turn over your phones. They can track us," Hector offered.

Hector had a command about him.

"Better do what he says," Thew whispered.

"Can I call home before –"

"Right. Fucking. Now." Master Chief Hector Gonzales glowered at the Private.

Clay dropped his phone into a box carried by the young SEAL Thew had first met when the *Bush* blew up.

Thew snickered. "Told you."

"Let's go, all of you!" the Master Chief bellowed.

Reluctantly, each of the Marines dropped their cell phones into the box.

Clay and the other marines looked on with dismay as the young SEAL put the box down in the sand and another SEAL squirted butane over it and set it aflame.

"You two, again," Hector said, looking to Thew and Skaggs. "You're with me."

Several Marines began barking orders, too, organizing them into squads and units.

Thew and Skaggs followed the Master Chief and gathered with the SEALs.

"The Fleet Kids," said one of the SEALs. He was the blond-haired guy who spoke up for them at the seawall, and a first-class petty officer. Köllner was the name stitched on his chest.

"Squid Punks," snickered another. It was the young SEAL. "Avellino" was stitched on his uniform.

"Welcome to Alpha Squad," said another young SEAL. "I'm Danny. Danny Liu."

"Thew," Thew said, and shook his hand. "Dave," Skaggs said, following suit.

"Henry," said the one with Avellino on his chest.

"Noah Hastings," said the next one. He seemed like a friendly guy.

"Christian Köllner." The blond guy again.

"Hector Gonzales." Thew nearly flinched. It was the Master Chief.

"Chief Bradshaw," said the last one, and Thew *did* flinch.

Bradshaw was downright scary. He had intense brown eyes, shoulder-length black hair, a black beard, and muscular arms covered in tattoos.

"You're with Avellino and Liu," Chief Bradshaw said to Thew, "and you're with Köllner and Hastings," he said to Skaggs. "Do *exactly* what they tell you *when* they tell you."

Thew nodded.

This Bradshaw dude is even scarier than the Master Chief.

The squad members turned their heads, and Thew followed their gaze. That English-accented officer was approaching them.

"I see that our forklift drivers have made it," he said, nodding to Thew and Skaggs. "Welcome to SEAL Team Two."

"Okay, gentlemen. Here's the plan."

25

Lieutenant General Abdulaziz al-Mutairi, Commander of the Saudi Land Defense Forces, sat stone-faced in the ornate Royal Defense Room of the sprawling Al Yamamah Palace in Riyadh, home to the King of Saudi Arabia.

The King was known to be mercurial, but today he was absolutely unhinged.

"I should have you fucking *hanged!*" he bellowed, his face beet red.

"Where are our soldiers?" he boomed. *"Where?"*

The King was not a small man. At six feet three inches and 220 pounds, he cut an imposing figure.

Some referred to him as the Lion of the Desert.

He's looking for somebody to blame. Somebody he can hold up to the public for being incompetent and then . . ..

Al-Mutairi stifled a shudder.

He focused his attention on the King. For his own self-preservation.

Look in the mirror, you pompous soft-handed sycophant of unbelievers. Whose idea was it to host the whole fucking army on one base?

He sat there on a large throne-like chair, just *glowering* at Al-Mutairi.

An aide stepped up and whispered in the King's ear.

The King looked startled.

He abruptly stood and walked to the large double doors before looking back at Al-Mutairi.

"I'm not done with you," he seethed, then left the room.

Al-Mutairi remained for a moment to gather himself.

Conspicuously absent from the King's court this afternoon was the commander of the Saudi Air Force which, from what he could gather, was largely destroyed in the overnight attacks.

Not a single aircraft had taken off to face the Iranian bombers.

But there was no Commander of the Saudi Air Force sitting here with Al-Mutairi.

Why not? *Because he's a royal.*

Abdulaziz walked to the double doors, his back ramrod straight.

He squinted as he stepped into the courtyard. The sunlight was bright, and the sky was crystal clear.

He understood why the King had abruptly, mercifully, ended his meeting.

The sound of air-raid sirens rose and fell across the capital city.

A pang of fear momentarily gripped him. The Palace of Al Yama-mah would doubtlessly be a target of the Iranians.

His phone buzzed in his pocket. He kept his head turning like a swivel as he pulled his phone out from his pocket. He half expected a Royal Guard to come at him with a sword in hand. Not *even* half expected.

"Hello?" he answered.

"Abdulaziz al-Mutairi, do you know who this is?" the voice asked.

Mutairi stopped, frozen.

The voice was young. It sounded somewhat familiar, but Mutairi couldn't put a face to the voice.

"Who is this, and what do you want?" he answered. He started walking again, his head still sweeping back and forth for the sword-wielding Royal Guard.

It was Prince Abdul bin Muhammad Al Saud, an impetuous fucking child. The son of the former Crown Prince, Muhammad bin Nayef, who was deposed in 2020 in favor of the current King.

Bin Nayef was forced into exile and died in Cairo. The circumstances behind his deposition – and death – were murky.

"You see how fat and soft the Fake King and his crew of lecherous hangers-on have become," the boy said. "They let the Iranians *walk* in." His voice *dripped* with derision and contempt. "And whom do they blame?"

He sounded smarter than the intelligence reports gave him credit for, this . . .

. . . *this boy who would be king.*

Abdulaziz cleared his throat.

"What can I do, Your Highness?"

No missiles had come. Hash kept an eye on radar, and his watch. Twenty minutes had passed.

He ordered his convoy to resume course.

They headed straight for the two American ships on his radar. Full steam ahead at forty miles per hour.

Am I sailing into a trap?

His whole convoy had been in range of the Americans' missiles for hours. They had radars that covered a much greater range than his own ships', and their missiles also had longer ranges, so it didn't make sense to draw him closer.

More than anything, Hash was curious.

26

The Port of Al Ruwais was full of shipping containers, flatbed trailers and multiple Mack and Mercedes trucks.

Get down to Al Udeid. I don't care how you get there, just go.

Thems were the orders, so Nigel ordered his men to commandeer as many trucks and trailers as they could handle.

They managed fifteen trucks with containers. That meant thirty soldiers crammed into each container.

Those things were *hot* inside. Only five had air conditioners.

The trip should take an hour and a half, unhindered. But with circumstances as they were, with Qataris fleeing Doha and no police, who knew how long it would actually take.

So they stopped every twenty minutes, and the soldiers took turns riding in the air-conditioned trailers.

Al Udeid Air Base was in the desert west of Doha, so taking Pitt's suggestion to avoid the capital city wasn't a problem.

Like Kuwait, Qatar was a city-state, with nearly ninety percent of the population concentrated in Doha.

The SEALs and Marines reached Al Udeid in under three hours. They could see the base from miles away. Multiple columns of black smoke still rose from the base.

Nigel didn't think they could just drive up to the front gate, but to his surprise, he found that they *almost* could.

About a mile from the base, there was a tank parked right in the middle of the main road, blocking their way.

Nigel got out.

The desert wind lashed his uniform.

"United States Navy and Marine Corps!" he shouted.

Nothing.

Nigel walked around the tank.

"Freeze!" someone shouted. *"Show me your hands!"*

Nigel did as he was told.

Several soldiers rose up out of the desert about fifty feet away.

Nice, thought Nigel.

Marines, Nigel noted, as they patted him down.

"Lieutenant Commander Nigel Woods," Nigel said, his arms still above his head. "United States Navy."

"Cheerio," he added.

"You talk funny," said a Marine, pointing his rifle at him.

Al Udeid was a small city in its own right.

Spread over fourteen square miles, it served as an air base for the United States, the United Kingdom and Qatar. It also contained Qatar's main Emiri Land Forces base, housing more than one hundred Turkish- and German-built tanks, armored vehicles and artillery pieces.

Roughly 14,000 Americans were stationed there. They were split between aircraft squadrons on deployment to Qatar – usually for six months at a time – and base support personnel.

Although the squadrons included pilots and flight crews, most squadron personnel were support staff: maintenance crews, logistics specialists and records administrators.

The base personnel managed the Mess Hall, recreational fa-cilities, base housing, the base hospital, the fuel depot, armaments, warehouses, and higher-level maintenance workshops.

A young Marine captain, Todd Wakefield, was the highest-ranked officer of the 400 Force Protection Marines sent to Al Udeid.

Two hundred and ninety were left. Twenty-five had been killed and another eighty-five injured.

Wakefield gave Nigel a quick tour of the damage.

It was extensive.

The burnt shells of aircraft lay in pieces, scattered across multiple tarmacs.

The long runways were pockmarked by hundreds of craters, large and small.

Aircraft hangars and warehouses were demolished. Wakefield reported endless shock waves from missiles and bombs and then, afterward, the arms caches cooking off.

Though the arms storage bunkers were a mile away across the runways, there had been nothing to blunt the shock waves, thanks to the absence of hills, trees or buildings.

Then there was the fuel depot and the rows of KC-46 aerial refu-eling tankers lined up on the tarmac.

It was hell on earth, according to Wakefield.

From what Nigel could see, there was no base left to defend.

However, one part of the base was mostly untouched: the Emiri Land Forces base. Their tanks and artillery pieces were lined up in neat rows behind a fence.

Nigel had 400 – make that 690, now – Marines under his com-mand, plus the Air Force and other service personnel at Al Udeid. Nearly 700 Marines and fifty Navy SEALs.

That was a potent fighting force.

They could make a stand here, Nigel thought, and wait for the calvary – General Pitt, the Navy, *somebody* – to come to the rescue.

But contending with ballistic missiles and stealth bombers? Nigel didn't like that prospect. *No way, mate.*

Nigel looked to the sky.

It would be dark soon.

They had to move.

But to where?

★ ★ ★

A good SEAL knows his Geography – one would hope.

The SEALs laid out a paper map of the Persian Gulf, and Nigel studied it in silence.

The Iranians had come down through Kuwait and eastern Saudi Arabia – right down Highway 5, no doubt – and taken Bahrain.

Qatar was about half as far from Bahrain as Kuwait, and the Iranians had covered *that* distance in a day.

The Iranians *were* coming, Nigel was certain. They might already be trekking up Salwa Highway from the southwest corner of Qatar.

If we could stay to their east and head down to the Qatar-UAE Highway.

From there, east into the United Arab Emirates. It was only seventy miles between Qatar and the UAE.

What then?

What is this? Nigel thought, as he focused on the UAE.

There, right on the coast – on the *Gulf of Oman,* at the top of the Indian Ocean – was the UAE city of Fujairah.

Those were *open* waters, not hemmed in by any chokepoints like the Strait of Hormuz.

It would be a race.

"Alright, gentlemen," Nigel announced. "We have a destination."

Nigel informed General Pitt of his plans.

He *didn't* tell him, however, about their raid on the Emriti Land Forces base.

There had been only a few Emriti soldiers on hand, and they offered no resistance. They were startled, more than anything, as their American guests pointed rifles at their faces and raided their armory stores.

The American officer had apologized in broken Arabic.

So far, so good.

No Iranians. Not yet.

After that, Alpha Squad sped southwest on Salwa Road in privately owned Land Rovers, courtesy of the Emeriti Land Forces base. It took only fifteen minutes at eighty miles an hour to reach the junction of the Qatar-UAE Highway.

They scouted for several more miles before giving the green light for the convoy to continue to the Qatar-UAE Highway. Bravo Squad was tasked with speeding down *that* highway to within five miles of the border – if they could get that far.

The Marines, meanwhile, had commandeered a couple of Emeriti tanks and parked them in the middle of Salwa Road a mile southwest of the Qatar-UAE Highway junction to block an Iranian advance, even if the tank amounted to nothing more than a speed bump.

An hour after sundown, Nigel gave the green light, and the main convoy of Marines and Air Force airmen drove off in Mac trucks and Emiriti Army vehicles.

A young Emiri soldier watched as the two-mile-long convoy of Americans snaked away from the base.

I should call someone.

But who? The cell phone network was jammed, and rumor had it that the Emir himself had fled the country.

Ten miles from the border, Nigel's satellite phone buzzed.

It was General Pitt.

A Navy MQ-45 Devil Ray stealth reconnaissance drone from the USS *Barack Obama* loitered over the Qatari-Saudi-UAE border region.

Iranian special forces operating ahead of an advancing column of tanks and troops had seized the Al Ghuwaifat border crossing on the UAE side.

Nigel and the convoy stopped and huddled.

The Devil Ray's digital signal was fed to the SEALs' encrypted electronic tablet.

Thew and Skaggs were jammed inside a container with Marines and Air Force airmen.

Fun.

The SEALs scouted ahead of the stopped convoy. Thew and Skaggs waited in their packed container. And waited. It was getting hot.

A Marine sergeant opened the container back door and consulted with somebody on the outside.

He whistled, and everyone scrambled out.

"Pssst." Thew looked to his left after jumping out of the container.

It was Clay, the Marine private.

He motioned for Thew and Skaggs to join him.

"What's going on?" Thew asked as he and Skaggs jogged over.

"I dunno," Clay said. "But they told us to get down."

Something caught Thew's eye, and he looked up.

Movement amid the darkness above.

Then a red flare, a gush of fire.

27

I n Tampa, General Pitt watched, via the satellite link to the stealth Devil Ray drone, as explosions erupted along the length of the mile-long convoy of trucks and Emiriti military vehicles.

Pitt felt sick. He was helpless as he watched the carnage unfold.

"Where are our F-35s?!" he demanded.

Along with the MQ-45 Devil Ray, the *Obama* had launched a squad of four F-35 Lightning II stealth fighter/attack jets to keep tabs on the convoy's progress.

The General had spoken too soon. The F-35 Lightning IIs had launched a string of missiles as soon as their radars detected the open bomb bay doors of the Iranian FC-31 Gyrfalcons.

The four Lightning IIs fired four air-to-air missiles apiece, each missile targeting an independent radar signature.

There were ten Taklamakan Squadron fighters on this run and sixteen American Sidewinder missiles.

The "air fight" was over in seconds. Despite their low-signature radar returns, the AI-assisted targeting apparatus of the American planes easily homed in on the Iranian aircraft – and in the case of six of the ten Gyrfalcons, *two* missiles apiece zeroed in.

Not that it mattered. One Sidewinder was enough.

Fourteen flashes of light.

Ten blooms of sparks and fire.

Ten Gyrfalcons were destroyed.

Thew didn't see the fireworks show. The last thing that he remembered was pointing to a strange light in the sky.

He didn't know it, but what he'd seen was the after-burn of a Gyrfalcon's engines after it dropped its bombs above the American convoy. The Iranians had spotters near the Al Udeid Air Base, and they'd been keeping tabs on the convoy every step of the way.

Thew didn't remember, but he had instinctively dropped to the ground.

For the Iranian Gyrfalcon pilots, it was a turkey shoot. They even had a "Convoy" option on their target display which, of course, the lead pilot had selected.

Their aircraft were networked, too.

The lead aircraft's computer identified the line of vehicles and, networked with the other Gyrfalcons, spaced out their bombs along the length and narrow breadth of the long convoy.

From out of the darkness, eight 1,000-pound bombs fell from the lead plane.

One detonated as it struck the container truck behind the one that Thew had just left. So when Thew came to his senses, he ran.

Others ran, too. Marines and Air Force personnel. *Hundreds* of them. Through hardscrabble oven-baked sand.

The farther he got from the roadway, the more beach-like the sand became. The pathway had turned into sand dunes.

Thew struggled in the loose sand, lifting his knees higher to drive himself forward. He worked hard, but barely made any progress.

The more his memory put the pieces back together, the harder his legs worked.

The wind had been knocked out of him. His diaphragm had seized up, and he'd silently but desperately gasped for air.

He remembered thrashing about, trying to get air. And then darkness.

He must have passed out which, in turn, must have relaxed his body, allowing him to breathe again.

Then his eyes had snapped open.

Clay, the Marine kid, stared. *Gawked* at him, his mouth open.

Focus on your feet.

It was odd. The kid was smart. His eyes had shone with a gentle light. But now they were dull. He looked stupid, the way his mouth was open.

Just run.

"Clay?" Thew had asked. But there was no response, no movement.

His uniform was ripped open, his pale stomach bare.

Keep going.

The night flashed bright, just the blink of an eye, and, like a wipe-out on a wave in Ocean City, Thew tumbled head over heels amid a whirlwind of sand and limbs.

It was another explosion.

RUN.

There were jets above, invisible in the darkness. But their engines roared.

KEEP RUNNING.

As he ran, he went through a mental checklist of sorts.

Legs working? *Check.* Arms? *Check.* Trouble breathing? *No. Check.* Bleeding? *Not that I can tell. Check.*

On the ground, amid the sand, there were clumps of gore and the fabric of uniforms.

Don't stop.

Another flash, and Thew face-planted into the sand. There was a roar, and another whirlwind washed over him.

Thew pressed his face further into the sand, tried to merge with it, as more explosions ripped the air above and shook the ground beneath him.

The sand seemed to embrace him, parting for him as finer particles sifted down into the trembling ground.

Then there was silence.

Thew waited.

And waited.

After a while, he rolled over.

The night sky was brilliant before him. Except for the fires behind him, there was no light pollution here. The stars and galaxies of the universe burned bright, vast and all-encompassing.

Thew thought that he might fall into it.

The roar of jets was long gone.

Silence.

The light of the moon and stars cast an eerie white glow on the desert.

A land of ghosts.

He could just turn around and walk back the way he had come, through the desert.

But that thought chilled him. It was a land of ghosts now, and of ghostly predators.

And of the things he had seen.

Thew walked, then broke into a jog, then sprinted until he reached the road.

It was a multi-lane highway, like the one the convoy was traveling on. Thew ran out into the middle of it.

He stopped and placed his hands on his knees. He calmed his breathing.

He began walking down the highway in the general direction of the convoy, whose orange glows had now disappeared.

Maybe it isn't a good idea to walk in the middle of the road. What if a car was driving fast with no lights on?

Thew looked over his shoulder to scan for movement in the darkness before heading to the side of the road.

Headlights appeared in the distance.

They were mesmerizing, like distant jewels.

He heard the car gun its engines, though it was still far away. It was driving *fast*.

Oh shit.

Thew booked.

Straight into the land of ghosts he went, into the bush, throwing himself into the sand.

He waited for the sound of the car speeding by.

It never came.

Silence.

Did I imagine the car? Did it stop?

Thew raised his head, slowly, and peeked over the sand.

There was no car. No headlights.

Am I making too much of this? he asked himself.

Did your convoy just get bombed? was the answer that came back to him.

Good point, Thew.

Thew froze. He thought he heard something.

His heart pounded in his ears. Surely, if someone was out there, they could hear it too.

He lay down and stayed as quiet and still as he could.

A wash of light blinded him.

Thew raised his hands to block the light and show that he was unarmed. Several figures moved in the darkness behind the light.

This is it, he thought, and led a silent prayer. *Dear God . . .*

"Well, I'll be buggered," said a familiar voice.

"It's our forklift driver, yeah?"

Among the advancing Iranian soldiers in eastern Saudi Arabia were next-generation Russian S-500 and Chinese HQ-22 anti-aircraft missile batteries.

These anti-aircraft systems were preprogrammed with the radar signatures of the Gyrfalcons. It was postulated that the American F-35 produced a similar radar return.

The Chinese and Russians had guessed right.

The F-35 signatures were close enough to the Gyrfalcon's that they registered as enemy aircraft.

Four enemy aircraft were detected.

Six missiles launched within seconds of each other.

The four American F-35 Lightning IIs immediately detected the initial radar locks and then the missile launches. They enacted evasive maneuvers.

Because of the F-35s' minuscule radar signatures, the missiles had trouble maintaining their radar locks after they were airborne.

Two of the missiles, however, were able to get close enough that, when they detonated, their shrapnel shredded their targets.

One of the F-35s went down in flames over the desert of the United Arab Emirates. A second exploded offshore near the UAE's Yasat Islands in the Persian Gulf.

The other two turned tail and raced back to the *Obama* in the Indian Ocean. The four remaining missiles streaked harmlessly out to sea and into the desert.

The Devil Ray stealth drone captured streaks of light and an explosion in midair.

"Can someone tell me what the hell just happened?" General Pitt demanded.

It was nearly midnight in the Persian Gulf, and Iran was not yet aware that they had lost ten more Gyrfalcons.

Fifty of their remaining 138 Gyrfalcons lifted off into the night, as another fifty prepared for missions of their own.

General Mohammad Yaghani had returned to the front after his detour to Lebanon to meet with the head of Israel's Military Intelligence Directive.

Yaghani was in Dammam now in what was formerly eastern Saudi Arabia.

The Western media had dubbed it "Occupied Saudi Arabia."

What a joke.

The encampments in Dammam and Al Hofuf were established to fend off a Saudi counterattack.

They were following Hash Ghavam's "white paper" almost to the letter. Based on the events of the past week alone, the man deserved a place amid the greats of Iranian – nay, *Persian* – generals. He would see to it that Hash took his place in history.

Never mind that Hash is an Admiral.

Yaghani allowed himself a smile.

Then it was back to work.

The fifty Gyrfalcons raced down the spine of the Persian Gulf to where the Arabian Peninsula jutted out to the northeast, forming the Ruus Al Jabal, or the Musandam Peninsula.

Rather than turn with the Gulf, the Gyrfalcons went straight inland over the United Arab Emirates.

This was the trickiest part of the operation.

The United Arab Emirates was a dangerous foe. *Very* dangerous.

Not that Saudi Arabia wasn't.

The UAE had over 150 combat aircraft – American F-16s and French Dassault Mirage 2000s and Dassault Rafales – most of which were probably under hardened bunkers at this point, or preparing to strike his advancing army.

Saving the UAE for this stage of the plan, Iran had lost the element of surprise. That much was a given.

Drones and satellite images shared by Beijing showed that the UAE was scrambling for a fight.

Their army was busy setting up defenses outside Abu Dhabi and Dubai, including anti-aircraft systems, American Himars long-range artillery and other systems.

Their aircraft had scattered to various airbases and airports.

It didn't matter.

Every airport runway in all of the UAE was a target.

And unlike the Gyrfalcons of Iran's Taklamakan Squadrons, none of the UAE's aircraft were stealth.

No, it wasn't the *armaments* that made the UAE dangerous. Rather, it was the geography.

The distance from Kuwait City to the UAE border at Al Ghuwaifat was roughly 360 miles. From Al Ghuwaifat to the Gulf of Oman coast – thereby surrounding the coastal Persian Gulf cities of the UAE – was *another* 360 miles.

They had already pressed their luck, Yaghani thought. To go the distance was courting trouble.

But Hash had a theory that he'd included in his white paper.

The UAE had a population of over twelve million. Over ninety percent of them were foreign workers, primarily from South Asia: Indians, Pakistanis, Bangladeshis, Nepalese and Sri Lankans alone accounted for almost fifty-five percent of the population.

The next largest group were UAE Arab nationals themselves. At only ten percent.

The rest were from a range of disparate countries, the most prominent of which were the Philippines, Egypt, Syria, Jordan and even Iran. Residents from Europe, Africa and South America rounded out the rest.

The UAE's military – though skillful, well equipped and well paid – was likewise composed mostly of foreigners.

They were, essentially, an army of mercenaries.

Hash's theory? That mercenaries look good on paper, but in actual combat – *real* combat in which the outcome could go either way – their loyalties falter.

God willing, let Hash be right.

The first attacks would be two waves of Gyrfalcons to take out their anti-aircraft missile batteries and communications systems.

Then would come the missile attacks. Just like before in Bahrain, Qatar and Saudi Arabia.

Except in this case, *every* missile and *every* air strike would be concentrated on the UAE alone.

A thousand bombs.

Shock and awe – to borrow a phrase from the Americans.

Would the mercenaries hold up?

Yaghani allowed himself to hope not.

In two hours, Hash and his convoy of twelve ships had just about closed the distance on the American ships.

He stood on the bridge of the *Sabalan*, peering through binoculars.

There. An American *Arleigh Burke*-class destroyer, on the horizon. He recognized the shape of the class almost instantly.

A cloud of smoke trailed the destroyer.

Hash swept the area until . . . *there.* The second ship. Also an *Arleigh Burke*-class destroyer.

The American Navy had reverted to flying its original ensign following the 9/11 terrorist attack decades ago. That flag contained the thirteen red-and-white stripes of the American flag, but with no blue quarter or stars. Instead, it depicted a snake amid the stripes, with the words "Don't Tread on Me" beneath it.

The flag and its message befit the *Arleigh Burke* destroyers. They were not to be trifled with, and Hash had worked his whole career to avoid any run-ins with those American beasts.

Just one *Arleigh Burke* destroyer could wipe out Iran's entire fleet. Not that this said much. Heck, a pimple-faced Iranian cadet sank the *Kharg,* an oiler and Iran's largest ship at the time, with a carelessly discarded cigarette in 2021.

From the looks of it, these two *Arleigh Burke* destroyers were not in fighting condition.

At the same time, he had fired thirty-six missiles at the two ships. If they were truly out of the fight, they would be sitting at the bottom of the Gulf.

"All stop," Hash ordered.

Hash continued to peer through his binoculars. Both ships had sustained at least one missile strike, if not more – though he wasn't sure if the strikes were from *his* ships.

The Americans had their automated Phalanx close-in weapons system that defended against missiles and fast boat attacks.

Indeed, the radio silence from the IRGC Navy speedboats told the story.

While their anti-ship missiles might be inoperable – for the moment – their Phalanx systems were up-and-running.

"Forward ten knots," Hash ordered. "Take us to their starboard, then bring us around to their port side."

Hash could see American sailors looking back at him with binoculars of their own.

Hash kept his distance, giving the American ships a wide berth as he came around.

"Debris in the water!" shouted a sailor.

Remains of Iranian speedboats. And bodies.

Hash ordered that the bodies be recovered by two ships of his convoy. The rest would continue with Hash and the *Sabalan.*

"Sir," an enlisted radarman alerted. "Multiple returns to our port."

Hash looked over at the radar. They were coming from the west. From Iran.

More IRGC Navy speedboats.

Hash picked up a radio transmitter. "This is Rear Admiral Hash-emi Ghavam of the Islamic Republic of Iran Navy. I order you to stand down." He spoke with authority.

There was no reply. The speedboats kept coming, and then more of them entered radar range.

"Ready the Mark 8's," Hash ordered. The Mark 8's were the British-designed high-caliber, high-rate-of-fire machine guns mounted on the bow and stern of the *Sabalan* and all *Moudge*-class frigates.

"Sir?" asked his executive officer, Captain Cyrus Farsad.

"Do it," ordered Hashemi. *You ass of a donkey!*

"Rear Admiral Ghavam," said a voice on the radio. "I am Soroush Nazem, Commander of IRGC Navy Speedboat Squadron 20."

"Hello, Captain Nazem," Hash said. "Stand down."

Nazem took his time responding. The speedboats, meanwhile, kept coming.

"Sir, speedboat at 9 o'clock," said a watchman.

"Fire the forward Mark 8 across their bow," Hash ordered.

Farsad looked askance at Hash. Hash returned a withering look.

"Fire across their bow," ordered Farsad. Hash continued to glower at him. Farsad straightened and shifted on his feet.

"Admiral Ghavam, what are you doing firing on my boats!" demanded Nazem.

"Captain," Hash said, "I'll say it one more time. *Stand. Down."*

Once again, Nazem took his time to respond. The speedboats continued to advance.

"Fire another burst," Hash ordered.

The ship shuddered with another round of cannon fire.

Another tense moment passed.

"They are turning around," announced the watchman.

"You will be court martialed, Hashemi Ghavam!" railed Nazem on the radio.

Hash looked out on the Americans. They had witnessed the showdown – with confusion, no doubt.

"Signal the Americans," Hash said. "The signal is, *'follow.'"*

Best to keep it simple.

The Americans didn't respond. Hash didn't expect them to.

He ordered the *Sabalan* to take the lead ahead of the American ships, and ordered the rest of his convoy to fall in behind the two *Arleigh Burkes.*

Hash believed he understood, now. The two American ships had escaped the strikes on their base in Bahrain, perhaps sustaining some damage in the process, only to run into the IRGC Navy speedboats. And his thirty-six missiles.

He could easily sink them. That much was clear two hours ago.

But they were operating under their own power and were going . . . *where?*

Home, of course. Back to America.

Those sailors were a long, long way from home.

Any sailor in the world could relate.

28

Americans were panicked.

From coast to coast, grocery stores shelves were stripped bare. Gas stations were running out of fuel.

Local news stations reported on the whereabouts of dusty old Cold War-era bomb and nuclear fallout shelters. *Find one near you!*

Commercials for potassium iodide pills – for protection against radiation – saturated the airwaves. Gold, too, was in great demand. And, of course, guns were flying off the shelves.

And then there were the calls for blood. How dare a foreign country bomb American cities after the USA had bombed *theirs*.

It wasn't supposed to work that way.

For nearly a century and a half, it *hadn't* worked that way.

Daddy Longlegs led the way from his bunker beneath Number One Observatory Circle in Washington. He went on the twenty-four-hour cable news shows via his bunker studio to lobby for a new nuclear posture for the United States.

"In 2020," Longlegs would repeat, "Russia announced that it would perceive any ballistic missile attack on its territories as a nuclear attack. Consequently, any ballistic missile attack must, as a matter of course, warrant a nuclear response."

"We should – we *must* – do the same," he argued. "There is no way to tell whether an incoming ICBM is nuclear-armed or not. We do not have the luxury of assuming that they are *not* nuclear-armed."

"I'm afraid we have to cut you short, Mr. Vice President," interrupted the cable-news host. "Air raid sirens are sounding in Los Angeles and New York City."

Boooop.

That sound again.

The rotating red beacon light high on the wall lit up and started spinning, like before, and the klaxon alarm started.

The 2nd Space Warning Squadron at Buckley Space Force Base in Aurora, Colorado, had, for the second night in a row, detected a series of missile launches from Iran.

Once again, multiple intercontinental ballistic missiles – twenty-five this time – were detected.

Six of the ICBMs appeared aimed at Diego Garcia and Guam again, as well as Hawaii. Two missiles each, if they remained true to the night before. That meant six warheads for each target.

At Guam, the previous night's attack was concentrated on Anderson Air Force Base. More than twenty strategic bombers were damaged or destroyed: ten B-52 Stratofortresses, five B-1 Lancers, three B-2 Spirits and two B-21 Raiders. The B-2 and B-21 were stealth bombers, and cost half-a-billion dollars each. The U.S. had less than forty of these two aircraft combined.

The remaining nineteen ICBMs appeared headed to the continental United States. As the missiles made their way into the Earth's upper atmosphere, the Space Force computer algorithms became more confident by the second. They concluded that the targets were the Navy bases at San Diego, California, and Norfolk, Virginia; Tinker Air Force Base in Oklahoma City, Oklahoma; Whiteman Air Force

Base east of Kansas City, Missouri; and perhaps the oil refineries in New Jersey across from New York City and Philadelphia.

Whiteman was the home of the B-21 Raider stealth bomber. Tinker was the home of critical early-warning radar aircraft like the E-3 Sentry and the newer Boeing 737 AEW&C (airborne early-warning and control), as well as strategic telecommunications aircraft like the E-6 Mercury.

The United States maintains a ballistic missile defense system based out of Vandenberg Space Force Base in California, and Fort Greely in Alaska. The system was designed to defend the West Coast against ICBMs from North Korea (and, unofficially, China).

An East Coast-based system would, by default, be designed to defend against ICBMs from the Soviet Union – now Russia – and would violate treaties between the two countries.

However, after Russia invaded Ukraine in 2022, the United States Congress authorized an East Coast ballistic missile defense system.

However, the system hadn't been built yet.

All ten of the incoming ICBMs aimed at Los Angeles and San Diego were successfully intercepted over Nevada. Each of their warheads – thirty of them in total – fell harmlessly into the open deserts of Nevada and eastern California.

The remaining nine missiles – or twenty-seven warheads – struck the refineries in New Jersey, as well as an area of Philadelphia between its downtown and the airport.

Several warheads fell wide of their targets, landing in the densely-packed, working-class neighborhoods of South Philly, and in the nearby suburb of Folcroft, Pennsylvania.

Rescuers in the coming days would count more than 800 killed and 3,000 injured – the largest number of civilian casualties in a foreign attack on American soil since 9/11.

★ ★ ★

After her on-the-street reporting in Washington, DC, following the first ballistic strike, CNN flew Bernice Hamandawana to Dubai to report on the war from what was thought to be an oasis of peace in a region roiled by war and terrorism.

She had arrived the day before and stayed at the Radisson Blu Hotel, just across from CNN's Dubai regional headquarters, in Dubai Media City. It was more opulent than anything she had ever experienced.

Her room window faced a concentration of skyscrapers in southern Dubai that seemed taller than anything she had seen in Chicago or New York.

Her assigned team was very courteous, insisting that she sleep off her jet lag – until they banged on her door in the middle of the night.

The airport and nearby Minhad Airbase were being bombed.

The SEALs picked through the carnage of the bombed-out caravan just north of the Qatari border with Saudi Arabia.

Charred and shredded bodies lay up and down the length of the caravan. Body parts were scattered on either side of it.

Almost all of the vehicles were burned-out shells.

It was a wonder that the supply kid, Thew, had survived at all, let alone unscathed – at least physically.

Fifty others had also escaped the carnage. Like Thew, they had run into the desert.

As for the King of Bahrain, there was no sign of him.

Nor the other supply kid. Skaggs.

Thew was stoic when Master Chief Gonzales broke the news to him. He had probably already known.

Nigel relayed the news to General Pitt, who did some quick math. More than four thousand soldiers and airmen – mostly noncombatant

Air Force personnel – were likely killed. That would be the largest number of American military casualties in a single day since the Battle of Antietam during the Civil War.

This doesn't help, Pitt told himself. *Get your shit together.*

"You have to move," Pitt told Nigel. "The Iranians are progressing as we speak."

The two lead trucks, and the last two, were still in working order. Almost all of the rest were burnt wrecks.

The SEALs and surviving Marines and Airmen loaded the wounded into two trucks, and a volunteer force of Marines and Airmen filled a third. They headed back to Doha.

The SEALs and nearly 200 Marines pressed forward.

SEALs from Echo Platoon had already secured the border crossing into Saudi Arabia, and the convoy blew right through it.

Although they were near the coast, this was open desert, far from any major city.

An hour after crossing into Saudi Arabia, the convoy approached another border crossing, this one into the United Arab Emirates.

Ahead and to their right, a vehicle burned brightly in the night.

"Iranian scouts," said the whimsical young SEAL manning the post. "Permission to come aboard?" he asked. The rest of Echo Platoon was already well ahead of the convoy.

Soon, Highway 5 in Saudi Arabia became the E11 Highway in the UAE. It paralleled the coast for about 300 miles all the way to the rugged Musandam Peninsula exclave of Oman.

The night sky at their twelve o'clock flashed like lightning, again and again.

Any hope that they had somehow *made it,* that they could let their guard down, vanished.

The war had followed them to the United Arab Emirates.

"Alpha, Echo, over." It was the radio.

Nigel responded with a single squawk, signaling acknowledgment.

"Trouble, mate," said the SEAL on the radio.

The convoy caught up with Echo Platoon.

The burnt-out shells of cars and trucks littered the highway and the desert on either side of it.

UAE military vehicles were among them.

It appeared to have been a checkpoint. The bodies of UAE soldiers lay scattered about. More than twenty of them.

Someone had come through before the SEALs.

"Probably Sepah Special Forces," the Echo Platoon leader surmised.

"Alright," Nigel said, "let's keep it tight, yeah? We've got 200-plus Marines with us. Whoever they are, they won't want what we're bringing."

Headlights appeared in the distance behind them.

"Step on it, yeah?" Nigel commanded.

The convoy moved forward, and Echo Platoon once again sped in front.

In the meantime, Nigel phoned CENTCOM in Tampa, Florida, to ask about the Devil Ray.

The first one was returning to the *Obama* after its brief encounter with F-35s and the Iranian Gyrfalcons that had bombed the convoy in Qatar. Another one, this one from the USS *Doris Miller,* was on its way. It would be on station within the hour.

Echo Platoon radioed.

Their message over the radio was cryptic. Just . . . *keep your eyes open and your head on a swivel.* And a request for acknowledgment. Nothing else.

To make things worse, traffic was beginning to fill in. That meant that they were getting closer to Abu Dhabi, the capital city of the United Arab Emirates.

And dawn was beginning to break.

Chief Buck Bradshaw spotted brake lights ahead. Nigel broke out his night-vision binoculars.

Echo Platoon's assemblage of Land Rovers, Jeep Grand Cherokees and Ford Broncos – all commandeered in Qatar – was about a
mile ahead of them.

"I don't see anything," Nigel said as he peered through his
binoculars.

"Hold on," he said. He adjusted the zoom feature.

Nigel picked up the radio handset. "Echo, is that . . .?" he asked,
leaving the question unfinished.

A single squawk responded.

Yep.

"What is it?" asked Bradshaw.

"There's a line of military vehicles in front of Echo Platoon,"
Nigel said.

Buck looked at Nigel, wanting more.

"They're heading east, like us," Nigel said, still looking through
the night-vision binoculars. "Troop transport trucks, artillery pieces
and tanks on trailers."

"Okay, so . . .?"

"They're *Iranian.*"

In Dammam, "Occupied" eastern Saudi Arabia, the orange rim of
the sun appeared on the horizon at 5:40 a.m.

It was odd to schedule a ceremony of this magnitude at first light,
but General Yaghani had places to be. Besides, the rising sun was
a metaphor of sorts: a new beginning for eastern Arabia, Bahrain,
Qatar and Kuwait.

The assembled VIPs – the Mayor of Dammam; the Saudi com-
mander of the Eastern Police; the commander of Bahrain's Public
Security Forces; Saadi Yaqoob, the Governor of the Iraqi Basra
Governorate; and various imams of Shi'a mosques in Dammam and
Manama – applauded as the sun grew brighter.

"Today marks the return of our people and our land to the arms of God," said Ayatollah Fahad Al-Ghamdi of the Al-Anood Mosque in central Dammam.

He wept as he spoke.

A new flag arose on the tallest flag pole of the Qasr Khaleej Palace. The green flag of Saudi Arabia – with its inscription "There is no god but God; Muhammad is the Messenger of God" in white Arabic script with a white sword beneath – had been removed the day before.

The new flag was red, with a large green oval at the center. The oval was the same shade of green on *Iran's* flag. In the center of the oval was a white, upright sword with two white curves on either side.

The flag was clearly a replica of the flag of the Lahsa Eyalet of the Ottoman Empire which, from 1560 until the withdrawal of the Ottomans in 1670, included most of the territory of Basra, Kuwait, Dammam and eastern Arabia, Bahrain and Qatar.

The shape of the sword and four curves together resembled a tulip, an early symbol of ancient Persia. The five shapes also represented the five pillars of Islam.

The same emblem adorned the center of Iran's flag.

Iran was, after all, the cultural hearth and traditional leader of Shi'a Islam, and the entire region was, except for Kuwait, majority Shi'a.

"I proclaim the Islamic Republic of Al-Ahsa," Ayatollah Al-Ghamdi said.

"Allah Akbar!" he boomed. The growing crowds responded with equal zest.

"Allah Akbar!"

A thunderous unison of thousands of voices.

"Allah Akbar!"

"Allah Akbar!"

"Everyone stay cool, yeah?" Nigel said into his earpiece microphone.

The SEALs – *all* of them – were geared up and wearing mics.

The Marines had painted their faces and brought their weapons to bear.

Everyone was on edge.

The American convoy had somehow managed to get hemmed in by the lead vehicles of advancing *Iranian* forces, with the back half of the Iranian convoy closing in from behind.

They were stuck.

Fortunately, the Iranians didn't seem to be any the wiser.

For now.

Traffic had slowed to a crawl. Civilians lined the highway, waving at the Iranian convoy that the Americans had accidentally joined.

Nigel's satellite phone buzzed.

"Wood here," he answered.

"That's *brilliant,* sir," Nigel said. He was cheerful.

Apparently, that the was the end of the conversation.

"What's up?" asked Hector from the back seat.

"Nothing to get bothered about, mate," Nigel said. "The Emir of Abu Dhabi Emirate declared Abu Dhabi to be an 'open city,' then took a holiday to Muscat, Oman."

"Why is that *good* news?" asked Hector.

"It *isn't.* I mean, *honestly,* mate."

Hector shook his head and stifled a smile.

To their right, black smoke rose in several clusters. It was the Al-Dhafra Air Base of the UAE Air Force.

It was a familiar sight for the Americans at this point.

At the Al Salam Royal Palace in Jeddah, the King held court with his national security team. His mood from the previous day had not improved. In fact, it had only darkened as he watched the so-called Islamic Republic of Ahsa Proclamation Ceremony on Al Jazeera.

What truly infuriated him was the legitimacy that Al Jazeera afforded the occasion. They depicted old maps from the days of the Ottoman Empire outlining the old Ottoman eyalet that the invaders had seized. They even suggested that an Iranian client Shi'a state in eastern Arabia was a return to the natural order of things.

Lieutenant General Abdulaziz al-Mutairi, Commander of the Saudi Land Defense Forces, had seen the King behave like this before. He knew the fate that awaited him. Worse, he knew what it meant for his family . . . for generations.

If the King were *Abdul bin Muhammad Al Saud,* however, things could be different. Maybe not for him, but certainly for his family.

What else could Mutairi do?

"General *Abdulaziz al-Mutairi,"* the King said. He carefully enunciated Abdulaziz's name.

Abdulaziz stood.

"You are *relieved* of your duties, Abdulaziz al-Mutairi," the King said. He said it slowly, as if savoring the words.

"Further," the King said – but he never finished the sentence.

Abdulaziz pulled out his SIG Sauer P226 standard issue sidearm and opened fire.

The young Crown Prince, Salman bin Mohammed, sitting at the King's right, jumped to his feet to aid his father. He threw his arms up to defend against something invisible before stumbling backward and falling to the floor.

The King slid down his chair and crumpled to the floor.

Ministers dove for the floor, under tables and behind chairs, as more gunfire erupted.

It was over in less than ten seconds.

Abdulaziz emptied the SIG's fifteen-round magazine before he himself was gunned down by Palace Guards.

29

Traffic moved forward at a snail's pace as the Iranian military convoy, with an American center, snaked around a traffic circle at Bawabat Al-Sharq.

Nigel had turned the radio on and found the BBC. It presented a long report on how ordinary Americans were coping – i.e., freaking out – after the ballistic missile strikes from Iran.

It was downright embarrassing to the SEALs.

"Fucking A," griped Chief Buck Bradshaw as he followed the Iranian convoy.

He wasn't complaining about the radio report. Rather, the Iranians apparently had the same idea as the Americans: to head inland, away from the suburbs of Abu Dhabi, before heading northeast again to parallel the coast.

Nigel's satellite phone buzzed.

He listed for a moment.

"'Bout fucking time, mate," Nigel finally spoke. He powered up his tablet.

"Man, that's a *General* you're talking to," Bradshaw whispered.

"It is, innit?" Nigel whispered back, smiling ear to ear.

"Taking control," Nigel said into the satellite phone.

Bradshaw glanced over. On Nigel's tablet there was footage from a high-altitude aircraft or . . . drone.

Nigel spread his thumb and pointer finger on the screen, causing the camera to zoom in.

It was real-time, Buck realized.

Nigel zoomed in to the long – *really* long – slow-moving convoy.

It took him a minute, but he found his own Land Rover, and the other American vehicles, sandwiched between the Iranians.

Using an identification tool, he electronically marked all the vehicles of the Americans. It easier said than done. There were now a lot of civilian and commercial vehicles woven into the Iranian convoy.

The sound of jet aircraft.

A formation of four Iranian Gyrfalcons flew at a leisurely pace along the highway before turning toward Abu Dhabi. A second formation of four Gyrfalcons soon followed.

It was a daytime show of force.

It also announced to the denizens of Abu Dhabi that the Iranians had arrived.

"Okay," Nigel said into his satellite phone. "There you have it, mate. Now try not to get us whacked, yeah?"

"Thank you," Nigel said after a moment. "Good shooting, mate."

He hung up the phone.

"Okay, gentlemen," Nigel announced. "I hope your affairs are in order. Things are about to kick off, yeah?"

"Do you guys see what I see?" It was the young SEAL, Henry Avellino, from a few vehicles back. "Look to your right, two o'clock."

Nigel, Bradshaw and Gonzales spotted it.

It was a large billboard advertising a Ford dealership. A few yards up the road was a *sea* of 4x4 pickup trucks, SUVs, Jeeps and Land Rovers – row after row of them, right off the highway.

Al-Wathba Auto Mall.

Nigel quickly marked the Al-Wathba Auto Mall corner as friendly on his tablet.

"Okay, *Doris Miller,* I just marked a new friendly zone. That's where we're headed," Nigel said into his earpiece microphone.

"Got it, Team America," said a voice over the earpiece. It was an F-35 pilot.

"Take cover, brother," said the pilot. "Helleth unleasheth."

Bradshaw put his turn signal on and, when incoming traffic lightened, he turned into the parking lot of the Al-Wathba Auto Mall and parked.

Then he ducked.

The other Land Rovers, Grand Cherokees and Broncos followed suit. The length of tractor trailers carrying Marines and the remaining Air Force personnel awaited their turn, holding up the rear of the Iranian convoy.

Wump wump wump.

Nigel didn't hear it so much as he felt it.

Wump wump wump wump wump wump wump wump wump . . .

All the windows of the vehicle shattered.

Move, Nigel commanded himself, even as explosions from the F-35 bombing run erupted along the line of the convoy.

"Move!" Nigel bellowed into his earpiece microphone. "Yeah?" he added.

Nigel rolled out onto the parking lot pavement. Fires crackled. There was shouting. Nigel wasn't sure what language it was, but it wasn't English.

Nigel brought his Colt M4 to eye level and approached the burning trucks and buses ahead of him. Alpha and Echo Squads formed up behind him.

He fired at anything in his sights that moved. A single shot. Same for each of the operators of Alpha and Echo Platoons.

Then it was on to the 4x4 trucks and jeeps. *Let the Marines deal with the remainder of the convoy for now.*

The Al-Wathba Auto Mall had just opened for the day. It didn't take much talking to get the staff to fuel up all their 4x4 vehicles – sixty-five of them – and check their tires and so on.

There were even several dune buggies.

Then it was go time.

Four wheeling time.

Was there a male on Earth who wouldn't take a turn at four wheeling?

Nigel smiled.

"Whoop!" It was Buck Bradshaw, the tattooed SEAL chief.

He fired up a brand new rugged-version Ford Bronco. Nigel and the SEALs climbed in.

"Let's go, yeah?" Nigel commanded through his earpiece headset. To everyone.

Within minutes, a fleet of brand new 4x4 pickup trucks and SUVs was heading northeast along the E75 – away from the burning Iranian convoy.

Rear Admiral Habibollah Nasirzadeh stood amid the smoldering wreckage of the Iranian military convoy.

They had been nearing the End Game until this – this first significant engagement with an enemy force.

Curiously, three different segments of traffic – all comprising civilian vehicles – had been left untouched.

Even more curious, *all* the vehicles – mostly tractor trailers, with a few Land Rovers and other SUVs mixed in – had Qatari license plates.

Habib had watched a slew of U.S. Navy SEALs and Marines escape the U.S. Navy base in Bahrain, and they had apparently taken the King of Bahrain with them.

This very morning, he heard about the long convoy of American soldiers and airmen bombed by Iran's Taklamakan Squadron, which, according to initial reports, killed thousands.

In Qatar.

Truth be told, Habib was saddened to hear about the fate of the Americans that had escaped Bahrain. They were the vaulted American Navy SEALs and Marines, after all – the best fighting forces the world had ever known.

To be done in by an air attack in the desert in the dark of night? That was not a fitting end to warriors of that caliber.

Just as curious, the Iranian dead not killed in the initial air strike were apparently killed by close-range small arms fire. Witnesses described the shooters as coming from the same convoy.

They were very professional. Just one or two shots per dead Iranian soldier.

More than a hundred Iranian soldiers were killed that way, if not *two* hundred, yet it was all over in a matter of seconds according to witnesses.

A very lethal force, indeed.

Finally, there was the car dealership. The poor owner wept. Ruined, he said. Almost his entire inventory of 4x4 vehicles was stolen in a matter of minutes.

The American SEALs and Marines had survived the air strike in Qatar after all.

Habib was pleased.

But, *what was that American saying?*

Habib looked at the tracks on the ground. Some burnt rubber, but mostly deep rivets where vehicles' tires had dug into the sand, leaving a trail out onto the E33 and the Abu Dhabi Desert.

He looked out into the void of open desert. The air shimmied and warped as the young day's heat took hold.

Be careful what you wish for.

"I got here as soon as I heard," said General Yaghani.

He watched solemnly as soldiers pulled the charred remains of their friends and comrades from the blackened shells of troop carriers.

Given the length of the convoy, upward of a thousand casualties were wrought by the American air strike and subsequent firefight with their special forces.

"You are sure that these Americans are the same ones that escaped Bahrain to Qatar?" Yaghani asked.

"I believe so," Habib said. He pointed to the Qatari license plates and registration numbers on the commercial trucks.

Yaghani looked to the open desert, to where Habib thought the Americans had escaped.

"Clearly, they are on the run," Habib said. "I am of a mind to let them go."

Yaghani didn't answer. He studied the destruction of the convoy.

The bodies of Iranian soldiers were being laid out in rows. Yaghani walked slowly along the line of bodies.

Habib and Alamouti walked at his side.

Yaghani stopped and looked skyward.

He was reminded of a phrase that Rear Admiral Hasehmi Ghavam had written repeatedly in his white paper.

Deny the space.

He turned to Habib.

"They are a wedge," Yaghani said, "these SEALs and Marines."

"Look at what they have done," he continued. "Clearly, they have the means to coordinate with their carriers in the Indian Ocean. If they are not secured, then they allow the Americans a toehold from which to stage their offensive. We must deny the Americans the space to regroup."

"We don't know where they are heading," Alamouti offered.

"Don't we?" said Yaghani. He turned to Habib.

"Habibollah Nasirzadeh, you are *Sepah* Naval Special Forces. Where do *you* think they are going?"

"The coast," Habib answered. He didn't hesitate. "The coast of the Gulf of Oman. Sohar, Oman, or . . . more likely . . . *Fujairah*."

"We've got company." It was the young petty officer, Henry Avellino, on the radio. "We hear jets."

Chief Buck Bradshaw turned down the radio – it the was the BBC again, now reporting that the Emirate of Dubai had declared *that* city open.

According to the BBC, the United Arab Emirates was no longer united. One Emirate after another had unilaterally declared itself neutral and "open" as Iranian troops approached.

Bradshaw, Wood, Gonzales and Köllner craned their necks and looked up at the sky even as Bradshaw continued to drive.

And drive *fast*.

He drove up to 110 miles per hour along certain stretches of the straight-line highway.

They'd been on the road for an hour after the air raid on the Iranian convoy and the subsequent firefight.

Nigel knew it would be a race to the Al-Hajar mountains.

"Do you hear anything?" asked Bradshaw.

"No," said Gonzales from the backseat.

Nigel picked up the radio. "Do you still hear jets?"

"No," Avellino replied. "We heard them for a few seconds, but not anymore."

Bradshaw, Wood, Gonzales and Köllner still craned their necks, looking skyward.

Trust your men.

Nigel had to work on the assumption that a jet – *Iranian* jets – had spotted them and reported their whereabouts. They could expect company at any time.

They had covered a lot of distance, but they were running out of time.

Nigel picked up the satellite phone.

It was time for Tampa to perform some more magic.

★ ★ ★

Master Chief Hector Gonzales handed the binoculars to Lieutenant Commander Nigel Wood.

A crescent from their north to their east was saturated with paratroopers falling gracefully through the clear blue sky.

Like leaves on a breeze.

It was a beautiful sight, really, if one were to be objective. One could admire the athleticism of a leopard, for example, while acknowledging its lethality.

The convoy of SEALs and Marines had just passed UAE Highway E44, which a half-mile to the east became *Omani* Highway 5. Omani Highway 5 cut through the Hajar mountain range to Aqar, Oman, on the coast of the Gulf of Oman. The Hajar Mountains were only fifteen miles wide, but rugged. Highway 5 followed a wadi – a dry riverbed that runs with water only a few times a year – called the Wadi Hatta, which cut a valley through the Hajar Mountains to the coast.

From what Nigel could tell, Oman was a half mile to their east. Unfortunately, Iranian paratroopers were landing in the foothills before the Hajar Mountains . . . *in Oman.*

Nigel made a calculated decision.

They were going to Oman.

The convoy stopped, and Nigel conferred with the Marines' officers.

They all agreed that the best defense was a good offense.

After a brief drawing of plans, they climbed back into their vehicles.

"Gun it," Nigel said into the radio. "Let's roll right up on them before they can think. *Tallyho!"*

Bradshaw turned sharply and went off the road. The Ford Bronco bounced and heaved in open desert.

The other vehicles in the convoy followed suit.

Thew lay face down in the back of a Land Rover as he was told to do, with SEALs Henry Avellino and Danny Liu.

The Land Rover tore through the open desert. Orders were passed back and forth on the radio. Thew couldn't make sense of them.

"Okay, everyone out and *stay down!*" Henry ordered, then brought the Land Rover to a skidding stop at the foothills of the rocky Hajar Mountains, kicking up a cloud of dust.

Thew clambered out and was immediately shoved face-down to the ground. "You're with me," Danny Liu – the other young SEAL, said. "Keep your head down at all times. *Do not* stand up."

"Okay, let's go," Danny said, and the two sprinted forward while hunched over.

Thew could hear machine gun fire, muffled and distant.

First one, then several sounds of . . . *bees?* . . . and Danny shoved Thew to the ground again.

Bullets, Thew realized, cutting through the air. And *close.*

They were being shot at.

Then all hell broke loose, at least sonically.

Danny and multiple SEALs and Marines opened up with their rifles.

It was deafening. And unnerving. Thew tried to scramble away from the sounds but was held down.

"Stay down," somebody whispered with urgency. It was Liu again.

Thew did so, but quietly seethed. He was tired of being thrown to the ground and treated like . . . *like a fucking burden.*

"Come on," ordered Liu, who helped Thew up – but Thew pushed him away.

"I'm not a fucking kid," Thew protested, and stood up while keeping low.

Thew followed Liu and the others. His legs were noodles, and he quietly cursed himself for barely keeping up. *Fucking move, Thew!*

Within minutes, the heavy gunfire seemed to ease up a little.

The sky was now full of parachutes.

Just keep going, he told himself.

The jackhammers started anew.

Just keep going.

The jackhammer gunfire didn't stop.

Thew was thirsty.

He sprinted past a body. He only got a glimpse of it, but he saw enough: a pair of legs, a bare stomach – flat, pale and youthful beneath a ripped and bloody uniform.

The dead body of an *Iranian* youth.

He was immediately reminded of Clay, the Marine kid.

"Everyone down!" someone yelled, and the order was repeated.

Somebody counted down: *3 .. 2 .. 1.*

The *BOOM* resonated in Thew's head and chest, and he rolled onto his back. Sand and pebbles rained down on him. Dust was kicked up above him.

Don't move, he commanded himself.

The dust above him drifted away, slowly, revealing blue sky.

Thin white lines etched across the sky caught Thew's attention.

Contrails.

The white lines turned, twisted and intertwined.

Thew saw an orange flash.

"Where the fuck did our air support go?" someone demanded on a radio.

"Petty Officer Avellino," Thew whispered.

Henry looked over. Thew pointed to the sky.

Distant thunder washed over them.

It was a dogfight – dueling fighter planes high in the sky. The aircraft themselves could not be seen from this distance.

"Ah *shit,"* said Henry.

"There's a dogfight above us," Henry said into his mouthpiece. "I don't think we'll be getting another round of help anytime soon."

Far to the east, a plume of black smoke rose from the ground. Another to the north.

Planes were falling out of the sky.

Most likely Iranian jets.

Fingers crossed.

It had been twenty-four hours since Hash and his fleet came upon the two American *Arleigh Burke*-class destroyers.

After signaling for them to follow, there was zero communication between the two Navies.

Hash plowed ahead, first at twenty knots; then, after repairs (no doubt) allowed the Americans to speed up, he upped it to thirty knots.

Hash followed the centerline of the Persian Gulf, navigated through the meandering Strait of Hormuz, and finally reached the Gulf of Oman, the gateway to the open seas of the Indian Ocean.

The American fleet was out there somewhere.

"Signal the *Arleigh Burkes*," Hash ordered. "The signal is, *'Goodbye.'*"

Best to keep it simple. Like before.

As his signalman flashed the message repeatedly, the *Sabalan* and the rest of the Iranian fleet turned back toward the Strait.

In Jeddah, the largest Saudi city on the Red Sea, Rear Admiral Abdulaziz Al-Zahrani watched the news.

Just three miles north of his office on the King Faisal Navy Base was the Al Salam Royal Palace, where the King and his Crown Prince were assassinated the day before.

Thirty-year-old Prince Abdul bin Muhammad Al Saud, son of the *former* Crown Prince, held a news conference during which he claimed to be the rightful Heir to the Throne.

The second son of the recently deceased King, seventeen-year-old Khalid bin Mohammed, also claimed to be the rightful Heir to the Throne – as did various other Princes of the House of Saud.

It was a classic crisis of succession, one that often befell absolute monarchies throughout history and throughout the world.

For the Saudi armed forces, it was time to pick sides. If you *didn't* pick a side, you were suspect to *all* sides.

Abdul bin Muhammad, known colloquially as ABM, was the first to make his move following the assassination of the King and Crown Prince – which, of course, he had successfully engineered. A handful of officers at the bombed King Faisal Air Base in Tabouk threw their lot in behind ABM, and Tabouk was his.

The teenage Saud, Khalid bin Mohammed – or KBM – had wider support from legal experts. *He* was considered the rightful heir in terms of succession, but his young age and his asthma were problematic.

The poor, sickly kid never saw it coming. His very own bodyguard was a secret adherent of Wahhabism – the strict fundamentalist religious sect that dominated much of central Arabia. When he found himself alone with the young prince, he strangled the boy with his bare hands until he was dead.

It was a gruesome affair.

The skinny boy had barely put up a fight. He died swiftly with his eyes wide open and his tongue sticking out.

Pathetic.

The bodyguard had then sworn his allegiance to Imam Omar Farook, a Wahhabi cleric in Riyadh who saw the opportunity to stop the slide into Western-like debauchery led by the boy's father.

Then there was Abn Al Aziz Al Rashid, of the ancient Rashidi Dynasty that historically ruled the Emirate of Jabal Shammar in north central Arabia. A royal prince himself, of the Rashidi branch, he seized the opportunity to reclaim the family's former glory.

It had been thirty-six hours since the assassination of the King and Crown Prince, and Saudi Arabia had already descended into civil war.

"Saudi" Arabia didn't even fit anymore.

There *was* no more "*Saudi*" Arabia.

Meanwhile, in the Hejaz Mountains along the Red Sea coast of western Arabia, armed members of the historically and regionally prominent Zahran tribe seized the village of Hajar (not to be confused with the Hajar Mountains in Oman).

Commander Abdulaziz Al-Zahrani of the Special Navy Security Units – a special forces unit trained by U.S. Navy SEALs – was born in Hajar and was, perhaps, the most prominent member of the Zahran tribe.

Should he pick sides with one of the claimants to the Throne? Or should he go home and lead his tribe?

30

They sprinted again.

The SEALs and Marines had taken the fight straight to the closest contingent of Iranian soldiers.

In conjunction with the other SEAL squads and marines, Henry Avellino and Danny Liu tried to outflank the Iranian paratroopers. Each took turns firing while the other ran behind the rocks and desert shrubbery ahead.

Even as they advanced, Avellino and Liu did their best to protect the young forklift driver.

They picked off four Iranian paratroopers. In turn, the other Iranians concentrated their firepower on the two advancing SEALs, believing them to be the vanguard of a much larger force.

Avellino and Liu scrambled behind some boulders and covered the supply kid as a hail of bullets was unleashed on them. The diversion worked. Other SEAL squads opened fire from the west and pressed forward, killing nearly a dozen Iranian paratroopers.

It was terrifying to witness, and hard to keep up with.

"Violence of action," Thew had heard Chief Bradshaw say.

The SEALs and Thew made it to a place that looked out on a flat desert plain that stretched forty miles to the Persian Gulf.

It looked like the entire Iranian Army – tens of thousands of troop carriers and tanks – had filled the plain, kicking up sand and dust.

They stretched as far as the eye could see.

Meanwhile, to their north and south, the rest of the Iranian para-troopers picked their way through the rocks. They would soon be close enough to direct artillery at the SEALs and marines.

Above the horizon to their northwest was a skyscraper. Its top was like a needle piercing the clouds. Its bottom was obscured by the desert haze. It was the 2,722-foot Burj Khalifa skyscraper in Dubai, the tallest building in the world.

It looked like a great sword standing upright, above the clouds. It shone bright, its windows reflecting the sun.

And then, the sun itself seemed to materialize above the plain between the Burj Khalifa and the SEALs.

Thew was confused. *Did the building do that?*

"Get down!" yelled Gonzales.

"Don't look!" yelled another SEAL.

Thew was slammed to the ground again (*Fuck!*), his face thrust into the sand.

Although his eyes were clamped shut and his face buried in the sand, the blazing light shone through his eyelids.

Then came a *BANG* so loud it sounded like two locomotives collid-ing just feet away. Thew was thrown upward as the ground convulsed and buckled. Then he skidded and bounced along the rocky floor.

"Ahhhhhh!" Thew screamed into the deafening roar of earth and wind. He reached out and tried to grab onto something, anything, as he was dragged along the rocks.

Then another *BANG,* and he was flung backward in the opposite direction like a ragdoll, was dragged along the ground toward a boil-ing cloud of sand and dust.

He wound up flat on his back, staring at a brown void, coughing and hacking.

The deafening roar continued. Hot air and sand lashed his face and body.

Thew grunted, then moved his arms and hands.

Arms are okay.

Next, his toes. Then his legs. Nothing. *No pain.*

Nothing was broken, as far as he could tell.

He rolled onto his side and sat up, bracing himself against the roaring wind and whipping sand.

He could see only a few feet in front of him.

Shadowy alienesque figures emerged from the orange haze, slouching toward him.

Thew's breath caught in his chest. *Iranians. What do I do? Surrender?*

Will they shoot me?

Another sun materialized over the desert, even closer, and the brightness cut right through the dusty haze.

Thew felt the heat and threw his arms up.

That was the last thing he remembered.

"Bryson! Can you hear me?"

A shadowy alien – its face and head completely covered – hovered above Thew.

Oh, right, the aliens.

"He's turning blue!"

How do they know my name? They speak English pretty good.

Thew was dreaming.

Then, quite suddenly he was awake. There was no air.

He was on his side now, and his chest *burned* liked fire.

Chief Bradshaw shoved the blade of a Swiss knife into Thew's mouth – as far as he could.

Thew convulsed, violently, and wretched.

Bradshaw opened a water bottle and shoved it into Thew's mouth, gagging him.

Another violent, convulsive spasm, and the supply kid vomited sand and water.

A wave of nausea wracked Thew as Bradshaw, or someone, pounded on his back. He thrashed, involuntarily, but was held down. He gasped desperately for air.

Another wave of nausea and Thew, on his side, projectile vomited a muddy mix of water and sand.

He coughed deeply, incessantly, and uncontrollably.

Thew's lungs burned, and his abdomen seized with cramps.

Painted faces . . . *aliens* . . . peered down at him, their foreheads furrowed in concern.

Thew curled into a fetal position as he was wracked by another wave of uncontrollable coughing. It passed, and Thew breathed in deeply, making a wheezing sound.

The SEALs let him breathe for another moment.

"Can you stand?" asked Master Chief Gonzales.

Thew sat up, slowly, and was pulled to his feet. He was unsteady. Dizzy.

SEALs on either side propped him up.

"What's wrong with me?" Thew asked in a whisper.

Henry Avellino chuckled. "You were buried under the sand for at least two minutes," he said. "You're lucky to even be alive. Give it a few minutes, and you'll be okay."

"We don't have a few minutes," snarled Chief Bradshaw. "Carry him until he can walk on his own."

Thew remained the charge of Henry Avellino and Danny Liu, as they hiked up the foothills of the Hajar Mountains, following the wadi that ran alongside Omani Highway 5.

He pretended, as best as he could, not to struggle, though his lungs burned and his heart pounded like a bass drum. He was determined, and his strength seemed to be returning.

"Come on, Fleet, you can do it," Henry Avellino encouraged. His voice was barely audible below the continuing roar of wind and sand. If they could just get far enough into the foothills before the approaching Iranians were in range, they would have ample cover.

The trouble was getting there.

"Get down!" Gonzales yelled. Thew ducked behind a rock.

He remained still, not daring to raise his head or twitch a muscle. Jets roared overhead.

"Stay down!" yelled someone else.

Thew waited. *Are we being bombed again?*

"Move!" yelled Gonzales.

Thew stood and walked, trying to keep up with the SEALs.

Mercifully, the SEALs soon came upon a cropping of boulders that were large enough to shelter behind.

Thew collapsed against a boulder. He coughed deeply and uncontrollably. His chest and stomach ached.

"You good?" asked Henry. Thew was out of breath, but gave a thumbs up.

"Good man," Henry said, slapping Thew on the back, which prompted another fit of coughing.

"Fucking A," breathed Chief Bradshaw. He was perched atop a boulder, scanning the plain with binoculars.

Everyone clambered up the rocks, including Thew.

The entire plain, as far as the eye could see, was a mass of hovering dust and sand. Above it, two massive mushroom clouds reached high into the sky. A wall of sand appeared to be pouring down from each of the mushroom heads.

The sound of the falling sand was a roar, like twin waterfalls.

Thew could see soldiers and vehicles moving down there before disappearing beneath the rain of sand.

Thousands – tens of thousands – of Iranian soldiers were being buried alive. From atop the boulders, the view was biblical.

Nuclear, Thew only now realized.

Bullets ricocheted amid the boulders. The Iranian paratroopers had resumed picking their way toward the SEALs and marines.

"Let's move!" ordered the SEAL commander.

Thew found himself trying to keep up with Liu and Avellino again. He was successful, but only barely, until he was slammed to the ground. Someone had their knee on his back, shoving him into the sand, as they fired their rifle.

The knee was removed, and Thew turned over and gasped. He was wracked by another painful coughing fit.

It was Liu again. Thew shot him an angry look.

"Sorry, kid," Liu whispered, "but you're my responsibility right now."

"Look," Danny said, trying to explain. "We thought you were *dead.*" His face cracked with an emotion that surprised Thew. "Your eyes were open."

Half of Liu's face, then, disappeared, showering Thew with blood and brain matter.

All the athleticism and grace of the twenty-year-old SEAL evaporated in an instant. His lanky body crumpled to the ground. His misshapen face fell onto the hard desert.

What was Liu a moment ago was no more. What remained was a heap of inanimate flesh and bones.

Thew still lay against a rocky mound. He stared at the heap of Liu's body.

After a hail of bullets against the rocks around him and Liu had subsided, Henry resumed repressing fire. But he was alone.

"Danny," Avellino said into his mouthpiece.

No response.

Out of the corner of his eye, he could see Danny sprawled on his back. "Eagle down," Avellino said into his mouthpiece as he continued firing.

"Stay put," ordered Wood. "Keep up covering fire. We're coming to you."

"Hurry!" said Henry. He kept firing as the rest of the team worked their way to Henry, Liu and the supply kid.

"Oh *fuck!"* exclaimed Bradshaw.

Köllner and Hastings tended to Danny.

Henry stopped firing and turned. He caught a glimpse of Danny's face for the first time. He turned away and dropped to his hands and knees.

Danny's face was covered in blood that streamed out of his nose; his. His head was misshapen and his right eyeball dangled from its socket. It rested on his cheekbone. Hastings was trying to put it back into place.

Danny had a tiny bullet hole beneath the eye socket, next to his nostril. His left eye stared straight ahead. A mess of blood and brain matter lay splattered on the rocks and dirt beyond his head and covered the young forklift driver who stared at Liu's body with wide eyes.

Henry gripped the ground. He was trying to stop the world as it spun around him.

He dry-heaved and gasped for air, then bellowed a long and wrenching *"Unghhhgh . . .,"* as he fought against the wave of emotion coursing through him, his fingers digging hard into the soil.

"Stay alert," ordered Nigel in his soft-spoken accent to the rest of the men as Hastings, Köllner and Bradshaw worked to secure Danny's body.

"Alex," Nigel said to a member of Alpha Squad, "take up a suppressing position. Shoot anything that moves, yeah?"

"Smith," he said to another, "why don't you go up on that ridge?" Nigel nodded to the top of the hill behind him. The suggestion, of course, was an order.

Making eye contact with Master Chief Gonzales, he nodded his head toward Henry.

Hector walked to Henry and knelt down beside him, gripping his shoulder.

"Just *breathe,* Avenue" said Hector, calling Henry by his nickname.

The wave of emotion passed, and Henry, breathing deeply, re-gained his composure, or a semblance of it. He stood, wiped his eyes and nose, slung his rifle over his shoulder, and walked off to take a suppressing position along the perimeter. He kept his back to Danny's body.

Several of the Alpha Platoon men gave Henry a gentle, knowing pad on his shoulder as he walked past.

After securing Liu's body, Hastings, Köllner and Bradshaw turned their attention to the young forklift driver.

Hastings opened a packet, and removed a moist antibacterial wipe. He cleaned Thew's face and arms of the blood and brains.

Chief Bradshaw knelt in front of Thew.

"What's your name, sailor?" he asked.

Thew didn't respond. He stared ahead, wide-eyed, as if the Chief weren't there.

Bradshaw smacked the teenager's face.

Thew blinked, and a flash of anger crossed his face. *Good sign.*

"Your *name,* sailor, what *is* it?" Bradshaw demanded.

"Thew," Thew said, almost defiantly. "Um, Seaman Apprentice Bryson," he corrected.

"Well, Seaman Apprentice Thew Bryson," Bradshaw said, "get your *shit* together, *capisce?"*

"Yes, sir," Thew whispered.

"See this here?" Bradshaw pointed to his rank insignia on his uniform. "I'm not a 'sir.' I *work* for a living. That guy over there . . ." Bradshaw pointed to Nigel, *"he's* a 'sir.' That's what I'm talking about. Get your shit together, sailor."

"Yess . . ."

"Yes, *Chief,*" Bradshaw offered.

"Yes, Chief."

"Good," Bradshaw said. "Now, are you injured?"

Thew wore a stupefied look on his face.

"Are you *injured?*"

"No," Thew said. "No, Chief."

"That's good," Bradshaw said. "Because we've got a long way to go, and we're not out of the woods yet. So man up, okay?"

"Yes, Chief."

Bradshaw stood and offered a hand to Thew. Thew grabbed it and stood.

"We're good, yeah?" asked Nigel, watching from a few feet away.

"Yes, sir," said Bradshaw.

"Fantastic," Nigel said. "Let's move, then, yeah?"

Thew had enjoyed his time as a cross-country runner in high school, but it hadn't prepared him for this. And the sand particles lodged in his lungs didn't help matters. His wheezing grew more labored.

Omani Highway 5 became UAE Highway E44 again. The borders here meandered like a drunken sailor.

They followed the wadi into the village of Masfut which, together with neighboring Hatta, was hemmed in by red, sharp-edged mountains.

Traffic stopped and people gawked. The SEALs and Marines walked right through the middle of town.

No one said anything to them. Just blank stares and hard looks.

They weren't welcome here.

Not that it mattered. The SEALs and Marines had no intention of hanging around.

They continued to follow the wadi until they crossed back into Oman.

It was a three-hour trek through the knob of UAE territory that Oman bent around.

It would be dusk soon, but the SEALs and Marines had no intention of bedding down for the night. The trek before them was downhill now, and they would reach the coast in another four hours.

Thew, lagging behind, fell down.

When he didn't get up, the SEALs gathered around.

He was semi-conscious. His breathing was labored.

Hastings shined a light into Thew's eyes. His pupils were slow to contract, his eyes glassy.

Worse, the kid was burning up.

A Marine-embedded Navy Corpsman administered moxifloxacin. It was an antibiotic used to treat infections, including pneumonia, which the corpsman suspected as the cause of the wheezing.

After conferring, the SEALs and Marines agreed to press on. They rigged together a stretcher to carry the young logistics specialists down to the coast.

As they prepared to resume their march, Chief Bradshaw saw the silhouettes of armed men on a ridge above.

Bradshaw raised his rifle and took aim, and the other SEALs followed his lead.

It wasn't just a few armed men.

The entire ridge was full armed men looking down on them. Same for the ridgeline a tier above, and all sides.

They were surrounded.

Someone called out to them in a crisp, British accent. "Is there a Lieutenant Commander Nigel Wood among you?"

Master Chief Hector Gonzales looked to Nigel and held his index finger to his lips.

Hector stepped forward and did his best impression of an English accent.

"Why, *yes,* old chap, *I* am left-tenant Nigel Wood. So very pleased to meet you, I do say, mate. *Cheerio.*"

"You better pray that you didn't just get us all bloody *killed,*" whispered Nigel. "That was the *worst* attempt at an English accent I've ever heard, yeah?"

The silhouette of a young man, a kind of shawl wrapped around his narrow shoulders, stepped into the wadi from behind a large rock.

"I am Colonel Haitham bin Theyazin, Royal Army of Oman," he said. "I spoke with General Pitt of the United States Central Command a few hours ago."

"He's the Crown Prince," Thew said, slurring his words. "Son of the Sultan."

Nigel looked askance at the delirious supply kid on the stretcher.

"I like geopolitics," the boy boasted, then drifted off to sleep.

The young man with a shawl stepped forward, glancing down at the kid on the stretcher.

"Indeed," he said in a flawless English accent. "I am *Prince* Haitham. At your service."

As Commander of the Saudi Special Navy Security Units, Abdulaziz Al-Zahrani had loyal soldiers of his own.

And they weren't just soldiers. They were highly trained *commandos,* trained by the world's very best: America's Navy SEALs.

The geography of how things were playing out made it seem as if Allah had chosen him.

So, Al-Zahrani seized the moment.

He ordered his men to take Jeddah airport in the pre-dawn hours. Then they stormed the Al Salam Palace, which they found empty.

And just like that, Jeddah was Al-Zahrani's.

His tribe had already seized nearby Hajar.

The real prize lay just forty miles to the east: Mekkah.

Al-Zahrani wasted no time, and Mekkah was his before noon. His fellow Zahran tribesmen were already laying siege to Medina, a hundred miles north of Hajar.

Before the day was over, meanwhile, the officers who had sworn allegiance to the son of the former Crown Prince, Abdul bin Muhammad (or ABM) – the one who had engineered the assassination of the King and his Crown Prince – had turned on him.

ABM was hung naked from the golden palm sculpture at Sultan Good Field – the Palm Circle – in Tabouk.

The officers had switched their allegiance to Abdulaziz Al-Zahrani.

Abdulaziz Al-Zahrani declared himself King of the newly re-established Kingdom of the Hejaz, comprising the entire Red Sea coast of Arabia.

Saudi Arabia was no more.

31

The klaxon alarm.

The rotating red beacon light.

Personnel of the 2nd Space Warning Squadron at Buckley Space Force Base in Aurora, Colorado, hadn't enjoyed a moment's rest during the past thirty-six hours.

But this time was different.

Satellites had detected a mixture of gamma rays, x-rays and neutrons consistent with a nuclear explosion.

Two nuclear explosions.

The on-board computers and the computers at various Space Force commands, as well as at NORAD in Colorado Springs, had independently verified the data.

The yields of both nuclear explosions appeared to range between 300 and 400 kilotons. Both appeared to have been airbursts located in the far northeast of the Arabian Peninsula in the United Arab Emirates.

As before, analysts furiously navigated their computer software and followed emergency protocols.

The President was stunned. Sitting in the Raven Rock Situation Room, she put her hand to her mouth.

"Did we do that?" she asked.

The nuclear strikes were clearly aimed at the advancing Iranian army.

"We don't know yet," said the Chairman of the Joint Chiefs of Staff, Admiral Sorenson. "I've ordered all nuclear-armed commands to report in."

"Israel?" The President asked.

"We just don't have enough information," Sorenson said. "What we *do* know is that the yield was significant – about 350 kilotons for each bomb. That's big."

"Ma'am," interrupted Oscar Schwarz, the president's Chief of Staff. "The President of the Russian Federation is on the emergency hotline."

"Madame President," the President of Russia spoke.

"What have you done?"

Daddy Longlegs appeared on one of the TV screens. He was still in DC, in his bunker beneath Naval Observatory One, built by Dick Cheney after the 9/11 terrorist attacks.

"Madam President," he said – *was that disdain in his voice* – "I recommend an immediate nuclear strike on Tehran and its environs in order to end the *scourge* of that government once and for all, and to bring this war to a quick end."

"It's about American . . . *lives,"* he said, pausing to let the last word soak in. "Like Harry Truman, you can save the . . . *lives* . . . of tens of thousands of young American servicemen and women by ending this war . . . *now* . . . *today."*

On another monitor, CNN was showing stock footage of Chinese Navy ships at sea, stealth fighters in the air, and shock troops conducting exercises.

A ticker below read:

. . . Chinese military on highest alert . . . Russia declares state of emergency . . . NATO on alert . . . Global markets in free fall . . .

Things were spinning out of control.

"Madam President," interrupted Oscar Schwartz, her National Security Advisor. "I'm afraid I have more bad news."

Deep in the desert of central Iran, the government of Iran had detonated six – *six* – nuclear warheads, in succession, in an underground test.

The estimated yield of each warhead ranged from sixty kilotons to 300 kilotons.

Several messages were clear.

First, by detonating *six* warheads, there was no telling how many warheads Iran actually possessed.

Second, by testing various yields, Iran demonstrated a level of sophistication in nuclear weapons technology.

Third, their ICBM attacks on the continental United States were a demonstration of Iran's capability to *deliver* nuclear warheads, even though those attacks had used only conventional warheads.

As far as the carrying capacity of an ICBM goes, there's really no difference between a conventional warhead and a nuclear warhead.

In short, the President thought, *we're fucked.*

President Cynthia Belle paced back and forth as she read.

Seated in her Raven Rock office were her National Security

Advisor, Oscar Schwartz; her Chairman of the Joint Chiefs of Staff, Admiral Erik Sorenson; Martin Hartshorne, her Chief of Staff; and her Mandarin interpreter. Vice President Daddy Longlegs was on one of the TV monitors.

That was *her* team.

Seated across from her team was the Chinese ambassador to the United States and six of his staff.

Cynthia couldn't believe what she was reading. It was, essentially, an ultimatum.

China was demanding an immediate cease-fire between the United States and Iran. Iran had already agreed to it, according to the letter.

Further, the letter demanded that the United States *not* send a naval expedition to the region to help liberate eastern Arabia and the Gulf states.

"We cannot accept a return to the pre-war status quo," the letter read.

It was signed by the President of China and the President of the Russian Federation.

On another TV monitor, the English-language China Central Television – CCTV – reported that China was mobilizing its entire fleet, including all five of its Type 4 aircraft carriers, each of which was the equivalent of a modern Ford-class American supercarrier, and their carrier strike groups.

Having declared a national emergency, China was also calling up all its reserve units to active duty.

In the hours ahead, pundits would draw parallels with the Cuban Missile Crisis.

Would the United States defy China and attack the fleet currently scrambling to block American access to the Indian Ocean?

Sir Jonathan Galloway, the British Ambassador to the United States, rode in the back of his armored SUV in a small entourage escorted by the Maryland State Police.

They drove from Washington, DC to Frederick, Maryland, which sat at the foot of Catoctin Mountain. Catoctin Mountain was the home of Camp David, the American presidential retreat.

But Camp David was not the destination. In fact, the motorcade drove right past the usual turnoff to Camp David and continued to the northern tip of the mountain.

The motorcade crossed into rural Pennsylvania.

A moment later, they pulled into Raven Rock.

Sir Galloway was led to a mine car. It was like being at Disney World.

The deeper into the mountain he went, however, the more claustrophobic he became. The walls were close, the ceiling low.

The American President is in a bunker, and the whole world is closing in. And she's got that warmongering twat of a VP whispering in her ear.

It's a goddamn wonder American, Russian and Chinese ICBMs weren't already passing each other in the heavens, like ships passing in the night, to deliver destruction to each other's countries.

What a dog's dinner this has all become.

The Ambassador waited on a single, unsteady chair in a room with a concrete floor and ceilings. *A bloody prison.*

"Mr. Ambassador?" It was the President's personal secretary.

Sir Galloway was led to the President's office.

"Madam President," Sir Galloway said. He removed his hat and bowed before the American president.

"Sir Galloway, it is a pleasure," she said.

A bloody pleasure, is it?

President Cynthia Belle led the British Ambassador to a sofa. She sat on the sofa across from him, legs crossed.

"Madam President," Sir Galloway began, "my government has asked me to meet with you personally."

"We enjoy such a close and historic relationship that the two of us – our two countries –should always be candid with each other."

"Particularly when a situation may be difficult for one or the other to objectively comprehend."

"The British Empire – and the French, for that matter – found itself in a very uncomfortable situation during the Suez Crisis of 1956, a painful crisis of our own making," he continued. "It was the United States that came to us with clear eyes, insisting that we withdraw from Egypt.

"Emotions had run high. Egos were rubbed raw. But, in the end, we recognized that only a true friend would lay out the truth in such stark terms."

"America brought us back from the precipice of a very dark place."

"Madam President, the United States *must* step back from the brink. With the introduction of nuclear weapons –"

"We didn't do that," Cynthia snapped. "My Generals *assure* me that we did not employ nuclear weapons."

Galloway paused.

"That may very well be true –"

"You don't *believe* us?" Cynthia interrupted. She appeared to be genuinely hurt.

"It's just that, we're all in a very difficult place," Galloway said. "Iran says that they did not attack your aircraft carrier –"

"Oh, *please,* " Cynthia spat. "How can you sit there with a straight face?"

"Madame President, please, if you could just see –"

"Et *tu*, Judas?" Cynthia said, her arms folded against her chest.

Galloway blinked. "I didn't mean to –"

"Get out," snapped the President.

Her words were like a slap to the face.

She's too emotional.

Cynthia stood, and marched to the office door, her back ramrod straight.

"Good *day,* Mr. *Ambassador."*

"Madam President, *please . . ."*

On the ride back to Washington, Galloway typed his report on his encrypted laptop.

Did that just happen?

His phone buzzed.

It was the American Vice President.

Bloody hell.

"Mr. Vice President," he said, a plastic smile on his face, "how very nice to hear from you."

"You stabbed us in the back, you *asshole.* You and your government," Longlegs growled.

Galloway recoiled. The accusation wasn't entirely unexpected. But hearing it, especially the way Daddy Longlegs delivered it, was unnerving.

In fact, it was downright hostile.

They've all gone mad.

Galloway struggled to find the right words and tone to sooth the Vice President.

"Hear me out, George, if you will –"

"Fuck you, asshole," Longlegs interjected. "Don't think for a *minute* that I will forget this."

"Please, Mr. Vice President . . ."

Daddy Longlegs had hung up.

Sir Galloway looked out the window as his motorcade headed back down I-275 to Washington.

Galloway's heart skipped a beat. He started to worry. *Really* worry.

He tried to remember, but he never paid attention to such things.

Was the basement beneath our Embassy a bloody nuclear shelter or not?

Multiple troop transport trucks of the Royal Omani Army were lined up on the other side of a ridge, just across the border from Hatta, UAE, all waiting along Omani Highway 5.

Crown Prince Haitham bin Theyazin of the Omani Sultanate had personally supervised the special operation of the Royal Omani Army to retrieve the American operators seeking protection and shelter from advancing Iranian troops.

It was a personal favor to General Alexander Pitt, Commander of the United States Special Operations Command . . . and to Daddy Longlegs.

It was a surprisingly short trip from the eastern foothills of the Hajar Mountains to Shinas Port along the coast.

Just thirty minutes.

When Nigel and the SEALs disembarked from their Omani trucks, they saw two American *Arleigh Burke-class* destroyers in port, a huge flag of the United States tied to one of the ship's masts. It was a stirring sight.

When they saw that it was the USS *Richard Lugar* and *Telesforo Trinidad,* both from Bahrain – that the ships had survived and come back for them – several of the men wiped away tears.

"Let's not faff about, yeah?" Nigel said. "Let's go home."

Nigel stayed behind to make sure every last man made it onto the ships before he himself stepped aboard the *Trinidad.*

The ship's crew untethered the ship, and it immediately lurched forward.

Nigel braced himself as the ship's bow rose high in the water, lowering and leveling as the ship gained speed.

Sea legs. He still had them.

His SEAL squad and several Marines had tossed their equipment against a bulkhead in the helicopter landing area of the ship's stern, and literally crashed there on the deck.

The young forklift driver was taken to the ship's infirmary.

Nigel faced aft and watched as the coast of Oman – and Arabia – faded into the distance amid a brown bluish haze.

A pair of F-35 Lightnings screamed toward the coast on a bombing run.

Master Chief Hector Gonzales walked up and stood beside him.

"We'll be back, yeah?" Hector said.

"I'm not so sure," Nigel said. "One thing I *am* sure of, though."

"What's that?" asked Hector.

"Another war," Nigel said.

Habibollah Nasirzadeh – now Admiral – stood at the footbridge to the IRIS *Sabalan,* along with an entourage of aides.

It was the dead of night. Three o'clock in the morning.

The ship was tied up in Saqr Port in the Emirate of Ras Al Khaimah, one of the smallest of the seven Emirates that made up the United Arab Emirates.

"Permission to come aboard?" he shouted. The officer on deck, now *Vice* Admiral Hashemi Ghavam, saluted.

"Come aboard," he answered.

A whistle blew.

"Admiral on board," an officer announced, and the sailors snapped to attention.

Hash climbed down from the watch deck, and the two embraced.

"I am very sorry to learn of General Yaghani and Brigadier General Ali Alamouti," Hash offered. The two were among the tens of thousands of Iranian soldiers killed in the American, or maybe Israeli, nuclear strikes.

Or maybe they were Saudi nukes. Or . . .

"It is a shame," Habib said. "They brought glory to Iran."

Hash couldn't add to the sentiment.

Glory . . . is that what that was?

Or just 40,000 meaningless deaths?

Hash was tired.

Sleep . . .

He was certain that Habib must be, too.

"Let me show you to your quarters," Hash offered. He led Habib's aides to their sleeping berths, and Habib to his room.

"Why don't you get settled in," Hash said, "then come visit me in my quarters."

"Thank you, my friend," Habib said. He grabbed hold of a bulkhead as the ship lurched.

They were under way.

Habib lay in his rack and closed his eyes.

His mind raced. There would be a lot of pomp and circumstance upon their return to Bandar Abbas in the morning.

He wasn't ready for it. He supposed he never would be.

Just put on a smile and get through it. *Soldier up.*

He focused his breathing to calm his mind.

He started tumbling. It was like he was in a washing machine, just tumbling head over heels.

He cried out, trying to find something to grab hold on for leverage.

The tumbling stopped. He couldn't see. He didn't know if he was upside down. He tried to move but couldn't.

He was *suffocating.*

He tried to calm himself, stifle the panic setting in.

He wiggled slightly, and a little more, and then his hand punched out into air.

Now he struggled and threw everything he could into loosening the invisible grip on him.

He climbed out of a hole and lay coughing and hacking.

A roaring wind lashed him.

He labored to his feet, bracing against the unrelenting wind. A thick orange haze kept visibility to a foot. As his eyes adjusted, he could see further.

All around him jutted the limbs of his men, sticking out of mounds of sand. An extended hand. A leg. The more his eyes adjusted to the orange haze, the more limbs there were sticking out of the sand.

One lad was buried from the middle of his torso down, his arms pinned to his sides. Habib went to help pull him out. But when he looked at the lad's face, it was frozen in a silent scream, dust clouding his wide-open eyes.

Habib snapped awake.

His memories no longer waited. They've invaded his dreams, which have become so vivid of late.

He was drenched in sweat. He looked at his watch.

Shit.

Four hours had passed. They were less than an hour from port.

He noticed the dress uniform hanging in the open closet. Hash must have seen to it.

He smiled. He still had time to visit his friend.

A young soldier led Habib to Hash's quarters.

Habib knocked.

"Come in," Hash shouted.

Habib stepped in and closed the door behind him, then paused.

The soldier. Was that the lad with the silent scream?

Habib shook off the thought and turned around.

The room was dark, except for a burning candle, which lent the room a cozy, homey ambiance.

The candlelight flickered with wind, which filled the room.

Habib spotted Hashemi and gasped.

Hash sat Indian style on a room-sized Persian carpet. He was out of uniform. He wore sweatpants and a T-shirt and was barefoot.

Maybe it was the lighting, but his eyes looked . . . *dusty.*

A large blue crystal hookah pipe sat at his knees, and he pulled deeply from the hose. He let out a long, deep exhale, emitting a blue cloud of smoke that filled up half the room.

The window along the starboard side was wide open, letting in the cool night wind. Outside, the ship was shrouded in thick fog.

"Hashemi Ghavam," Habib hissed, *"what are you doing?"*

He couldn't let this go on. Not now that he was the Commander of the General Staff of the Armed Forces.

"I am sleeping, my friend," Hash said, then laughed a genuinely deep, joyous laugh.

"You should try it sometime," he said, and laughed again.

Hash and the whole Persian carpet on which he sat lifted off the ground, then, and levitated.

Habib's jaw dropped and he stood wide-eyed.

"May God have mercy on our souls, Habibollah Nasirzadeh," Hash said. He took another deep hit of the hookah pipe.

The Persian carpet – with Hash sitting on it – slowly turned around and drifted toward the window.

The window was barely wide enough for someone to climb through, but Hash ducked, and he and the carpet exited the cabin with ease.

Hash paused and hovered in the night air. He and the carpet turned around to face Habibollah.

Hash leaned forward and stuck his head back inside the cabin through the window, his arms reaching in for anchorage, and his dust-covered eyes bored into Habib's.

A chill traveled down Habib's spine. He stood paralyzed with fear.

"Mind your ship, Habibollah," Hash said. "And beware our friend to the east."

He backed out of the window.

"But where are you going?" asked Habib.

"Home," Hash said, "where dreams last through the dawn."

Hash laughed, a deep and thunderous laugh as he and the carpet turned away and vanished into the foggy night.

"Mind your ship, Habibollah!" Habib heard out of the fog.

"Mind your ship!"

And then laughter.

Deep, soulful laughter.

Habib bolted awake, drenched in sweat. It took him a moment to gain his bearings. Hash's laughter lingered and then it was gone.

It was replaced by an insistent knocking, and Habib stumbled to his cabin door.

It was the young officer of the deck. He looked pale, as if he had seen a ghost.

"What is it?" Habib demanded.

"Sir, it's the admiral."

Made in the USA
Middletown, DE
23 November 2024

64968668R00166